Wife Overboard

Steve Colbourne

BenLiv Publishing
Brighton, England

PRAISE

Wife Overboard has been given the **'Cruise Bruise Editor's Choice Award,'** and in their review they called *Wife Overboard* a very clever fictional **Blueprint For Cruise Ship Murder At Sea.**

They also went on to say:

'Kudos to Colbourne's use of fictional character Michael's thoughts, observations and commentary on the specific details of so many cruise ship overboard cases, it is both brilliant as well as a refreshing and enlightening evaluation on cruise ship deaths, overboard passengers and crew and the cruise industry as whole. Fictional character Michael thinks in print, what others wish they could say publicly, without fear of being sued.

There is a very important moral to the story, something you will need to figure out on your own, through reading Colbourne's extensively researched, very dark, yet clever work of intrigue, woven into one of the best cruise ship murder mysteries of all times.'

COPYRIGHT

Wife Overboard, Second Edition, Copyright ©2015 Steve Colbourne

Wife Overboard is a work of fiction set in the cruise travel industry with a fictional cruise line. Names, characters, businesses, places, events and incidents are either the products of the author's imagination or used in a fictitious manner. Any resemblance to actual persons, living or dead, or actual events is purely coincidental. The author loves and recommends cruising, and went on three cruises last year.

All rights reserved. Without limiting rights under the copyright reserved above, no part of this publication may be reproduced, stored, introduced into a retrieval system, distributed or transmitted in any form or by any means, including without limitation photocopying, recording, or other electronic or mechanical methods, without prior written permission, except in the case of brief quotations embodied in critical reviews and certain other noncommercial uses permitted by copyright law. The scanning, uploading, and/or distribution of this document via the internet or via any other means without the permission of the publisher is illegal and is punishable by law. Please purchase only authorized editions and do not participate in or encourage electronic piracy of copyrightable materials.

ISBN-13:978-1507853740

DEDICATIONS

I started writing this book after coming out of hospital having just undergone my first chemotherapy session for my Chronic Lymphatic Leukaemia (CLL). I would therefore like to thank all the following for their support.

My wife, daughter, Olivia, and son Ben. I would also like to give a special dedication to Dr Tim Corbett and his complete team of doctors, nurses, and support staff, of the Haematology Unit at the Royal Sussex County Hospital in Brighton. Absolute professionals and friends one and all.

Thanks to them I am now able to live a very normal life. As a small thanks part of **any net profit from this book will be donated to Leukaemia CARE.** Steve also runs a Support Group for Leukaemia sufferers and their families and carers. Please contact him for further details.

I would also like to thank Dianne Purdie and her husband David who edited my book, and became my friends across the pond. Also to Douglas Williams, again from the USA, who formatted the book, and helped with the technical aspects of putting it all together.

Wife Overboard

ONE

Michael and his wife love their holidays. In particular, both Michael and his wife love cruising holidays. Michael, however, does not love his wife. He had often thought how much more enjoyable a holiday might be on his own or with another person that he really wanted to be with. In fact, Michael was sure that life would be much more fun if his wife were not around altogether. Michael had a plan.

Michael's plan had come to him in his own 'Eureka' moment. He had almost congratulated himself that his discovery was nearly as significant as the Archimedes one. Michael had also been lying in the bath when the thought came to him. 'Genius', he wanted to proclaim. Archimedes discovery had involved his body and the displacement of water. Michael's moment was just the same. His idea would also work. Yes, exactly as the old Philosopher had discovered over two thousand years ago. The principle was still the same. It would still involve a body and the displacement of water. The only difference being it would not be his body.

Like the Greek, Michael wanted to jump out of the bath and run around the streets naked. Even though he lived in the City of Brighton in southern England, which was probably more cosmopolitan and understanding than any other in the country, and he lived less than half a mile from a nudist beach, he realised his excitement had to be curtailed. Nevertheless, there was one person that he wanted to share it with. One person he hoped would be as enthusiastic as he was. He looked towards his mobile phone on the three tier glass upright storage unit, on which various colours of Egyptian towels sat immaculately folded. He wanted to call her and tell her how easy it would be. Did she realise just how many people a year fell off, died, or went missing, on cruise ships? He was astounded. No wonder the cruise companies did not publicise it. It was truly amazing, and it seemed almost too easy. He remembered the chart he had found earlier on the Internet that detailed exactly how many people from each cruise line had actually died or fallen off last year. He couldn't remember the number exactly, but he recalled that over twenty passengers or crew had gone overboard, and that was only taking into account about sixteen of the cruise lines. Many of the incidents had probably been suspicious circumstances, but whatever the way, accident or suicide, medical or murder, all had ended up the same way. Dead.

It gave cruising a whole new dimension. No wonder it was the fastest growing holiday sector. It was a different world that was promised when you booked, but they didn't tell you what the odds were of you ending up in a different world before your cruise was complete.

Michael continued to sit in the bath for a little while longer. The water had gone cold, but his body tingled with excitement. Michael was actually a shower man. Normally it was a quick in and out of the shower. A bath took too long. The bathroom was really his wife's domain. Sharon loved to spend hours in there pampering herself and talking and laughing with her friends on the telephone. Well she would not be laughing much longer. She would laugh at him no more. Yes, it almost seemed a cliché, but he would have the last laugh.

Michael raised himself up from the bath and found himself looking at his reflection in the large mirror on the opposite side of the wall to the corner bath. Sometimes he recognised the man staring back at him. Other times he did not. In some respects the past fifty six years had not been that unkind. His weight and the trimness of his body had not changed much from his younger days. He liked to keep himself fit and running was his chosen method. It was a solitary pursuit and it also provided him with a challenge. Not a challenge against anyone else, but just against himself. It was him against the clock. Michael always liked to measure everything that he did, and for him a run was no different. Just him and his smart phone recording the time and distance with a constant feedback on how he was doing through his expensive sports earphones. How he loved the run along Brighton seafront, especially in the summer evenings. He would jog from the Marina along to the rusting and neglected West Pier and back again. Sometimes, he would pass runners considerably younger than he was, and he would allow himself a smile. Life was good. Life was great. However, life could get even better, and with running he had much time to think, and much time to plan.

Michael glanced down at his chest in the mirror. He was thankful that he did not have a very hairy chest, but he noticed that quite a number of the hairs that nestled there had turned grey. He then moved his hand to his head. That was the problem. Michael did not feel his age. He did not think he actually looked his age, but losing his hair was one of his biggest disappointments. Yes, he realised that lots of men lost their hair years before they reached his age, but that did not help. Perhaps he did not want to take the crowning glory of his new romantic youth through to middle age, but it would have been nice to have had some hair to style or even colour. Now he kept it cropped in a trendy, sort of modern stubbly way, but it was a tribute rather than a triumph. He also wore a small, fashionable and neatly trimmed beard. He knew that if he dressed well he didn't look ancient, but nevertheless he would have still liked to have retained his hair. Of course, he knew his wife didn't help. She had recently taken to nicknaming him, 'Hedgehog,' to some of her friends. She would laugh, and pat his stubbled head fondly in front of them as they stood at a bar. 'Yes,' she would say, 'Michael's my own little hedgehog.' Her manicured hand would pat him twice on top of his head like some kind of ritual, and then she would announce to all that she had once studied French. 'Yes, he is my own little Erinaceous. He is of the hedgehog family, and he can also be a bit of a prick sometimes.'

Everybody would laugh. Michael would pretend to laugh, but he could not wait for that day when she would laugh no more.

Michael walked across the bathroom floor picked up a luxurious towel and rubbed himself down. His heart was racing, but he knew he also had to dampen down his growing excitement. His hand reached for his mobile smart phone. Oh how he loved that phone. Oh how it could be so useful. He went to tap in the four digit code that protected any other person from picking it up and gathering any information from it. Then he thought better of it. From now on everything would have to be thought out carefully. They had been married for over thirty years. Thirty years. Like two life sentences running consecutively. He did not want to serve life. He wanted to live life. Another few months would not matter. Another few months and he would be free. He could not afford to slip up. He would not slip up. It would be her that would slip. Slip quietly and gently into the sea. Michael finished drying himself and stepped into his striped leisure suit trousers, and a plain white T shirt. It was time to think. It was time to plan.

TWO

'I'll call you tomorrow,' Sharon said quietly, as she heard Michael in the hallway. Quickly her red painted finger pressed down on the red digital button, and she terminated the call. She glanced briefly at the screen of her smart phone. It was a different one from Michael's. His mobile phone was on a rival network, and up until now had been the mobile market's biggest seller for quite a number of years. Sharon's mobile phone company had recently launched a market winner with its much larger screen. Yes, she thought, as she placed it on the wooden coffee table. It's much bigger than Michael's, and she thought back to a time once when she had wished in other ways that Michael had been bigger. Now, of course it did not really matter, and soon it would not matter at all. The size of his bits had not been very important now for years. Now the size of his bits would not matter one little bit.

Michael had obviously gone into the kitchen, and Sharon settled down on the three seater leather sofa looking out onto the balcony and all the boats. One thing she did have Michael to thank for was the view. Their flat was in Brighton Marina. Michael had always been fascinated with the sea, and so it seemed natural that they would live overlooking the English Channel that provided a spectacular backdrop whatever the season.

Their apartment was quite an expensive one, and for the money certainly not that spacious. Though, as there was only the two of them, it was certainly roomy enough, or at least it had been once. Of course, what you were really paying for was the view and the convenience. The ground rent maintenance that also included reserved parking, left them with desirable, but dear accommodation.

Nevertheless, it was probably as near as England gets to a luxury gated community. It was a little bit, arguably to some anyway, a gateway to heaven on the south English Coast. Not only were they afforded fantastic views of the sea, but all within walking distance were designer and factory shops, eateries of every type of cuisine, a large supermarket, bowling alley, cinema, and a favourite haunt of both of them, a casino. Just a short stumble home after a heavy or losing night.

'Do you want a tea?' Michael called through.

'No thank you,' Sharon replied quickly without even thinking. 'I was thinking of having something a little stronger. I might well take that bottle of red wine that I opened yesterday out on the balcony. It's such a nice evening.'

Sharon found herself staring at the photograph of the two of them together on the display unit opposite her. It had been taken not long after they were married. Both of them were smiling, and looked happy in the picture. Of course, it had been taken a long time ago. Longer than she cared to remember, and so many things had changed since then. The deceptive thing, she thought to herself, was that outwardly, she hoped that she had not changed that much at all. At least not from a distance.

Sharon's hair was still blonde, but a bit darker now, and helped by her regular longer visits to the hairdressers. Her body was still very trim, and at least she had not suffered from any stretch marks. That was a benefit of not having had any children. However, she would never have conceded that not having children could be labelled as a benefit. She would have willingly paid the price if she could have done. It was certainly one of her biggest regrets.

Sharon still wore her hair long. Her friends had always said that she looked like a well-known, middle aged, pop star that still had attitude. Sharon did not really think that she did, but she could see how they had come to that conclusion, and she was flattered. The star, at least if you were a fair distance from the stage, looked as she had always done. It was only when you got up closer could you see that time had not stopped.

Sharon thought that was much the same for her. She still thought that she looked like the young woman in the photograph opposite. She didn't feel any different, but she knew that a closer inspection in the mirror revealed that her oval green eyes were now framed by tiny lines, and her soft features looked a little harder. She always tried to look her best, and nature with the help of the creams that promised so much, had been kind to her.

Michael came back into the room moments later carrying a mug of green tea and the bottle of wine with a fluted wine glass. He slid open the French doors to the balcony, and placed the wine bottle and glass on the wicker and glass table.

'Thank you,' Sharon said automatically. She managed a

brief smile as they faced each other. Michael did make her laugh sometimes, even if most of the time he did make her want to cry. Yes, he would often, if not always, do something that she asked him to do. But he was not normally so attentive nowadays, and eager to please.

Michael smiled back, and for a brief moment he seemed like the man that she used to know all those years ago. Though now that man was without hair. He looked relaxed. More relaxed than she had seen him for some time. It was difficult to work him out sometimes, Sharon thought, as she settled on the balcony and poured her first glass of wine. He was both a poker and chess player, and because of his interests she was never now quite sure what went on behind his painted smile.

She looked out to sea. Out to the horizon. It was a calm spring evening. The time of year when it normally felt good to be alive. To look to the future. To extend your horizons as the summer was coming. The whole town, or city as it was called nowadays, came alive, and although it was busy in the winter months it woke up again to welcome the numerous visitors of all persuasions over the summer months.

Sharon picked up her wine glass and drained the glass. She wished she could share in its enthusiasm for the future. She poured another glass and continued to stare at the horizon. She remembered once when she was a young girl nearly four decades ago when she had had dreams. Didn't all young girls have dreams? The painted pop stars of the period who were pinned to her bedroom wall had stared down at her. Great looking boys that would make the perfect partner. Magazines like Jackie and Smash Hits had promised it all. That seemed so long ago. Long before

Michael. She could see Michael though the French doors. He was sitting on the sofa with his iPad tablet. His fingers caressing the screen in short strokes. Sharon laughed to herself as she thought that Michael definitely loved that computer tablet more than he loved her. He and the tablet never seemed to be parted for long. She wondered what he was looking up, as he cradled it in one hand and caressed it with the other. She could have almost been jealous of the inanimate object if she had cared. But she did not. It had been a long time since they had had a loving caress. Longer than she cared to remember.

Sharon went to pick up her glass, and she wasn't sure how, but like her dreams it quickly slipped through her fingers and fell to the floor. It smashed to tiny slithers. The red wine ran between the groves of the decking, like blood from an abattoir trickling down the drain channels.

Almost instantly, and as if by magic, Michael appeared by her side with a dustpan and brush.

'Did you cut yourself?' he asked in a concerned tone. 'Do you need a plaster?'

'No. No thank you,' Sharon answered automatically. 'That was one of our best glasses.'

'Glasses can be replaced,' Michael stated.

Sharon was probably more shocked by how attentive he had been rather than what she had done. What had come over him? Had she misjudged him or was he simply making a big effort? She decided to give him the benefit of the doubt. Maybe that would be easier than to keep sniping at one another. 'What were you looking up?' She nodded towards the tablet that had been abandoned on the sofa.

'Oh just looking at holidays,' Michael replied casually.

'As your next birthday is the big Five O I thought we could do something special.'

'Like what?' Sharon asked. Michael never failed to surprise her.

'Oh I was thinking of a cruise,' Michael answered. 'A nice big ship, and a cabin with a balcony.'

THREE

Michael could not believe it. At times he felt in advance of his years, and could easily understand the principal actor in a television situation comedy of recent years, who played an older man named Victor. Victor was at odds with the world, and always displayed a complete bewilderment of what the world and the people in it had become. The character was always exclaiming, 'I don't believe it!' Michael shook his head in disbelief, and then realised that even his lack of hair was helping to morph him into Victor. It was something that he knew he must suppress for many reasons. Not least because Victor was quite a bit older than him, and if Sharon picked up on it she was likely to give him yet another nickname. The Erinaceous one was bad enough. A cheap laugh at his expense, but one of a man probably supposed to be over twenty years his senior was not something that he wanted to be associated with. Sharon knew he was sensitive about losing his hair, but if he mentioned it she only told him not to be so silly, and it was only a little joke.

He would give her a little joke, he thought, as he continued to stare at the screen on his notebook computer. He glanced down at the clock in the right hand corner of the screen, and realised that he had at least another hour before Sharon came home from the gym, which was a walkable distance from their apartment in Victory Mews in the Marina. The gym seemed to be her second home. She was always there most days as she too tried to stem the tide of age.

Michael liked to pride himself that he was quite up to date, and especially up with technology. He wasn't a technical wizard, but nor was he a Luddite. Admittedly, he was not like Bob, who was Mary's husband; he liked to think he was a bit more interesting than that. He likened himself to a car driver when it came to computers. Yes, he could drive them, and get what he wanted from them, and he knew the basics under the bonnet. He didn't need to know what drove the engine or how the computer worked. Of course, over the years computers had become a lot simpler, and he loved his tablet, but he still found it not enough. When it came to reports or accounts for his business he found that he still needed a traditional PC.

In fact, Sharon quite often used to amuse him when she tried to get to grips with technology. It was about as much as she could do to look something up on the Internet, let alone use the full facilities of her smart phone. To Sharon they were merely forms of entertainment. She loved Facebook, and she was always writing things on her wall or other people's walls. Michael sarcastically put it down to her childhood because Sharon had been brought up in Whitehawk, which had been a notorious Brighton council estate where once perhaps graffiti on a wall might have been considered art or even being literate. Over recent years the area had benefited from regeneration, and had virtually been rebuilt, but Sharon could still be sensitive about her roots. It was a scab that had only ever briefly healed, and it did not take much to knock it off again when they were in one of their duelling arguments. Why did they do that to each other? Did every couple, he wondered? Each person over the years storing up personal intimate little details about each other. Then when the bickering started and the fencing begun out came the pre-sharpened rapiers, as each one tried to score points against the other. He and Sharon had almost turned it into an Olympic sport, and both were highly skilled in hurting the other. Michael did consider however that over time it was Sharon that always won the gold medal.

Perhaps it was payback time, and Michael knew that he must not become careless. He should leave nothing to chance by leaving his iPad or Notebook open so that Sharon might see what he was researching or what pages he had been looking at.

He glanced at the clock again and briefly thought of Mary and when he might share his discoveries with her. Almost certainly she was trapped in her house with Bob at present. Although they only lived up the road in Queens Park, and their Victorian house was rather large, there was a good chance that each was in separate rooms and most probably on different floors; even so, a call to her would have been too risky. An email, he decided, would be safer.

Michael cast his eye back to the screen and the website that he had recalled when he was in the bath. The Internet site was called Cruise Junkie, and it listed each and every person that had gone overboard on a cruise ship since 1995. It also provided an account of each incident, and quite often details if that person died or survived. It made fascinating reading. Some appeared to have jumped, some appeared to have been drunk, whilst others had probably been larking about, and some were attempted or just plain and simple murder. It covered both passengers and crew alike. The site also detailed pollution and environmental violations, ships that had sunk, ships that had grounded, and disabling accidents, collisions, and fires.

Michael found it astounding. Obviously, this site seemed in direct conflict with the ones he had used before when they had booked previous cruises. The ones that promised paradise. The Cruise Junkie site didn't really fit in with the love boat image that the industry tried to portray. He shook his head in disbelief again, and then checked himself when he remembered Victor. He really must remember not to do that.

Michael looked at the totals of the people missing at the foot of the table for each year. Consistently, it was over twenty. Twenty. It certainly made for interesting reading. How could it be that many? How come the papers did not cover it? Surely, if those numbers disappeared from Disney World every year they would have shut it down by now? He read some of the brief cases in point. Different nationalities. Some were crew from third world countries. Probably, he thought, that the news would be too diluted throughout the world to have the collective horror that the total numbers demanded.

Nevertheless, Michael realised he was on to something. Dare he dream that he had found the perfect murder? The perfect murder they said had never been written about because the person got away with it, and nobody knew. This was surely the next best thing. Anyway, he consoled himself as murder was a very strong emotive word. Were these not just simple accidents? Accidents from which sometimes others benefitted. Well wasn't that life? Weren't there always winners where there were losers? Yes, 'accident' had a better ring to it. All Sharon needed to do was to have a little accident. A little accident with tragic consequences, and if he benefitted from it then that was the way of the world.

He knew that he had a lot more planning and research to do. Research made perfect. He glanced at the clock again, and realised it wouldn't be long before Sharon returned, but did he have time to send an email to Mary?

He could picture her now. Her black hair cut in a bob that framed a roundish face with dark eye shadow and liner giving her an almost exotic Cleopatra appeal. He could feel his body stir just thinking about her, but there would be time enough for that later on. Mary did things for him, but he was only too aware that Sharon would do things to him if she found out, for Mary was actually her best friend. He shivered at the thought. He wasn't sure how it had come to this, but weren't both he and Mary just two lonely people trapped within the confines of their individual marriages. Were they not just comforting each other? Maybe it had gone a little too far or perhaps it had not gone far enough? And what he had just researched told him that he would do anything to be with Mary. The question was would Mary approve of what he wanted to do to be with her? Would she help and aid and abet him? Would she want to stop him or even shop him? Would the sacrifice of her best friend to be with him be worth it? Perhaps it might be better to not know exactly. Maybe, he thought to himself he had better hold back.

How could you broach a subject such as this? 'Oh I had a little thought yesterday. I am thinking of knocking off your best friend. Don't you think it's a great idea? Do you want to give me a hand?'

In the cold light of the computer it seemed such an evil concept. A fantasy to enable him to be with the woman that he wanted. Most people he knew would wonder what was wrong with a divorce. A simple legal break. But it wasn't as simple as that. It was far from simple. Some simply wouldn't understand. But some would see what had driven him to it. But the big question was would Mary? He opened the email programme and sat staring at the screen. Then glanced at the clock again. No, he decided the email would have to wait. His mind began to race. He had to slow down. Think it through. Was he really serious? How had it come to this?

Michael reached across the wooden coffee table, and picked up the television remote control. The large wall mounted screen sprung to life and quickly Michael navigated his way to the History Channel.

Almost immediately he heard the key in the lock and Sharon walked into their lounge. Michael looked up and smiled. 'Had a good workout?' he asked.

Sharon nodded. 'Yes. Thanks. What are you watching?'

It took Michael several seconds to realise what he had inadvertently tuned into. 'Real Life Crimes,' he answered.

FOUR

Sharon pushed the door entry button to their flat knowing that Michael was probably in. She put down the four bulging plastic shopping bags that she had just carried from ASDA, their local large supermarket, and rubbed her hands to bring back the circulation to her fingers. She looked hopefully towards the intercom.

Sharon hated the short walk back from the supermarket, but it was convenient, especially as she had just come from her gym and she had to pass it on the way home. She had only popped in for a couple of bits, and here she was four bags later. It had almost been a race to see if she could get home before one of the handles snapped. Green ideology might seem very good, but was it practical? If you actually asked for a plastic carrier bag these days you almost became public enemy number one, and were sometimes blamed for single-handedly trying to destroy the planet. So was it on purpose that the ones they were forced to give you were so thin that they were really not fit for purpose? Yes, Sharon realised that she could have bought one of those 'Bags for Life', but then you always had to remember it before you went out. Besides, wasn't the slogan supposed to be 'a dog is for life'? Caring for a bag just didn't have the same appeal.

'Hello!' Michael's voice came though the intercom.

'It's me,' Sharon said breathlessly, wondering if the time in the gym was actually benefitting her. 'Can you come down please I've got some shopping?'

She waited probably less than a minute and Michael came bounding down the stairs. He immediately took the bags like a faithful puppy dog, and followed her up the stairs to their flat.

'Shall I help you unpack?' he asked, as he placed them on the kitchen floor.

'Thank you, but no,' she replied firmly, knowing that if Michael did unpack them it would take her longer to find the items later on as he squirreled them in places that she wouldn't think to look in the future.

'Shall I make you a cup of tea then?' Michael volunteered.

Sharon shook her head. 'No thanks. You go and get on with what you were doing.' She didn't want him under her feet. Michael disappeared into the other room. He did not need to be told twice.

Sharon started unpacking. This wasn't her weekly shop, but merely supposed to be a couple of bits to tide them over. No, if she were honest her preferred choice would never have been ASDA. She much preferred to shop at Waitrose. Waitrose, she always thought, seemed to have so much more choice and so many more exotic items, and it provided much more entertainment with the characters who shopped there. Once or twice there she had seen Zoe Ball, the famous television presenter and the wife of Fatboy Slim, who only lived just down the road on the seafront. It was also rumoured that it was a bit of a gay pick- up and what was in the basket or the trolley was the sign. What the signals actually were, she was never sure, but it was fun looking at the guy carrying a basket and working out if it really meant that he was happy to purchase a meal for one.

Sharon always tried to go there once a week, but it was on the opposite side of the city near Hove, and they did have a free car park, but the traffic back along the seafront to the Marina could be bad. No, ASDA was much handier as it was right on their doorstep, although she did remember a time when it had closed as the adjacent white cliffs had started to erode.

The cliffs formed a natural barrier between the Brighton Marina Complex and the beginning or end of the city, depending on which way you looked at it. To the right and above the Marina you had probably the most expensive houses in Brighton located in Roedean. These were massive multi-million pound properties in what was locally known as Millionaires Row, and at the end of the road was the world famous boarding school, Roedean, where the wealthy from all around the globe sent their daughters.

To the east was the beginning of the notorious estate Whitehawk which stretched up to the racecourse. Whitehawk had once been a place to be feared. A place not to go near at night. It was also the place in which Sharon had been brought up. Just the thought of where she used to live made Sharon shudder. Geographically, she had only moved a couple of miles to where she now lived, but to her it felt like a million miles.

'I don't feel like cooking,' she called out to Michael. 'Are you hungry?'

'Well a bit,' came the reply. 'I didn't have much at work

today. Do you want me to do something?'

Sharon thought about it. Michael did seem to be particularly helpful lately. It was like a change had come over him. It was almost like an unofficial truce. They seemed to be getting on better. Why? She wasn't sure, but perhaps it was best not to question it. Go with the flow as her friends would say.

'If you like,' she called back. 'I want to have a bath and do my nails. My programme is on at nine.'

Sitting in the bath Sharon shuddered when she remembered how things used to be. The water was hot, but she felt cold when she recalled how difficult things had been when she had been a small girl. Her mother had been a staunch Catholic, and had ruled her with a will of iron. She certainly hadn't wanted to spoil the child. Her mother was a small fiercely independent woman who had appeared to have had grey hair as long as Sharon could remember. She had never worn any make-up, and her only concession to beauty or vanity had been the occasional perm.

Looking back now when she was older, Sharon realised that her mother had to be strong because of her father. Like all little girls Sharon could not really see that her father ever did anything wrong. All she wanted was for him to spend time with her, and to be there with her and praise her for how hard she tried at school. Though for great periods of her childhood her father was not around. Her mother always told her that her father was into property. It was a long time before Sharon discovered that he was actually into other people's property, and the reason he could not get to see her as often as she wished was because he was being detained at the pleasure of her majesty.

Quite often when Sharon was small, and he was home, she would lay awake in her bed upstairs and she could hear her parents arguing below. Sometimes she would hear a struggle and in the morning her father would be gone and her mother might even be sporting a black eye. Other times there would be a knock on the door and it would be the police who had come to question her father. Money had always been tight, but often when her father came home he would bring her a surprise present. It seemed to make everything right. It proved her father loved her.

Sharon picked up her luxury soap and the real sponge and subconsciously she almost tried to wash away those days. She and her mother had never really got on. Now it was too late. Now her mother was dead. Sharon had often wondered why her mother put up with it all. The answer she found was simple. In fact one word. Religion. Her mother was, always had been, and would always be, 'old school'. The word divorce was not in her dictionary. She was from the, 'made your bed and you had to lie in it' era.

Sharon both respected and hated her mother for it. Was that why she felt trapped with Michael? Why did these things always rub off? Even when you didn't want them to. She wasn't sure if her father was alive or dead. She had not seen him for years. She tried to cast her mind back to the embarrassing last time that she had seen him, which was more than five years ago. He had pitched up with an inappropriate present as though she was still the little girl that she once was, and then he had wanted her to put him up and lend him money.

Michael would not have any of it and they had argued. There would have been a time, Sharon knew, when her father would have simply punched Michael. He would have considered that he was family, and you looked after family. Now he was frail and less sturdy on his feet. Sharon had let Michael turn him away from their door, and she felt she had turned her back on her Christian upbringing.

Sub-consciously, she knew that Michael was right, but she hated him for it. He was her dad and he had always loved her she told herself. Now he had gone and she had no idea where he was in the world, and it was all Michael's fault. Was her father still alive? He was obviously getting on now, and in his late seventies. He could even be living on the streets, or he might not even be alive. She had no idea. She felt alone. So very alone.

FIVE

Michael put down his pen, and studied the 'Electrical Installation Condition Report.' He then shook his head and wondered how it had come to this. The electrical industry that he had joined as an electrical apprentice over thirty five years ago had changed beyond recognition. It had always been technical. That was probably why it had been the highest paid trade when he had started. Now the *Seventeenth Edition Electrical Regulations* were written in Lawyer's speak, and not in the simple language it once had been when he had begun with the Fourteenth Edition. Now the testing procedures were so complicated in their use of tables, values, readings, and calculations, that you almost needed to be a Professor to understand it all. And it all kept changing with new Amendments so that you had to buy more books and go on more courses.

He had always been happy in his chosen trade, and if he were honest it had always provided him a good living. For the last twenty years he had been self-employed running his own business, and he had made it work. It was a solitary profession, or could be. Michael had always found that to be an advantage. He liked being his own boss, and being his own master. He loved being in control and working on the jobs that he wanted to work on; and because he was always polite, neat and tidy, cleared up after himself, and honest, he found himself having to turn work down.

Now the times were changing. Margins were becoming tighter and tighter, and with the influx of Eastern Europeans, who were often prepared to work twice as hard for half as much, work was becoming harder and harder to price. So much unpaid time could be spent giving a quote or trying to win a tender, and when you lost it, and the next one, and the next one, the spirits sagged as well as the bank balance.

Michael picked up the report and turned to the customer who held his hand out.

'Thank you, Mr Staines,' Michael said as he was handed a cheque. 'Everything appears to be satisfactory, and I would recommend having the test done again in five years.'

Five years, Michael quickly thought to himself. Where will I be in five years? My business certainly won't last another five years, and I certainly don't ever want to work for anybody else again. Not after having run my own business.

Mr Staines smiled gratefully and shook Michael's hand. 'Thank you for doing such a thorough job! My wife Debbie and I are very grateful, and please call me Peter.'

Michael smiled. Another satisfied customer. Sometimes they almost turned into friends, but what was the point if he did not need to go back for another five years. Of course, he knew that either Peter or Debbie would be on the phone whatever the time, be it day or night, if it was an emergency.

Michael glanced at his G Shock watch. It was an early finish, and he could get home and do the accounts before Sharon got in. Something he was not looking forward to doing, and he quickly thought better of it. Better still he could catch a few moments with Mary. She was likely to be at home, and Bob, her husband, would still be at work. Excellent timing.

Back in his car he sent Mary a text. The reply was almost instant. Come right up Bob would not be home for nearly two hours. Michael could feel his excitement build as he drove along the seafront past all the large and smaller hotels. How many assignations were going on in them at this moment, he wondered. Brighton could still be known as a dirty weekend place, and you didn't even have to wait for the weekend. Besides, he was going to his own assignation, and he didn't even need to pay for a room.

He passed The Grand Hotel which had once been bombed by the IRA in their attempt to blow up Margaret Thatcher. They didn't succeed, but she was dead now anyway, he thought sadly. He had admired her. She was marmite Maggie. Many loved her. Many did not. She was probably the one politician, male or female, that had ever divided the opinion of the country on such a scale. Nevertheless, possibly because of her background, she was a champion of the small businessman. Where was her like now? The government of today didn't care how many businesses and shops went under. All they cared about was human rights.

He passed the awful architecture of The Brighton Centre, and before he realised he was turning left up Rock Gardens towards Queens Park.

Mary's house was a large Victorian one complete with a balcony and a small private drive that overlooked the park. Bob and Mary had lived in it for nearly twenty years and Mary had it just how she liked it with its polished floors and fur rugs. Bob was very successful in IT, and Mary did not even need to work. She had previously had one or two small part time jobs, but more for something to do than anything else. He knew that she was bored. He was bored. Just two bored people together, he thought, as he parked his van, and then immediately parked any thought of Bob, her husband or Sharon, his wife.

Michael rang the doorbell, and Mary greeted him in an outfit that told him she hadn't just been doing the cleaning, and that he wasn't there to fit a plug.

'Quick lover,' she said softly grabbing him by his company badged polo shirt. 'We have about an hour before Bob comes home.'

Their old dog, Bess, a big black Labrador, appeared to open one eye, and then obviously deciding there was nothing to worry about, and as it was not her master, went back to sleep.

Michael did not need to be told twice as he climbed the stairs to the Promised Land. It was an erotic exotic heady mix, and Michael felt almost giddy as he mounted the stairs. Michael loved the excitement of their time together. The snatched moments. The naughtiness of Mary as her outfit demonstrated. He reached across to touch her nipple through the flimsiness of the material, but she pulled his hand away.

'Patience darling,' she said teasingly. 'Let's get you undressed first.'

She pulled the polo shirt over his head, and began to unbutton his heavy tool belt that carried his tester, pliers, and screwdrivers. 'Honestly, I don't know if it's like sleeping with Batman in his utility belt or one of the Village People,' she jested. She ran her hand provocatively over the shaft of a large screwdriver then lowered the belt to the floor. 'I can see you won't need one of these to screw me.'

Michael could not wait any longer, and pulled her to him. Their lips met and Michael drunk in her scent. Suddenly she pulled away as if she had been shot.

'What?' Michael asked. 'What's up?'

Mary put her finger to her lips. 'Just heard Bess give a small bark. She only ever does that for Bob. She's like an early warning system.'

Michael looked quizzical, but he didn't want to stop now. He couldn't stop now.

Mary wandered over to the window and peered around the open curtain. 'Oh my God!' she exclaimed. 'It is Bob. He's home early. Thank God we didn't close the curtains. Quick, get out of the bedroom, but you won't have time to get downstairs. You don't want to meet him on the way down.'

Michael quickly put on his shirt and picked up his tool belt as he was unceremoniously dumped out of the bedroom.

In what appeared to be no time at all Michael heard a key in the door, and then Bob entered and looked straight up at Michael on the landing.

'Oh hello Bob,' Michael said, barely looking up and engrossed in what he was doing, as he knelt down examining the landing electrical socket outlet in his hand that he had just taken off. 'I think I've got a new one in the van. Don't touch it. It's still live,' Michael continued casually. 'I'll go and get one.'

Michael reached across and took his test lead from the tool belt that lay adjacent to it, as the bedroom door opened, and Mary appeared dressed in a simple white top and long floral skirt.

'Oh. Hi love,' she said quietly looking down at Bob. 'You're home early. Do you want a cup of tea? I was just about to make Michael one. Lucky he was in the area. Went to plug the hoover in earlier and it didn't work. Think Michael's cheap at only the price of a cup of tea.'

~

Michael wasn't sure if he should have laughed or cried as he sat down at his notebook computer and opened the Business Accounts software package. The accounts were even worse than he thought, and the order book for future work did not exactly fill him with confidence. He really was in trouble. Or was he? He thought back to the episode earlier with Bob and Mary. It was lucky that they had both managed to keep cool heads and Bob had not suspected a thing. Perhaps it was the danger that excited him. Well perhaps a little bit, he had to admit. But there was much more to it than that.

He glanced down at the accounts again. Why did everything come down to money? Perhaps The Beatles had been right, it couldn't buy you love. Nevertheless, you needed money to sustain it and enjoy it. If he had to part from Sharon, and if he had to give her half, he would lose an awful lot and not be left with anywhere near enough to enjoy life with, let alone just survive. Mary, he knew, was also very dependent on Bob. The prospects of an extremely messy divorce, would be that she would have to fight for every penny, and force Bob to sell their jointly owned home. It didn't bear thinking about. There had to be a way. It was money keeping them apart.

Michael closed down the accounts. He didn't want to be

any more down. He wanted to be with Mary. There had to be a way. There must be a way. There was a way. A way that he had already established. All he had to do was research that way. He opened his Internet browser and began typing in simple short sentences to help him in his quest to discover just how many persons went missing or were murdered on cruise ships.

Michael glanced up at the carriage clock which sat on one of the shelves within their lounge. It was a survivor from their marriage. Perhaps the only survivor. It had been a wedding present from Sharon's father. It had been expensive at the time and if he remembered correctly that type of clock had been quite fashionable. Michael had always wondered how her father afforded it and why did her father choose it in the first place? They were better suited as retirement presents. It had never occurred to Sharon that it might have been stolen, and it continued to hold pride of place in their flat. He noted the time and realised that Sharon was due home.

Michael thought of printing out the pages from one of the websites he had found, but thought better of it. No, he must not ever leave anything lying about that might provide a clue or evidence. Instead he bookmarked the Cruise Ship Missing site that listed missing person after missing person. All ages and both sexes. A short description of each missing person describing the month and year, the ship, and how they came to be missing. Their name was a highlighted hyperlink that could be clicked on for more details. The site, to Michael, seemed to be one of hope. For it appeared that the relatives might take comfort if their loved ones were listed as missing as there was always a remote chance that one day they might just turn up and walk in the door. The reality, for many, if not all, was that it was obviously unlikely, as they had been missing for a number of years. Nevertheless, and Michael laughed at his own joke when he thought it, 'Stranger things happen at sea.'

However, it did not take Michael long to also discover that when he clicked on the hyperlink, which was the missing persons name, that many of the people were now presumed dead and so their file had been moved to the Cruise Ships Death website.

Michael shook his head. It was unbelievable. Missing, but not murdered, but just simply now presumed dead. The answer was staring him in the face. It was time to plan properly. The seeds were now firmly sown.

Michael allowed himself the luxury of thought as he moved to close down his computer. How much longer would it be before they closed his business down? Suddenly he stopped and thought better of it. You could never be too careful. He went into the computer's settings and changed the password for the computer to a new one. A new password that comprised of letters and numbers, and upper and lower case letters.

Satisfied he sat back and allowed himself to dream of Mary. To dream of what might be. It was almost a nightmare with a happy ending, he smiled to himself. Surely he couldn't be thinking it, but he was. He could picture it clearly. He and Mary sailing into the proverbial sunset on this great big boat looking down over the railings at the stern of the ship towards the wash. And there, hundreds of feet below them in the water, was Sharon treading water, and waving at them furiously. They were both looking down towards her. Their arms around each other, and they were laughing. Laughing together as they looked down at her. The sound of Sharon's voice was lost to the sound of the waves, and the ship; she shouted up at them in desperation, as meanwhile the boat pulled further and further away.

SIX

Sharon pressed the button two times to increase the speed, and immediately felt the need to move her feet faster in order to keep up with the running machine. At this pace she still had another twenty minutes to go in order to keep up with her exercise programme. She glanced at the empty treadmill next to her and wiped her brow. Who was the wit, she thought, who once said that women don't sweat they only perspire? Still no pain, she told herself, and knew that she wanted to be in good shape for her trip to Spain with the girls. It was a long weekend. A kind of let your hair down and lock up your sons, affair. Not that she presumed anything like that would ever go on, but you could always live in hope. No it was for a bit of a laugh really and they were all getting a bit long in the tooth for it, but even so it was at least a break from her monotonous life with Michael. Even a trip to a North Korean Labour Camp would have probably been a welcome respite.

She glanced at herself in the gym's floor to ceiling mirror in front of her and was actually quite pleased with her reflection. The years, she thought, had been kind. Nearly fifty and still in good shape. Bloody good shape if she said so herself. She always wanted to look her best and keep trim. She still cared how she dressed and what she looked like. Nevertheless, Sharon knew that the secret was to portray a youthful look, but not pretend that you were young and 'down with the kids'. Although she was not sure what that meant? No, it was a fine female balance that she hoped she had achieved. She had for some time been considering cutting her long blonde hair, but women certainly seemed to keep it longer for longer these days.

No. She nodded at her reflection she was satisfied with how she had it now. At least for the moment, but she knew that she did not want to overdo her workouts. She wanted to be skinny, but not stringy. Her appearance had always been her pride and joy, and Sharon would have always been the first one to admit that she was nearer to beauty than brains. Well, perhaps not beauty. Not in the traditional sense anyway. Nevertheless, she was certainly a woman who knew how to make the most of herself. Even her close friends would have been shocked to see how different she looked without her makeup. Sharon would never dream of venturing out of their flat without her makeup on, and that included just popping up to the local shops.

Certainly most of her leisure time was devoted to pampering and conditioning herself, and she always knew that she took far more notice of her Body Mass Index than the Financial Times Index. To be fair, she thought, grooming had been her way of life ever since she had tried to make her own money. At sixteen she had left school and gone to Brighton Technical College in Pelham Street, to learn hairdressing, and successfully qualified. Over the years she had worked for several salons and developed her own loyal customer base. However, it wasn't until she had met Michael, and with his urging and encouragement, she had thought about opening her own business. Michael had even helped her find the premises and project managed it as the former grocery store converted into a hairdressers that had been named not very originally, 'Sharon's Salon'.

In the beginning it had made sense. Michael had his own business, and then she had hers. Double the income. Double the fun. Well that had been the dream. The reality had been somewhat different.

She reached to the front of the running machine for her water bottle and took a swig. Immediately she glanced back to her reflection in the mirror to see an athletic guy, a decade or more her junior approaching from behind. She noticed that he glanced at her behind as he walked across, and she was grateful for its pertness. Perhaps the workouts were working.

'Anybody using this?' he asked, with one hand on the vacant machine next to her.

Sharon shook her head. 'No!' she panted, and wondered if her reddening was from her exertion or if she was blushing like some silly schoolgirl. Surely though, he hadn't needed to ask. It wasn't the norm, and besides why had he not gone straight on to the next but one machine that was also empty. Was she kidding herself? He could have actually even been up to twenty years her junior?

He looked across and smiled, and as if to answer her thoughts he said, 'This is my favourite machine. I always like to keep on this one so that I know the timing is always accurate, and not jump from machine to machine.'

Sharon felt a wave of disappointment. What was she

really expecting, she wondered? Why would a younger man as good looking as him look at her once yet alone twice. Besides, she consoled herself, in this town he was probably gay. What a waste.

'I don't really take it that seriously,' Sharon answered indifferently, and perhaps a little too quickly. My husband goes running around the streets, and he can't do it without his timing App.'

'Really?' He laughed as he pushed his foppish black hair from his forehead revealing his very attractive green eyes. 'You must have some kind of old man if he needs an App to time himself with you.'

Sharon looked across, and his boyish smile melted her, and she laughed. Why had she told him she was married? Had it been her defence mechanism kicking into place? Was it a subconscious warning to him to stay away from her? She was happily married. Correction, she thought, quickly, she was married. Was it a subconscious warning from her to warn him that she was married, and for him to take note of that if he still wanted to pursue her?

She watched as his canter got effortlessly faster. What the hell was she thinking about? He was only using the running machine next to her. He wouldn't have wanted to chase her even if he was on a running machine.

Grow up, she chided herself. Sharon you are nearly fifty you need to grow up. But that was the problem nobody in this town could grow up or indeed ever wanted to. It was the magic of Brighton. Brighton was the town where not only the town constantly reinvented itself, but so did the residents. Yes, as Michael said, it would always be a town to anyone who had been brought up there. They would never properly acknowledge that others called it a city.

It was populated by thousands of Peter Pans. Peters, Pauls, and Marys that never wanted to grow up. The town could have so easily be twinned with Neverland. Michael had thought that he had been clever in calling them the, 'hope I don't get old before I die generation.' Michael always laughed at his own little twist on words from the Who's lasting anthem. He had always been a fan of both the band and the solo work of Pete Townsend and seemed to love the darker side to some of the guitarist's songs.

Sharon had always considered that the Who were mainly a man's band. They weren't really her cup of tea even if they sung about one in the later years with the lead singer pictured drinking tea on stage. But then again that was now the voice of rock and roll. They were examples of them all, not just Brightonians, that nobody wanted to get old anymore. Everybody wanted to stay young forever. They were all wanting to live life to the full.

All the old groups were still performing and going strong. They were still selling out arenas and headlining festivals. Where was it all going to end? They all seemed to have been going forever, and The Who were no different.

Although Sharon never had their music on, Michael often played it on his phone. No, the only song of theirs that had struck a chord with her had been the Substitute one. Yes, she thought, as her legs began to feel a little weaker, she had also been born with a plastic spoon in her mouth. They had been poorer than she cared to remember. But then so had the rest of the neighbourhood, and those days were gone. Well they certainly were for her. Well as far as money was concerned. She and Michael were not exactly going to make the Financial Times rich list, but then again they did not need to rob the meter to pay Paul. No those days were back in her childhood. She wasn't sure if her shudder was the belt of the running machine or recalling those times. No, she didn't need to worry about bills as Michael had always taken care of them. Michael had always taken care of her like that. Well, when it had come to her welfare anyway. She couldn't fault him there. Not as a provider anyway. But emotionally she felt so barren. Of course, not having ever had children together probably didn't help. After all these years, there wasn't that common bond. Why, really, were they still together? Was it really still to do with money? Is that why they were still together? Was it that she had always been scared to be on her own and to try and make her own way? Was Michael her blanket and her protection from the hostile world out there? But that was exactly the point. There was a world out there. A big world that had passed her by. A big world that was passing her by. Obviously, as her legs were now telling her, she wasn't getting any younger. Was it all about money? Is that how in later years she would measure her life? Wouldn't that be a waste? Didn't she have a right to deserve more?

'No, my husband, as you put it,' she said quickly, and thought, yes he does look old compared to you, 'loves his tablet and smartphone more than me. They certainly get more attention than me.'

He looked across at her, but didn't say anything, and Sharon stopped speaking. What was she thinking? Why was she volunteering such information to a total stranger? Why was she volunteering such information to such an attractive stranger? She allowed herself to smile.

He smiled back and then replied, 'Do you think he's looking for an upgrade?'

Sharon laughed, and then answered sharply, 'Oh no. Not at all. He's not like that.' Why was she defending him, she wondered? Michael might be many things, but a womaniser he was not. He would probably need to go online to find out how to seduce a woman. No, Sharon didn't think she had anything to fear there. Especially nowadays, as Michael was always stuck in front of his notebook or tablet. She couldn't begin to remember the last time that they had made love or even the last time Michael had touched her. She even wondered if he ever thought about sex now like he had a long long time ago. But now those days were gone. Now she was sure that Michael would not have been able to find her erogenous zones unless they were on Google Maps.

Sharon glanced down at the timer; there was less than ten minutes to go before the machine automatically stopped. She was feeling breathless. Was that just from her running? She doubted it. Her heart was pumping. Did she want it to stop? Would she be glad when it stopped? Could she keep going?

She looked across and smiled. 'No. I don't think he's looking for an upgrade.' Her feet seemed to be moving as fast as her brain. The machine seemed to be running away with her or was she running away with herself. No matter. She didn't want to give up and stop the machine.

He appeared to notice as he effortlessly asked without a hint of breathlessness, 'Keep going. You are doing well. How long have you got to go?'

Sharon glanced down at the clock, 'About six minutes. Time to boil two eggs.'

He laughed. 'And I haven't even told you how I like my eggs in the morning.'

Sharon smiled again and felt her face light up. Was that an invitation? Was he teasing her? How should she answer? It was just fun wasn't it? When was the last time Michael paid her a compliment? A total stranger was flirting with her. A man much younger. Younger he might be, but it appeared he found her attractive. When was the last time Michael had found her attractive? It was making her feel good. Michael had not made her feel good for far longer than she cared to remember. But that was all it was banter, she consoled herself. She glanced down at the timer on the running machine that was ticking down. But that was it, she thought instantly. It was her life that was ticking away. Life was passing her by. She looked across hesitantly. He reminded her of a young Jean-Claude Van Damme, and he had obviously been working on his body. He was fit, and Sharon instantly nicknamed him, 'The Muscles from Brussels.'

'You're doing well. Keep going,' he encouraged her again.

Sharon concentrated as hard as she could and watched the timer tick down, and then suddenly it was all over. The machine came to a halt. Holding on to one of the sidebars she stepped off aware that she did not want an undignified exit. She went to wave goodbye, but he held up his hand and smiled.

'You look hot,' he said. 'I'll be finished on here in a few minutes. Why don't we both shower up and then go for a nice cool drink? By the way the name is Justin.'

'Justin,' Sharon grinned. 'I'm Sharon.'

SEVEN

Michael glanced up at the carriage clock. He had expected Sharon to be home by now, but no matter. She had probably bumped into one of her friends, and he decided to put her absence to good use. It was time that he could use wisely. Time that he could use without the worry of Sharon looking over his shoulder. Not that she really cared what he did. She hadn't cared for years. She was not worried at all, and probably never had been. He could have been there sitting looking at porn all night, and she wouldn't have noticed.

Michael laughed to himself. He did not need pictures. He needed a full blooded woman, and he had that in Mary. He had never met such a woman. Not that Michael was a man who played the field. He was a man who had never played the field. He had never played away. Never looked at another woman after he had met Sharon. Never looked at another woman when he wasn't even looking at Sharon, but Mary had changed all that. Mary had changed him.

The very thought of her made him feel excited. He looked down at his mobile phone and wanted to call her, but thought better of it. She and Bob would be sitting at home together now. Two people sharing the same house, but not sharing anything in common. It was the same with him and Sharon. It was probably the same the country over. To death us do part. And that is a long time. A very long time. Certainly if you had to wait for natural causes to take their course, and even then it might be you going first or by then you would probably be too old to care. Why wait for nature when you could give nature a hand? Michael wanted to get back to the Cruise Ships Missing site. Of course, many of the victims had been the unlucky victims of violent behaviour or assault, and he couldn't also help wondering how many were really genuine accidents?

Michael thought that because he had been with Sharon for so long now, what was right or wrong did not matter. They were probably like millions of couples all over the country that were together. It had seemed that way forever and unless one of them enforced a change it was probably likely to be forever. They were just one of those couples that ticked along side by side. Both probably knew that it wasn't that bad, but both equally knew that it wasn't that good. The alternative for most, with all the emotional and financial toll, was probably too radical, so couples just carried on day after day until other circumstances took over.

Michael now knew that he did want to change and influence the circumstances. Yes, he would never have changed things before, but he had Mary now. Mary had made him a different man. She had shown him that life could be fun and that it did not need to be mundane. Although what Mary would be like to live with full time, he wasn't quite sure? Would they see out old age together or just both drift into separate retirement homes? Well surely it was worth a try. He wanted to show Mary that he was worth being with. They both deserved it and really they both deserved each other. Now it was up to him to show her how they could be together. However, should she be his partner in crime? Should he involve her? Did he want to involve her? He wasn't sure. The best laid plans of mice and men, and he was sure he knew which category Sharon would put him in. She would probably have made some such witty comment, and issued him with yet another funny furry little nickname. No. He would show her. He would prove just how masterful he could be and just how decisive.

His mobile phone started to ring and the Dr Who ring tone got steadily louder. He looked down at the screen noting that the number did not show and had obviously been withheld. It was a trick that the two of them often used if Mary wanted him urgently. She would call him with a withheld number. Michael would answer his phone, and if Sharon was next to him, he would get angry and loudly speak into the handset. He would say that never in his life had he actually taken out a loan, and therefore how could they possibly pretend that he was owed some fantastic sum on the insurance that he was supposed to have paid to protect him should something unfortunate have happened to him. He would then terminate the call and moan to Sharon that when would these people learn, and when would they stop pestering him, and what an infringement it was.

He was sure that Sharon had never once guessed, but he and Mary had always chosen to play it safe. Perhaps that was part of the fun. Perhaps it helped to bring in a little excitement into his mundane world. Obviously, Mary's normal number was listed in his mobile phone correctly. Why should it not be? It would have been strange not to.

In the same way that he was sure that Sharon had both Bob and Mary's numbers stored in hers. That wasn't the clever bit. Mary had actually bought a second phone for such a purpose. It was automatically set to withhold the number each time so that it was not something that she had to remember to do. There could be no embarrassing, 'Oh I forgot to do it.' Sometimes it was a snatched call for a very short time. Others could be longer. He remembered when she had sent him an email with her new number on. He could remember how pleased he had been. It had been complete with a very sexy message of why she had bought the phone and what it would allow them to do, and what she was going to do to him, and how she could send naughty texts. The naughty texts that brightened up his day.

Michael reached for the phone. Of course, it could actually be one of those PPI companies that all seemed to have his number.

'Good evening Sir. Can I speak to Mr Saunders please?' The female voice sounded foreign and completely unrecognisable although Michael immediately recognised it.

'It's OK,' he answered swiftly. 'Sharon's out at the moment we can talk. Is everything alright?'

'Oh yes,' Mary immediately replied in her normal voice. 'Bob has just popped out, and I thought I would give you call. Wasn't that funny how Bob came home? I was so impressed with your coolness, and the taking off of the socket whilst just laying your belt down was brilliant. Bloody brilliant. Bob didn't suspect a thing.'

Michael felt himself swell with pride. But then again sometimes it was just Mary's voice that made him swell. Yes, he had certainly surprised himself with his coolness under pressure, but then again Mary knew how to tease him so that he almost felt like a pressure cooker fit to burst sometimes.

'Thought I would call you to tell you there was nothing to worry about, and I know how disappointed you must have been to have been cut off in your prime, so to speak. Thought I would make it up to you.'

'Really,' Michael said excitedly. 'When and how?'

'Well put it this way Bob's also helping.' Mary stopped talking for a short intense pause knowing that Michael would be perplexed, and then she continued. 'Well as Bob is doing the shopping I asked him to get a large pot of yoghurt. I think you can guess the rest.'

Michael certainly could. Mary found so many ways to make him happy. Happiness to him was not through his stomach, even if it included food.

'Well we don't want it to go off do we? Can you pop in tomorrow? Bob is out all day.'

Michael nodded enthusiastically whilst mentally trying to recall his work diary for tomorrow. Although he knew that he did not really want to be fitting electrical bonds when Mary had other bonds in mind. 'I'll see what I can do,' he stammered. 'It will be in the afternoon about three.'

'I will look forward to it my lover,' Mary continued seductively. 'I will be hot and ready.'

Michael picked up his computer tablet, and held the mobile phone between his ear and his shoulder, whilst also looking at the cruise site that he had just been studying. His mind was racing. He quickly remembered about one of the cases he had been reading about on the Cruise Ship Deaths website. It had caught his attention because the accident itself had involved running. Both he and Sharon ran, though generally not at the same time, as he liked to run along the seafront, and she ran indoors. Nevertheless, it set him thinking. They could always start running together. They did not really have any common interests. Perhaps they never had. Quite astounding that even their common interest was done separately.

The woman Michael had read about on the site who died was called Karen and she was only twenty six. She and her husband were on their last day of their honeymoon cruise. Her husband had claimed that high winds had blown her off the jogging track into the sea. Originally, it sounded plausible as they were both fitness fanatics, even though he did not report it until the early hours of the morning.

However, the police became suspicious as it was not that windy that night, and also Karen was not very tall. In fact, she wasn't even two feet higher than the railing. What was particularly interesting was that the bride's mother actually suspected that her daughter's new husband had financial difficulties. She had even suspected that her daughter's pear shaped engagement ring was not the real deal. The ring was to be his undoing. When the police interviewed him they noticed a mark on his face that could have been made by such a ring, as she fought for her life. He told them that he had hit his head on a gangway control box, although no blood could be found on the box, and photographs showed that it had no sharp protrusions that could have caused his wound. Further evidence continued to point to the husband as one passenger reported finding hair and a piece of earring. Another passenger on their table noticed that they argued, and her lack of social skills regarding which cutlery to use, angered her new husband.

When they found her body it was proven that she was actually alive when she hit the water and there was also evidence of foul play including strangulation. Her husband changed his story again.

Michael had found it both fascinating and frightening. It really showed that if a basic mistake was made then the simplicity and innocence of the incident could easily become more revealing. What if he missed something? What if he hadn't thought it all through properly? Did he need another pair of eyes to help him see it through? Should he tell Mary?

'Are you still there?' he heard Mary ask. 'Michael!'

Michael blinked. 'Yes. Yes. Sorry I was miles away.'

Mary laughed. 'You often are. Where were you this time?'

'On a cruise. Do you realise…?'

'Realise what?'

Michael took a deep breath. It was now or never. He settled back on the leather sofa, but the sound of the buzzer took his attention. He looked across at the carriage clock. 'I've got to go,' he said quickly. 'Sharon's home.'

Michael pressed the intercom, and as Sharon was walking up the stairs he couldn't help wondering where she had been. She was certainly late, and it would certainly be interesting if she said that she had popped in to see Bob and Mary.

'Hi,' Sharon said with a big grin on her face. 'I'm home.'

Michael was not sure if he should ask the question as he was not sure how he might deal with the answer if she pretended that she was at Bob's.

'Yes,' she volunteered. 'I'm later than I wanted to be. Popped into ASDA and bumped into Julie. She was in there getting her son, Louis, some of those ready meals so he can eat if he gets home from college and she's not home.'

'You certainly look like you've had fun,' Michael said grimly.

Sharon smiled and swayed. 'Yep, we ending up going to the West Quay, and having a right old gossip and giggle.'

'Really,' Michael said looking at the carriage clock.

EIGHT

'Hi,' Mary said sweetly to Sharon as she kissed her on both cheeks and hugged her. Of course Sharon could not see Mary's face harden as the two women embraced and pulled each other closer. 'Have you had a good week?'

Sharon smiled and her expression was one of delight. 'Yes. Yes,' she beamed. 'Very very good.'

'Oh great,' Mary smiled back. 'Let me get the drinks, and then you can tell me all about it. Go and grab those chairs over there.'

Sharon obeyed, and settled into one of the wooden chairs, and rested her elbows on it. The pub they were in was called The Slug and Lettuce. It was situated on George Street in Hove, the town immediately adjacent to Brighton. In recent years Brighton and Hove have even joined Councils and their own identities were somewhat muddled. Historically it had become a bit of a joke that a person who came from Hove was always correcting a person who accused them of coming from Brighton by stating, 'Hove actually.' Sharon had always lived in Brighton, but tonight she and the girls were meeting to discuss their holiday plans, and then they were going up to the Greyhound Stadium where there was a Motown night.

Mary joined her and placed a red highly decorated cocktail in front of her.

'Thanks,' Sharon said gratefully. 'Strange isn't it? All those years ago in the seventies when cocktails were popular, and now they're back in.'

'That's because they have discovered that by pretending to give you some great discount if you buy two, they in fact, have doubled their profit. Pubs like this aren't stupid. I wonder how much he is being paid.' Mary pointed at the DJ in the corner who stood in front of two mixing decks and his computer. He always seemed busy doing something as he studied the screen, and then put the headphones to his ears.

'Not much I don't suppose. He probably does it for his love of music if you can call this music.'

Sharon laughed. 'Yes it does make you feel old doesn't it; I remember when DJs were paid because they talked and made you smile. Don't really understand this lot, and how a DJ can be the star?'

'Well you can always pop down and ask old Norman he only lives just down the road. I guess he was the one that virtually started it all. Yes, Mr Norman Cook has come a long way from The Housemartins.'

'Well I see his wife sometimes in Waitrose. Think they are Mr and Mrs Normal nowadays. Old Fatboy is now grey and hardly a boy. Guess it comes to us all.'

'Oh please,' Mary said. 'It's not going to be one of those nights is it? Thought we were going to have fun, talk about the holiday, and then go clubbing? I'm sure some nice guy later will cheer you up.'

'I don't need cheering up thank you,' Sharon said defensively. 'I'm perfectly happy thank you.'

'Really,' Mary said lightly. 'You could have fooled me.'

Sharon twiddled with her straw. 'Don't judge me by your standards. I can have fun without having a man around. Life for me does not revolve all around men.' Sharon stared at a group of three men propping up the bar. Did she really mean that? She knew she always wanted a man around. She could not function without one. She had Michael. Her point exactly. Perhaps she had once enjoyed being with Michael, but that was a long time ago. Such a long long time ago. There was a time when he had both moved and excited her. She remembered some of the little things that he used to do. There was a time when they were together in the beginning when they would sometimes do the shopping together. In those days Michael could turn a dreary trolley push into something erotic. He would come up right behind her when she was bending over one of the cold food cabinets and whisper to her how hot he felt and what he was going to do to her when she got home. Sometimes he would ask her to leave her knickers off when they went shopping. He was always coming up with ideas. Often the bags never did get unpacked. Well not straight away. They would leave them defrosting in the hall as a trail of clothes led to the bedroom and they melted together on the bed. It was always short but intense.

Nowadays, Michael would not ever dream of coming shopping with her let alone trying to seduce her amongst the frozen veg. It was her that was frozen or frigid now. Her feelings and emotions frozen in time, either on hold or gone away. The only shopping that he did now was online, and Sharon always thought you did not get the same touchy feely experience when buying off the web. It was not the same as handling the goods, but his touchy feely days had been shoved firmly in to touch. Michael was no longer interested in touchy feely whether it was shopping or her.

'Hi.'

'Sharon looked up. It was Julie standing in front of her. Julie was both tall and blonde. She was in her early fifties, but did not look it. She was the only one of them that was single. She was officially single as her decree absolute had just come through. She had been married to an Arab, and had a young teenage son called Louis, who was the product of both cultures. Although she was no longer married she was certainly not in any hurry to get into another relationship despite the other two sometimes urging her on.

As if on cue Mary said quietly, or at least as quietly as she could, against the music, 'What about those three over there. You have first pick, Julie.'

'Do you mean, The Good, The Bad, and The Ugly?' Sharon quickly commented. 'If that's the best we can do I'll get my coat.'

'You didn't wear one,' Mary laughed. 'But I bet they will look better when you've had a couple.'

'Please,' Sharon pleaded.

'And you've got Michael to go home to,' Julie chipped in.

'Don't remind me. I came out to forget and have a good time. Besides I thought we were going to discuss our long weekend.'

Both the other girls smiled, but Mary's smile faded fast, as she added, 'Let's get down to it, and then we can get down to the real business when we get to the club.

The three sat discussing different dates with both Julie and Mary consulting their phones. Sharon used her pocket diary.

'That's settled then,' Mary said two drinks later. 'The Thursday before Sharon's birthday, and we will go to Spain. Both the other girls nodded in agreement. 'Now we can get down to the real business. Let's walk down and get a cab.'

The three of them arrived at The Greyhound Stadium. Every last Friday of the month the complex held what they called a Motown night. Obviously, there is no dog racing on that night, and the front terrace facing the track became the smoking area. There was a separate dance floor and a DJ in each of the two bars, and the music ranged from a lot of the early Motown music to some Northern Soul. It was a venue that attracted a wide range of ages. The clubbers literally could be anywhere from their late twenties up to their early sixties. It was popular because it catered for the older 'not ready to stay at home and haven't lost it, or at least, think I haven't lost it' brigade. It also catered for the single again crowd, or even those that pretended they were single, if only for a few hours.

Some of the labels were a little unfair and some had even called it a meat market or dogs at the dogs. Realistically, it provided an outlet that suited all ages. It was somewhere to go for the older person. For some it was like stepping back in time in more ways than one, because Brighton is a town or city that few move away from. Many people even met others there that they had gone to school with probably over a quarter of a decade or greater before. Many of the punters were married and many of the married women went there to have a chat with their friends, have a drink and a dance, and then straight home. Some might even enjoy a brief flirt, but all in all it was mainly harmless fun.

The three girls went in with linked arms, almost feeling

a brief floatation back to their youth as if they were The Pink Ladies entering Rydell High in *Grease*. Julie went to the bar to order the drinks as the other two surveyed the scene.

'Not too busy at the moment is it?' Mary said. 'Mind you it's a bit early. Should fill up.'

'Oh definitely,' Sharon nodded, as the DJ announced the next song. It immediately got her attention, and she turned to Mary. 'Oh I love this one.' It was Freda Payne singing 'Band of Gold'.

It was one of Sharon's favourites. It was an evergreen song, but how many people had actually studied the words. Was it about a frigid woman or an impotent man? Or as Freda Payne herself thought, was it about a woman who was a virgin or sexually naïve? Whatever the true meaning Sharon loved it, and the song brought so many memories back. Most were painful ones. She remembered when she had married Michael. The ring had great significance and she felt then she had someone to look after her and comfort her. At first he had been so attentive. Nothing had been too much trouble. He took her on romantic picnics. He took her to art galleries and museums, and told her about things that she had no idea about. He made her feel special. He was so knowledgeable and she felt almost honoured that he had chosen her. She was completely under his charm. It was as if he had magical powers. It wasn't until much later that she realised that that was the beginning of Michael trying to manipulate her or Michael trying to control her. It had been a battle of wills. A battle that was still going on and had been for a number of years. However, now they were both in no-man's land. Both, even after all these years, still vying for position.

She often wondered why she had never walked out. But then again she had never really had anywhere else to go, and she was always scared of being on her own. But Michael had also always been so demanding. That was why the sex was probably so quick. It was always just for his gratification and satisfaction. They had never really made love. It had always been how Michael wanted it. It had always been where Michael wanted it, and when she rarely declined he accused her of being frigid.

Mary and Julie continued to sing about the significance of the wedding ring, in unison over her shoulder.

Sharon turned and smiled. She guessed all three of them were somewhat in the same boat. Julie was divorced, and she no longer wore her wedding ring. Mary was stuck with boring Bob. Yes, he was a very nice and clever man, but Sharon could not imagine a less passionate man. It had always amazed her that Mary and Bob had got together. Mary was a very sexy woman who gave out sexual chemistry even now in her later years. Bob looked like a man born to wear slippers and a cardigan.

'Wow!' Mary said suddenly. 'Have a look at him over there. He is fit.'

Sharon looked up as she realised that the man was coming towards them.

'You'll have to fight me to get him!' Julie added quickly. 'He could make me happy again, if only for a night. He's coming towards us.'

Sharon wasn't sure what to do as she fidgeted from one leg to another like an awkward teenager as the guy stopped a few yards short.

'Hi Sharon,' he said.

Sharon noticed that the other two stood there stunned like bunnies caught in headlights. 'This is Justin,' she announced. 'We met in the gym.'

NINE

It was Friday night and Michael knew that he had the evening to himself. There had been a time when Friday night meant something. What did they say, 'You can beat an egg. You can beat a carpet. But you can't beat Friday night.' Well nowadays Friday to him was just another night of the week, and because his business was struggling he often worked Saturdays. In fact, he worked them more often than not, because it gave him a chance to do the jobs for his customers who were out because they worked during the week.

Gone were the lay-ins and urges that had once been satisfied every Saturday. He glanced at the carriage clock and realised not only was it her centre piece, but it seemed to be the centre piece to his life. All he ever seemed to do was gaze at that bloody clock. Where was she? What was the time? When would she be home? How much time did he have before she was home? He remembered long ago when there had been a time when he had cared where she was. A time when he worried incessantly where she was. In truth at times he had almost driven himself sick with worry. The nerves tore at his stomach, and as he waited for her each minute had seemed like an hour. She hadn't known what she did to him when she was late home. She had never realised how much he cared for her. How she drove him mad with frustration simply because he cared. He recalled one such time many years ago when they had just got married when he had flown into a rage when she got home. She had returned much later than she had promised, and this was long before the time of mobile phones. He had spent hours worrying while she spent more time with her friends. She was having fun. She was safe. How did he know that? He had no way of contacting her. She was so precious to him. Hadn't she known that? Hadn't she always known that? Why did she do this to him? Didn't she know how much it hurt him? He was beside himself by the time she had come home. He hadn't meant to hurt her, and it had all happened so fast. Then there had been the tears. They had both cried, and he had promised her he would never ever do anything like that again.

They had gone to bed and made love. It had seemed to make everything alright. It had all been forgotten, or so he had thought. In the morning she had apologised to him for staying out late. She said she didn't realise what it did to him and how it made him behave, and if she was not late he would then not worry. She had promised never to be late again. That was years ago. Oh how it had changed. Now he was hoping she would be late. He had a lot to do.

What a difference two or three decades make, Michael thought, as he prepared for his evening. An evening on his own watching what he wanted to watch, and when he wanted to watch it. Perhaps most men might save a DVD to watch on their own when their wife went out. A

DVD that their wife didn't know about, and Michael was no different. He had saved this one for such an occasion. He went to the brown package that he had hidden from her and opened the cardboard sleeve. Carefully he slid out the plastic casing. To some, anyway, the cover might have surprised them for it did not show busty blondes or brunettes in various stages of undress. It did not have 'Censored' on it or say 'Adult Material'. It did not promise Danish Delights or Swedish Swingers. There were just two words for the title, *Deadly Honeymoon*.

No this was not exactly the kind of film that most men kept from their wife. The front cover pictured a happy smiling couple through a porthole. It was in reality a romance that had gone wrong. It was about a couple who had not even completed their honeymoon before disaster struck, and one of them was dead. Michael studied the cover he did not recognise any of the stars as it was a low budget made for American TV movie. Nevertheless, he was very much looking forward to watching it because he had also read the book, on which it was based or at least thinly disguised. The book was the real story of a young beautiful couple who were on their honeymoon when the husband, George, vanished. The book was subtitled, *Inside the Honeymoon Cruise Murder*. The case itself had gripped America and captured the public's imagination, and it raised many questions over many months about the dark side of the cruise industry. It was not just the case which was most shocking, but more regarding the cavalier, and 'what do you expect us to do' attitude of both the cruise lines and the authorities. It became quite apparent from this case that cruise lines need to do little to defend themselves as they did not need to do so. They were a powerful monolith that rolled on for the most part unregulated, and backed by their lobbying arm the ICCL. It seemed to Michael that the cruise lines had an almost standard defence to deflect any blame away from themselves. It was never their fault, and it was much easier to muddy the waters and blame the victim, whether that person was male or female, alive or dead. In this case the cruise line had even launched a website detailing what they said were the 'Top Ten Myths' regarding their handling of the George Smith case.

It was obvious that a family would be devastated if they lost a loved one on a cruise. That person was only going on a holiday. A holiday or honeymoon of a lifetime. It would not be expected that they lost their life. Therefore, was it not obvious that because the family had to not only handle the sudden death, but also find the energy to fight to find the truth, and find the funding to pursue a legal path, that most families settled with the cruise line, and the case just faded away.

It had certainly given Michael food for thought and been an eye opener for him as he sat in his van reading the book in between jobs. It was obvious that as the cruise industry was worth billions per year, it was extremely powerful and almost a law unto itself. This was actually helped because if a crime happened at sea it did not infringe on the peace or dignity of the country that the ship was visiting as defined by maritime law. What was more important was that the boat sailed on time and not held as a crime scene so that all the thousands could enjoy the holiday they had paid for.

Obviously on the ship when George Smith had disappeared rumours had spread amongst the passengers and crew. Therefore, to try to keep a lid on things the next day, when the boat sailed into the twilight, the captain of the ship, who was coincidently named Michael, announced over the ship's intercom system that they had been working with the local authorities to investigate whether a man may have gone overboard the previous night. He then went on to say that they hoped to have the issue resolved shortly, and that they all should enjoy the beautiful sunset.

Michael took the disc out of the box and opened the tray in the DVD player. He had recently purchased it as it automatically up-scaled the picture to near HD quality. He was absolutely sure that Sharon would not be home anytime soon, but just in case he slid the cover into his man bag so if she did make an unexpected appearance he could easily switch the channel.

Michael went into the kitchen to make himself a tea, and then allowed himself the luxury of a chocolate bar as he settled on the sofa to watch it. Firstly, he had to fiddle with the remote controls so that the picture changed from the normal cable one to the DVD screen. Sharon found it awkward to do and to switch back again, but as she rarely watched DVDs it did not appear to matter much.

Michael pressed the desired button, and within a few seconds the music began and Michael followed the plot intensely. He had to admit it wasn't the best acting he had seen, but he found himself comparing it to the book and recalling some of the more startling facts. Of course, it only loosely followed the story of the actual case, of a wealthy man meeting a very determined girl from, as the Americans would say, 'the wrong side of the tracks.' Nevertheless, the Lifetime Movie Network, had used both artistic licence and supposition in an attempt to make the movie very dramatic, knowing that the watching public would draw direct comparisons to the actual case that involved the disappearance of George Smith.

Michael tried hard to concentrate, but found his eyes drooping. He was having trouble staying awake. It had been a long week and he was only too well aware that he had to get up for work again in the morning. His head began to nod and then before he realised it he was asleep.

Sometime later he awoke with a jolt. He wasn't even sure where he was when he first woke up and then slowly focused on the room and then his mobile. He picked it up and noticed that he had a new text message from Mary. He quickly read it.

'Hi lover. In a cab now on way home. Boring night. Left on my own. Julie talking to some bloke that looked like Rod Stewart. Sharon very much talking or drooling over some bloke she's nicknamed Muscles from Brussels. Text me tomorrow. Would really like to see you if you can make it. Let's meet up. I will make it worth your while.'

Michael glanced at the clock and realised that the text had been sent nearly two hours ago. Mary would be home now. Home now in bed with Bob. Bored now in bed with Bob. Well that would not be the case for ever. It would not be the case for much longer. Not if it all went to plan. Up until then he would have to satisfy himself with seeing Mary when he could. He would have to make the snatched moments count. He could not afford to be careless.

He looked at the clock and then realised that Sharon was still not home. Where was she now? What was she up to? He was surprised to think that he did not really care. In fact if she did run off with someone it could save him a lot of trouble. But it would not make the break clean. They would still be tied to each other and after what he knew would be a messy divorce he would still owe her half of everything he had. Everything he had worked for. Oh the 'Muscles from Brussels' could have her, but he doubted that would be the case. He was not that lucky. Michael knew he needed to continue researching, thinking, and planning.

Michael felt his eyes grow heavy. He had to be up for work in only a few hours. He hoped Sharon would not wake him up when she came in. Knowing her she would probably sneak into the spare bedroom and tell him in the morning that she had done so because she did not want to wake him up. Did she think he was an idiot? Did she not realise that he knew she did it in the hope that if she left him fast asleep in his own bed then he would have no idea of what time she got in? Oh how some things never changed? The games over the years. Well soon the game would be over. They would play no more. Soon it would be checkmate to him.

Michael lifted himself up from the sofa. He was on automatic pilot. He reached for the remote control and turned the television off, and sleepily dragged himself off to their bedroom.

TEN

Sharon woke up and immediately realised that her surroundings were different. This was not where she normally woke up. She felt the bed as if she expected to feel another body lying next to her, but there wasn't one. She was on her own. She opened her eyes and tried to focus. The digital alarm clock blinked back at her with an unnecessary brightness, and she reached across and pressed the dimmer button on the top. Was it her being dim she wondered, as she began to piece together events of the night before?

The room slowly came back into focus. She recognised the pale blue and white paintwork and beach and boat theme that she once had it decorated in to please Michael. She knew how much he loved the beach and boats. She knew how much he loved naval things, and she had tried to combine them. She had always tried to please Michael in the same way that she had always tried to please her father, but now she knew that she had probably failed on both counts.

When she had the room first done he liked it and he had praised her, but that was typical of Michael. Sometimes he would be full of praise, and then he could be highly critical. It was as if he was trying to boost her confidence and then almost immediately take it away again. It was like that in the beginning until she was often unsure of herself. It had made her see how much she needed Michael, and how useless she would be on her own, and how lucky she was to have him.

At least that was how it had once been, and it had been that way for a long long time until she almost felt that she had no personality of her own. She had heard Michael talk about the military, and he was always watching historical programmes. She remembered one that he had watched about The Legion, and what all the new raw recruits went through in their basic training, and how gruelling and humiliating it was. Michael had told her that it was basically what all military training was based on. They would do their best to break a person, and when they had them at near breaking point they would build them back up to what they wanted them to be.

But that was what it had been like for her. She had been at near breaking point, but she could never understand if that was because of Michael or how much worse off she would have been if she did not have him. She had settled for an easy life. She wanted to please him and like all people she loved praise, and Michael could also be very generous. He could also be very charming to her and all her friends. Everybody had liked Michael when they first met, and they all seemed to fall under his spell. There were also times when he could become very angry and irate, but that was always when they were on their own. He would lose his temper and sometimes he would pick up something and throw it. It would normally be the first thing at hand. It wasn't that often, but when he did he would always be sorry. He would be beside himself with regret and he would beg her forgiveness, and he would promise her that he would never do it again. Sharon could always see that he was genuinely regretful and she loved him. She had always loved him then whatever the circumstances. She had to forgive him. How could she not?

Over the years his temper had got less and less, and she also realised that she had become stronger. Perhaps there was never too much wrong and now they were older and supposedly wiser. Perhaps their partnership was now much more of an equal match. She tried to picture a future with Michael, and found it hard, but then again she tried to picture her life without Michael, and that was just as difficult. Life was complicated, and she realised that her head this morning was certainly not up to thinking about anything heavy. She slowly got up and sat on the edge of the bed and noticed her discarded clothes on the floor. At least she had managed to remove them, and just jumped into bed in her bra and knickers. The spare room, she admitted, was handy. She had slid in silently in the silly hours, and at least by her sleeping here she was not in any danger of waking Michael up. She was aware that he would need to get up for work and would not have been best pleased if he had been woken. But perhaps best of all she was sure that he would have had no idea of what time she had got in.

Suddenly her bag which was lying next to her discarded skirt started to ring. It took her several seconds to realise that it was her mobile phone ringing. Should she leave it, she wondered? She did not feel much like talking. She reached for the bag and rummaged in it for her phone. Her standard ringtone got louder as if demanding attention. She finally managed to find her phone and pulled it out of her bag. She recognised both the name and number. It was Mary.

'Hi Sharon,' Mary said in a very awake voice sounding like she had been up for hours. 'You weren't asleep were you?'

Why did people always ask that Sharon wondered when they called early morning? It was as if they realised that they shouldn't really call as there was a danger of waking the recipient up, but then again they couldn't really resist, and if the person was asleep, too bad.

'No. No I wasn't,' Sharon said loudly, then lowered her voice as her head still hurt. 'No I was awake. I was just getting up.'

'I bet you were still dreaming,' Mary said teasingly. 'I can't say I blame you. He was such a hunk. I'm almost jealous. What happened after I left? I didn't want to get in your way. What happened? Where did you go? What time did you get in?'

Sharon thought quickly. She wasn't feeling her best and she certainly did not feel with it. She needed at least a couple of coffees before she could even begin to function. 'What is this?' she said lightly. 'Twenty questions.'

Mary laughed. 'Oh my dear. Please tell. Please give me all the gory details and don't leave anything out, and I mean everything.'

Sharon knew that Mary was a friend. They had been friends for many years, but she was unsure of how much to tell her. Mary was the kind of person that wanted to know everything about everybody, but when it came to herself she almost became a closed book, but defended herself by saying that there was not anything to tell. Sharon had often thought otherwise. Often without proof, but as the years passed Sharon had become wiser or at least she thought she had. But perhaps her behaviour last night had proved otherwise. Perhaps there really was no fool like an old fool, and she was about to compound it.

Sharon laughed. 'We did stay until the end when it wound down, and then I shared a taxi home.'

'With Julie?' Mary immediately seized on a suspicion of who Sharon shared the cab with like an interrogator.

Sharon thought for a moment. It was no good lying to Mary and telling her it was with Julie, for before she knew it Mary would be off the phone to her and calling Julie before Sharon had had a chance to warn her. Not that there was too much to warn Julie about, but if Mary knew she was not telling the truth Mary would put two and two together and come up with her usual six. Sharon decided that she could be economical with the truth, but she would not lie. She decided to make Julie the object of questioning. It couldn't hurt Julie as she was single. She had a right to do what she wanted to do. She was an adult, and it was up to her.

'No. Julie was talking to that bloke with the spikey hair. You know, the one I nicknamed 'Rod the Mod. She was really engrossed. I'm not sure if she went for a coffee with him or went back to his place, as I know they couldn't go back to hers because of her son.'

'My. My.' Mary quipped. 'She is a dark horse our Julie.'

'Oh I'm not saying she was going to do anything,' Sharon quickly defended her friend feeling guilty. 'I know she really liked him though.'

'Well it seems I missed all the fun after I left.'

Sharon bent down and picked up her skirt and top. It reminded her of her teenage years when her clothes used to be constantly scattered all around her bedroom. It would drive her mother to distraction until in the end her mother just used to close the door and let her get on with it and pretend all was well on the other side of the door. But then again her mother had always been good at pretending all was well.

Her mother had always pretended that all was well. She had always pretended that she was happy with her lot. Perhaps, Sharon realised, this was where she got it from. Had she pretended for too long? Had she really managed to persuade herself that she was happy? Life had been complicated then. Then she had married Michael, and he hated mess, and he had made her feel like the teenage girl she was trying to run away from. Everything had its place with Michael. It all had to be in order. Why did everything have to be so complicated? Why couldn't life be fun? Why couldn't she have some fun?

'You're not going to get away with it that easy,' Mary said. 'Are you still there?'

Sharon found herself feeling defensive. She knew Mary would not let go. Mary knew what she thought she wanted. Mary was well known as a woman who got what she wanted.

'So how did you get home then? What time did you get in? Who were you with? Did you share a cab with him? Did you go back to his place? What happened?'

Sharon's head began to swim. She had still not had the first coffee she promised herself let let alone the second. How was she supposed to function? She just wanted to get Mary off the line, but she did not want to say the wrong thing. She wasn't sure if she fully trusted her friend. She didn't know why. She had told her secrets in the past, but perhaps it was better to hold back now. After all she did not know how things would progress. Perhaps it was best not to lie, but not necessarily tell the whole truth. If she told Mary a little she might go away. She had once confided in Mary, but it appeared that Mary always took Michael's side. Everybody always said how charming Michael was. Besides, recently Mary had seemed more distant if not a little cold towards her. She had grown closer to Julie.

'Well,' Mary said. 'I'm waiting.'

Sharon thought for a second. 'Well we did share a cab. I dropped him off on the way.'

'Him. Do you mean the hulk? The Muscles from Brussels as you called him.'

Sharon realised that by calling him that it sounded so superficial. 'You mean Justin?'

'Just-in. Yes I bet he was last night.' Mary laughed at her own little joke. 'Was it good? Is he as big elsewhere?'

'Please,' Sharon said firmly. 'I dropped him off and nothing happened. I told you.'

'Did you arrange to see him again? Don't worry if you did. I can cover for you. I can be your alibi.'

Sharon thought better of it. 'No, nothing happened and nor will it? Now if you don't mind I need to get on. I've got a lot to do.'

'I bet you have,' Mary teased. 'Don't worry you can tell me all about it when you want to.'

'There really is nothing to tell.'

'OK. I get the message,' Mary said grumpily and then changed her tone. 'Are you on your own? Did Michael go to work?'

Sharon suddenly realised that she did not know. Michael could have overslept or changed his mind, and not gone to work. She didn't know. She had slept in a different room although she did not want to admit it to Mary. She did not want Mary to know all her secrets or even feel sorry for her. She decided to buy time as she opened the bedroom door and went towards the Master bedroom where the master slept. She hoped he was not still sleeping there. The bed was empty. He had gone. Relieved she said, 'No he's gone to work. I am not expecting him home until late afternoon.'

Sharon terminated the call and went into the kitchen. She went over to her coffee machine. It had been a present from Michael. He knew she loved coffee and he could be so thoughtful sometimes. While she was waiting for it she decided to go into the lounge and put on Sky News just to see what was happening in the world.

Within a minute she realised she could not get to the television channel. It was stuck on the DVD one. Michael must have been watching a DVD. She hated the complexity of it. Why was everything so complicated nowadays? Why hadn't Michael changed it back when he had finished watching it? She picked up the DVD remote and pressed the Open button. The draw slid open and before she could press any button it automatically slid shut, and the music started.

Briefly she wondered what Michael had watched last night. Some, interesting documentary, she suspected, on naval warfare or some such thing. Well interesting to him. Then the movie title came up, *Deadly Honeymoon*. Sharon made a face it did not appear to be his usual kind of viewing. Interesting. She found herself settling down on the sofa as the movie began.

ELEVEN

Michael sat in his van gazing down at his tablet computer and anxiously looked at the dashboard clock. Mary was only a few minutes late. Not that it really mattered, but it would eat into the time that they had together. He wanted to get back home at a reasonable time, as if he had been working, so that Sharon would not be suspicious. Besides, he and Sharon were supposed to be going out this evening, and he realised that they would probably end up at the casino. She would be doing her thing which was roulette. He would be doing his thing which was Blackjack.

Michael mused that even that mimicked their respective personalities. Sharon was prepared to have a little flutter, and it was all on the spin of a wheel. It was all down to chance. She would leave it to Lady Luck. Michael was a man who did not like to leave anything to chance. Michael was a man who liked to think things through. He liked to think he was in control and he could influence the outcome. This was why his chosen game was Blackjack. He had read that it was the only game where you had a chance of beating the bank, and that was without even counting the cards. Of course, casinos won in any case, because the decision of the player was often based on a gut reaction or how much they had had to drink and not a rational one that should have been based on published recommendations of what to play in any combination. Michael was probably an exception when he was playing Blackjack. He always knew what action he would take with regard to what cards he had been dealt, whilst also taking into account what card the dealer held. Stand, double, split, or take were the words that rolled off the tongue. He would just indicate to the dealer by hand signals. He had it down to a fine art. He had memorised each reply automatically, and the risk and reward of each new hand and what that combination promised. It was not a method that was ever going to make him rich, and certainly not on the amount that he bet, but it enabled him to play, and play for some time. He enjoyed the thrill although he never won that much. Best of all, he rarely lost. Michael did not like losing. More times than not he would leave the casino with some winnings. It did not matter to him how much he had won. The most important thing of all was that he was walking out as a winner.

Michael looked out of the van window. He felt conspicuous in the van with his business name 'Saunder's Sparks' written on the side, along with the NICEIC logo, which is the regulatory body for the electrical contracting industry. Michael was not a man who had worried about marketing his business. All his business was generally repeat business from satisfied customers or recommendations from word of mouth. At least it had been up until now; but work was becoming harder to get, with the only bonus being that if he had down time then he could use it for up time with Mary.

Sharon had insisted that he had the van badged which was why he had not really wanted to bring it, but he couldn't have used the car today as he was supposed to be working. Besides Sharon might have needed their car. So the van it was.

It was a bright sunny day and it made him smile to think that even in the casino he and Sharon were divided as they were in life. Well soon they would be divided forever. Soon he could be with Mary.

He returned to looking at his tablet, and decided to kill time, and kill the anticipation of seeing Mary, of feeling Mary, by doing some more research. The pleasures of her flesh could wait although he could feel his excitement build. Mary did that to him. Just the thought. No other woman had ever done that to him.

Almost immediately he chanced upon an article on the Internet about what happens if a person dies at sea, and he wasn't shocked to learn that over two hundred people a year did just that. Again, it wasn't really that surprising, because many of the larger ships were really small towns at sea. Some of them held over six thousand passengers, and that was without the officers and crew. That was more people than his football team Brighton and Hove Albion used to get for their home games when they played at Withdean, before they moved to their posh new home the Amex.

That was a lot of people to feed. A lot of souls in one place, and of course it stood to reason that they might lose one or two souls on the way.

Michael had already read that the average age of cruisers went up depending on the length of the cruise. For only a week long cruise the average age was 49, and Michael thought interestingly that was Sharon's age now. It seemed almost too convenient. She fitted the demographic perfectly. Michael reflected that if the cruise lasted longer than a week, the average age shot up to 64, and he briefly wondered if Paul McCartney would want to write a new song about it. Things had certainly moved on from the time when then young Beatle had pictured and penned what 64 year olds looked like and did.

The next fact compounded how much more fun people were having as they got older. On the longer round the world cruises, the average age was over 75. Not really that astounding if you thought about it, because realistically you had to have both the time on your hands as well as money to be able to go on a cruise of that length, and that was mainly the retired, he presumed. Some of these cruises could be for over a hundred days. One hundred days, two people locked together was a long time. Perhaps if one passed away it was not always from natural causes he chuckled. Perhaps two people pushed together in the close confines of their cabin pushed one over the edge or the balcony so to speak.

It did mean, though, that the cruise line's crew were used to dealing with death. Death would have been part of their training. A death would not have been anything that unusual. At least a death that had been caused by natural causes.

What he did find interesting was the next bit. The codes and alerts that ships used in their announcements to alert crew to a problem, but not worry their passengers. In fact it appeared that their passengers would not even be aware that an emergency was happening. The most common warning seemed to be, 'Operation Bright Star.' This would be announced over the ship's intercom followed by the exact place where the medical emergency was taking place. Michael found the second announcement interesting, 'Operation Rising Star.' This would mean that the medical emergency was now over, and the passenger had died. Probably in other words don't bother rushing. Michael wondered who came up with these and was the 'rising' almost a code for rising up to the stars and the heavens.

He tried to think if he had ever heard any of these announcements on any of the cruises they had been on. The trouble was there was often a bombardment of information that most people generally switched off to.

Michael glanced down at his tablet and continued to read. Then, his mobile rang and he noticed it was Sharon calling. Should he answer it, he wondered? He glanced out into the car park, and there was no sign of Mary. He supposed he should do, otherwise she might keep trying to call him throughout the afternoon. He was parked and didn't need to be on hands free. But he would need his hands free for Mary this afternoon, he smirked. He decided to answer it. He hoped Mary would not interrupt them.

'Hi,' said Sharon pleasantly. 'Where are you?'

'Michael thought for a moment. 'I'm sitting in my van at the moment. I'm between jobs.'

'What time will you be home?'

Michael wondered where it was leading. 'Why?'

Sharon waited a few seconds before she spoke. She sounded a little nervous. 'Well I've just had Mary on the phone. Well, to be honest she's called a couple of times. She wanted to know what we were doing tonight.'

'Why?' Michael said for the second time. 'I thought we were going to the Casino, possibly. Am I wrong? When did she call?'

'Oh the last time only a few minutes ago.'

'Was she at home?'

'Probably. Don't know really. Why? Does it matter?'

'Oh no not really,' Michael said quickly. Just wondered.' He didn't want to draw attention to it, but why was Mary on the phone to Sharon when she should have been meeting him? Was that why she was late?

'Did you want to meet them? Go out for a drink?'

'Eh, not sure. Do you?'

Sharon sounded less than enthusiastic. 'Well I can always call her back and say you're not feeling that well.'

'Oh don't do that,' Michael answered trying to buy time. He needed to question Mary before he answered Sharon. Why had Mary seemed so keen to get the four of them all together? 'Just tell her that I'm a bit tied up on a job, and not sure if I might be a bit tired when I get in, but we'll let them know.'

Sharon agreed immediately, and Michael hung up and went back to his tablet. What was Mary playing at? He looked out of the window. It was still sunny and he knew that she would be along shortly. He could ask her then. At times he was still not sure of her. At times she was a mystery, but that perhaps was the buzz. She had a certain mystique. It was like being in some kind of film that you were never too sure where it was going to go. It kept you on the edge of your seat. It almost reminded him of that Michael Douglas thriller *Basic Instinct*. Yes, Mary certainly had something, and she brought out the basic instinct in him. Alhough, now perhaps, it was moving more towards *Fatal Attraction*.

He continued reading the article that he started earlier and smiled when he read that most ships have a morgue capable of storing up to ten bodies. The bodies are then generally unloaded at the next port of call, but only if the country is willing to accept it, and issue a death certificate which creates a large headache and a great amount of paperwork. This usually involves the relation or friend travelling with the deceased. Only when a death certificate has been issued does the deceased's home consulate get involved.

But the biggest nightmare of all appeared to be the costs to fly the body home. These costs are the responsibility of the family, and not the consulate or the cruise line. Apparently sometimes it is cheaper to fly a body home than fly a living person. Michael briefly wondered if some of airlines might not be missing a trick as they tried to get more and more add-ons to the cost of the basic flight. Yes, 'Dead Cheap Flights', had a good copywriter's ring to it.

Of course, some travel insurances did cover such a cost, and Michael made a mental note to go into the fine print when he purchased theirs. Obviously, he was hoping that there would not be a body to bring back, but nevertheless, if she was found drowned it would be silly to waste money doing the decent thing, when the insurance could have covered it in the first place.

He remembered reading that over 75 per cent of bodies that go overboard are never recovered. That meant that there was still a one in four chance that the body would be found either as part of a search and rescue operation or washed up at a later date.

However, Michael was sure that with a bit of forward planning, luck, and a good tide, he could influence the odds further. He decided that it might be useful to research currents, tides, and the depth of the sea, on the route that the cruise ship took.

Michael did not want to have the added worry of a body, but he did have to hand it to the son that was travelling with his mother on a world cruise who featured in the article. Unfortunately his mother died on the cruise 36 days into the 114 night cruise. Her son dealt with the paperwork and arranged to have her cremated at one of their port stops. Both of them re-joined the ship, and they finished it together, although his mother was obviously in an urn.

Michael was busy laughing to himself when there was a tap on the window. He looked up to see Mary above him. She smiled then looked to her left and right. There was no one near apart from a man walking his dog in the distance. She beckoned to him to get out the van and join her in her car. But before Michael had had a chance to move she unbuttoned her coat and opened it. Michael's mouth fell open. She was completely naked.

'Don't be shocked, lover,' she said softly. 'Let's get in my car and go to our favourite spot. I thought you would like me like this.'

Michael nodded. Words appeared to be failing him. Mary had done it again. She always liked to surprise him. She had certainly done that.

'Come on, lover,' she urged him. 'Let's go. I want you now.'

They got in her car and Mary did up her coat. 'Thought that would excite you. Thought that would get you going.'

'Yes....Yes,' he stammered. 'I even thought you might not come. Then I knew you would be late because Sharon called me.'

'Oh. Yes. Sharon.' Mary undid another button and watched Michael's eyes follow her hand. 'When you have satisfied me I'll tell you all about Sharon.'

TWELVE

Sharon was waiting for the little shiny ball to stop spinning. It was like her world at the moment. It all appeared in a spin. Very shortly the roulette wheel would slow and then the ball would stop, and she would reap the benefits of what she had placed her bet on. Alternatively, she reasoned, she could lose the lot. Life was like roulette, she thought to herself. How much you put on depended on what you were willing to risk, but nevertheless it could all be taken away and lost in a moment. One foolish move or thought and depending on your luck or judgement your life could instantly change. But if you did not try, and if you did not bet, you could not win. If you did not try you stayed exactly where you were. Was life really that simple, she wondered? Did you have control over your own life? Sharon was sure that she had never ever really felt fully in control. Was it time she took control? She was not getting any younger, but was she getting any wiser? She was beginning to believe in fate. But should she resign herself to it or try to influence it? Her mind certainly felt like it was a roulette wheel at the moment.

The little ball bounced and teased and finally stopped.

Sharon had lost. She couldn't even get the colour right. Would it mimic real life, she mused? What did she really have to lose?

Sharon put down her wine glass on the table provided and looked across at Michael who was playing Blackjack just feet away. What was the expression? Sharon could not remember, but in modern parlance, he looked like he had lost a twenty five pound chip and won a five pound one. All evening he had worn a glum expression, and Sharon was not sure if it was because he was with her or if there were other things on his mind. She watched as he studied his cards. There were three other people on the same table as him, and they were all men. All seemed to be betting much more than Michael, as they sported higher denomination coloured chips or simply placed three or four chips to Michael's solitary one. All seemed to be having a better time than Michael or at least they appeared to be happy, even as more often than not, the Dealer relieved them of their chips so that they had ever diminishing piles. It did not seem to be a problem as when they ran out they simply produced another note or notes that the Dealer changed for them so they were able to get back into the game.

Sharon was sure Michael was still sitting there with his original chips. Michael always played the game safe. He was a safe person. Perhaps that was why she had married him. He had made her feel safe. He was not really a gambler and it had not felt like a gamble marrying him all those years ago.

Sharon walked across and placed her hand on Michael's arm just as the dealer announced that he had Blackjack, and which obviously beat Michael's hopeful two pictures.

Michael immediately recoiled as if she had given him an electric shock and made a face.

She watched as he lost the next two hands. 'Well at least you can't lose the taxi fare home,' she tried to joke. 'It's only a few hundred yards to home.'

Michael gave her a quick smile that instantly vanished, and he picked up his chips. 'Come on I need a drink. I might try again later. I'm not having any luck tonight.'

'Tonight? You've looked glum all evening. What the hell is the matter? We could have gone out with Bob and Mary, but you didn't want that, and you obviously don't want to be with me.'

Michael hesitated as they walked towards the bar. It was obvious he was measuring his words. He ran his hand through his stubbled hair. 'Well to be honest Sharon I am disappointed.'

'Disappointed? What about?'

'Let's get a seat.' Michael ordered a beer as Sharon accepted another wine.

'Well?' Sharon asked after they were seated. 'What do you mean?'

Michael thought for a moment. 'It's this holiday with the girls.'

'What about it?'

'Well, why didn't you tell me about it? Why did you not discuss it with me first?'

Sharon laughed, which she quickly realised was not the best response. 'Ask your permission do you mean?' She took a sip of her wine. It was like turning back the clock. Turning back the clock to all those years ago when they had argued fiercely when she felt that Michael tried to control her. Michael had been a master. A master at making her feel guilty. He always managed to turn an argument around so that it looked as if she was in the wrong. When they had first met, Sharon had wanted to continue going out with her friends. She hadn't seen anything wrong with that. She wasn't sure if it was a Brighton thing or if the practice continued throughout the country, but most of her friends still continued to go out together, whether married or single, on a Friday night. It was fun. It was harmless. What was wrong with it?

Michael had not agreed. Michael would never agree that it was normal. Sharon was his wife. The wife he treasured and loved. Why would she want to go out without him? Why should she want to? Was he not enough for her? She was enough for him. He did not want to go out with his friends. He did not want to go out without her. Why should she want them to spend an evening separately? Did she not like being at home? Why had they even got married? Didn't they get married so that they could be together? More often than not Sharon had given in. Her white wedding dress could easily have been used for a surrender flag. If that was what white symbolised in the ceremony, and not just like one of Michael's other poor jokes, 'It was white so that it matched the kitchen appliances.'

Michael, she liked to have thought when she got married, was very old fashioned in many ways. Traditional even. That had a certain attraction back then. A certain protection. He almost could have been a father figure, and one that replaced the father she had always hoped she had, but who had never really materialised. But that was then. This is now. In any case she knew through their time together that nobody would have ever accused Michael of being a 'New Man'. No, she was at the moment very much stuck with the old man.

Sharon rotated the base of her wine glass looking down into the red liquid as if it might reveal an answer. 'Disappointed? How can me going away for a few days upset you? I would have thought you would have been glad? It's not even for a week.'

'Aren't I allowed to be upset?'

'Upset at what? Why? I'm sure you and the microwave meals I can get you in will mean you can manage quite ably.'

Michael put down his beer forcibly on the table so that a little shot over the side. 'I would have thought you would have had the decency to talk to me about dates first, and you didn't tell me that Mary was going with you. I thought it was just you and Julie.'

'Mary? What difference does it make if Mary comes?'

Michael's expression quickly turned to one of concern. 'Well it's only that I will worry. You know that.'

'Worry? Why? We don't even go anywhere near each other when we are together. Do we?'

'You don't understand,' Michael said in a hurt voice. 'Oh. All right I might as well tell you. In any case I did mention it to you some time ago, but I suspect you weren't listening as usual. It was going to be some kind of surprise. Well I suppose it can still be.'

'Tell me what?' Sharon's tone softened.

'Well it is the big one your next birthday. You are 50. I wanted to make it special. I wanted to celebrate it with you. Make it unforgettable.'

'Go on,' Sharon urged. She could feel the all too familiar feeling of guilt creeping in.

'Well I wanted to book a cruise to take you on, but if your heart is set on going away with the girls, I will have to concede.' Michael sat back and lifted his beer glass watching Sharon and waiting for her response. He had played his cards. It was her turn now.

Sharon smiled. But she knew Michael had won. How could she argue? How could she resist? Michael would win. He always won. Michael knew how to play her. He had always known how to play her. She could see how she had disappointed him. When she told him earlier in the evening he had not looked that upset. Either that or he masked it well. Sharon could not understand where the sudden anger had come from, or had it been brewing. Mind you, when she thought back, Michael always had a bit of a temper. Admittedly, it wasn't that obvious when they first met. Michael had been charming and appeared to be very even tempered. He always considered her wants and needs. He always appeared to put her first. When they first got together she could not believe her luck. Michael had almost been the Prince that she had been brought up to expect.

Sharon always loved fairy stories when she was a little girl, especially the ones where her father read to her when he was around. Her favourite had always been Sleeping Beauty, at least the first part anyway. Her father would sit on the edge of the bed and hold open her fairy tale book that had the most wonderful coloured illustrations. It was quite an old fashioned book, and was probably second hand when her father gave it to her. But that did not matter. He brought it home to her late one night. She knew it was not new, but to her it was, and it had instantly become one of her most prized possessions. She ignored the scribbled message that had been written in pencil to some other little girl in the inside cover. The words of the stories appeared to almost leap from the page as her father read them to her. He would sit on the edge of the bed and ask her what story she wanted him to read. There were probably over 20 stories in the book, but she chose 'Sleeping Beauty' over and over again.

She never really wanted her father to finish the story or to turn out the light. He would laugh lightly and call her 'his little Princess.' He would stroke her hair and tell her he had to turn off her bedside lamp to save the pennies. She had to be a brave girl. He had to go out and there was a chance that he might have to go away. He had to work away sometimes he told her, but she had her mother. Her mother was downstairs now so she should not worry. She should close her little eyes and go to sleep. She should close her little eyes and dream, and one day her Prince would come.

Was that really her Prince sitting opposite her now, Sharon wondered. Life could be such a disappointment. Life was certainly not the fairy tale she had been led to believe it was. Certainly the crown on the man opposite her had slipped. It had slipped many years ago and was now extremely tarnished. Perhaps she wasn't being fair. Had he not just told her he was booking a cruise for them? Perhaps it was the wine? Perhaps she might have had one too many? She remembered telling him earlier about the break she was planning with the girls, but she could not remember telling him any more than the date, and where they were going to go. She hadn't, she thought, mentioned Mary. She was certain she hadn't mentioned her. Originally it had only been her and Julie planning to go as Mary had declined, but then Mary changed her mind. Strangely, that was what seemed to upset him the most.

Sharon put down her wine and looked at Michael. Perhaps she had had one too many after all. She was beginning to feel tired. The drink was making her sleepy.

She wanted to sleep. She wanted to go home to her bed. She wanted to dream. She wanted to dream of what might be. Life could be too complicated sometimes. Perhaps she made it too complicated? Perhaps it was over ambitious to want more than she had? Even at her age was she wrong to want a little bit of happiness? Was she so much different to that very young girl all those years ago? Did dreams die with age?

She looked across at Michael. Was he such a bad man? Was she that unhappy? Could she live without him? Had he just talked about planning to take her away for her Birthday? Wouldn't most women settle for a man like that?

'I'm sorry,' Sharon said softly. 'Perhaps I should have asked you first. I'll speak to the girls and see if I can cancel it. I am sure they will understand.'

THIRTEEN

Michael had always loved Sunday mornings. If he were honest that wasn't strictly true. When he was a teenager he had been encouraged to play Sunday morning football. It wasn't a particularly high standard, and sometimes they did not even have a referee. Other times they had to put up the goal posts and take them down themselves. Perhaps worst of all were the changing rooms that were always freezing. That's if there were even changing rooms, because for some games they used to have to go to them in their kit, and then go home still caked in mud. The worst thing of all was that the season was during winter. Sometimes the pitch was so hard that the game was called off, but other times they played at their peril. The other unbearable thing was the times when they played in the pouring rain.

Michael had never really been a team player. He had never really wanted to be part of a team, and rely on other people. No, Michael had hated those Sunday mornings and he had soon hung up his boots when he discovered a world of girls and drink, and wanted to stay out late on Saturday nights. His parents had been disappointed, but Michael had never regretted his decision.

Now Sunday mornings were precious. Sunday morning was the one day of the week when he was not a slave to an alarm clock. The one day when his world seemed to stop, and the one day when he wanted to catch up with the world. Normally he would start the day with the Sunday papers.

Today, though, had been a little bit different. He had not been able to sleep properly, and when he had woken up just after six, he had been unable to get back to sleep. Perhaps it was because he was used to getting up for work that early, but he doubted it, and he was sure that it was the night before that had got to him.

He was thinking back to yesterday when he met Mary and how exciting that had been. Again she had managed to shock him. It had been a mad afternoon of daring and surprise that was mixed with danger. It was a heady mixture, and he had been completely under her spell. She was like a drug that he could not get enough of. Not that Michael had ever taken drugs or even tried them. Even in those days when he was young, drugs were always freely available in the south coast town, but Michael had never been tempted. Michael had never wanted to risk not being in control, and never wanted to let go and make a fool of himself. He had always stayed true to himself, and now he knew he would stay true for Mary. He was hers. But he knew that in order to have her he had to work hard.

That was what he wanted to do this morning. The papers could wait. The papers were not important. He wanted to make use of his time as best he could, especially as Sharon was still asleep. He wondered what kind of mood she would be in when she eventually woke up. She had certainly had too much to drink last night. Not that it really mattered to Michael, but the days when drink had made their sex life that much more exciting and passionate after a Saturday night out had long since gone. Equally so were the days when Sunday morning meant more than a chance to grab more sleep.

Michael went into their second bedroom which also doubled as their study and pulled down one of his bank folders as he had remembered that he was already entitled to holiday insurance for European travel. It went with his current account, and the beauty of it was that there was no need to register before they travelled. It did not flag up a large insurance sum that might raise an eyebrow at a later date. Nevertheless, he wanted to know how much he might be likely to receive. He thought about calling his bank, but thought better of it. Not only would he have to negotiate the wonderful button game, as you have to guess which option you need and which button to press in order to get the answer for which you had called. But also before the game began you were often informed that the company was keen on monitoring the calls for training purposes. Michael laughingly wondered that if he called to ask if he was covered for flying his wife's body home would they be able to rewind to the call at a much later date if someone should recall the conversation. He doubted it. He wondered if in the history of call centres had one call ever been retrieved? Certainly not if it was to the benefit of the customer, he suspected. With a police request it might be a different matter. No, he would definitely have to look into the small print.

Michael began thumbing through the folder and the first sum he noticed in the Summary of Cover was that the Death Benefit was for thirty thousand pounds. Not exactly a king's or queen's ransom, and certainly not an amount that would keep Mary in the lifestyle to which she had become accustomed. He drilled down further to find that he would receive five thousand pounds for a burial or cremation outside the United Kingdom. Further, it was seven thousand and five hundred pounds for repatriation of remains from outside of the United Kingdom.

Certainly his travel insurance policy would not solve the financial crisis that his business was going through, and also it would not lead him to a better life with Mary. After all he and Sharon still had a mortgage, and the property was not entirely theirs, well not for a few years yet. He would need to look up exactly what other policies they already had. He knew that when they had moved down to the Marina they had taken out at least four policies so that each was covered if something should happen to the other one. He wasn't sure if he and Sharon had then wanted to care for the other or if it had been one of the Building Society's requirements in order to take out the mortgage. Either way it did not matter. The love was gone, but he hoped the policies were still solid. He recalled that two of the policies, one for each of them, had been worth a diminishing sum, and would simply cover the rest of the mortgage outstanding. The other two policies were simple Life Insurance ones that paid out on the death of the first one to pop their clogs.

Michael laughed to himself as he remembered wearing clogs a long time ago. Life had been simpler then. It had been about the time when 'Schools Out' came out by Alice Cooper. Michael had only just left school himself, and was about to start his Electrical Apprenticeship. He had been a young man with long hair and plans. A young man with hope. Now the long hair had gone, but he still had hope, and although the plans were entirely different to what he envisaged all those years ago, he was still planning for his future. His future with Mary.

Michael was normally very organised, but he couldn't exactly remember where the policies were. It had been such a long time that they were signed and arranged, and he could not remember where he or Sharon had put them. He pondered for a moment as he sipped his coffee. He did not exactly want to wake Sharon and ask her if she remembered where her life insurance policies were or even who they were with. This certainly was going to take a lot of thought. It was like some of the crime programmes that Sharon liked to watch on the television. It was always the little mistake that the clever, but pretending to be dumb, detective picked up on. The devil was always in the detail, and not just in insurance policies and their like. Michael knew that he had to get even the smallest detail right. If he was not careful and overlooked even a small detail it might prove costly. That was why he knew he needed to involve Mary. Two pairs of eyes were better than one pair. He might miss something, but Mary might well pick it up. Mary was clever. Not in an educated way, but she was street wise. She understood people. She could play people. She had played him.

By coincidence he looked down at his mobile and noticed that he had a new text from her. He opened it up, and it simply said:

'Did you have a nice evening with Sharon? Are you having a lay in? Am I not enough for you?'

Michael studied the words. They seemed harsh almost sarcastic. Was she being sarcastic, he asked himself? He was never quite sure how to take her sometimes. She certainly could be a bit like that, and she was unarguably forward when it came to straight talking. It was also the fault with text messages he had found. Text messages could often be misinterpreted and read in the wrong way. The sender might well be trying to be funny, but it might not read like that. He read it again and knew that he wanted to talk to her. He picked up his mobile and sent her a short message asking if she was free to talk. The reply came back almost instantly saying that Bob was in the garden and she could speak if he was quick.

Michael went out of the bedroom and glanced to where Sharon was sleeping in the main bedroom. The door was still closed. He then went back into the second bedroom and quietly closed the door, and then dialled Mary's number.

'Hi Mary,' he said softly. 'What was that message all about?'

Mary laughed. 'Well did you have a nice evening with Sharon? Is she still asleep?'

'Yes. Yes she is,' Michael replied defensively.

Mary laughed again. 'Did you shag her silly? Is the poor girl having to have a lie in?'

'Don't be silly.' Michael said quickly. 'You know we don't do anything anymore.'

'I only have your word to take for that, don't I? But I suppose I could ask her.' Mary said seriously, but then her tone lightened. 'We could compare notes. We could both mark you out of ten. Not sure you would get a good mark from me. Not after your performance yesterday. But I suppose you would get a high score for finishing quickly.

My, you were an excited boy.'

Michael was silent for a moment, then realised that she was joking. At least he hoped she was joking. Michael was never quite sure with Mary. She was certainly a woman that kept him on his toes, but that was what he liked. 'Can we have a replay? I would do better in a rematch. I understand your dirty tactics now. I would be ready.'

It was Mary's turn to laugh. 'I'll have a think, but I will have to be quick now and can't talk long as Bob is in the garden. Oh shit. I think he's coming and not like you.'

Michael listened intently and then Mary's voice at the other end said, 'OK Sharon. Great. Glad you had a good night last night. We'll catch up in the week.'

The line went dead and Michael realised that Bob must have come into the room. Mary was a quick thinker and Bob was probably slow on the uptake anyway. Nevertheless, Michael knew they were both treading a dangerous path, but it wouldn't be for much longer. His thoughts turned to the insurance policies and he recalled that each one was a direct debit taken from his account each month for all the policies. He was sure that there were four different policies and at least two different companies. Nevertheless, he could call them and get the value and expiry dates.

Michael picked up his coffee and took a sip. Then again if he did call them, not only would he face the same problem as calling the travel insurance, but it might even prove worse. He would not only have to drill down to the right person, but then he would have to prove who he was. This, he could presumably do, by quoting the code against the deduction from his bank account statement. But then when they had asked him to prove who he was with ridiculous questions such as what was the maiden name of his cat, or his favourite wife's name, they would probably agree to send him out a copy. Firstly though, as he was sure the call centre would be manned by people simply following a script and not able to think for themselves, and with English almost certainly not their first language, experience told him that they would only be able to deal with the policy or policies that were attributed to him, and not the ones that had Sharon's name on them. Which way round it was, he wasn't sure? It could have either been the one that would pay out on his death or the one that would pay him on Sharon's death. It did not really matter which way round it was, but he was sure that they would only be able to deal with one. They would probably quote him the most misquoted quote in the history of any jobsworth.

'I am very sorry Sir, but I cannot give you that information under The Data Protection Act.'

The Data Protection Act. Just four little words that could bring the world to a halt. He did not know anybody that had ever read The Data Protection Act, even the people quoting it had never read it. He would often ask them as to what page and paragraph were they referring, but his sarcasm was wasted. It never did any good. The world had gone mad.

Michael knew that he would think again because not only would he be unable to get the full information, but they would also have a record of having sent a copy out to him which might look fishy. Michael laughed at his pun. Yes, if there was an investigation into her death, if she went missing in the sea, this sort of thing might well be taken into account.

Michael heard the bedroom door open and realised that Sharon was awake, and he went into their lounge.

She entered looking like she had been asleep for a

hundred years. 'Did you get the papers?' It was the first thing she asked.

Michael stood up from the leather sofa. 'No I haven't had time. I'm just going now.'

Walking up to ASDA Michael sent a quick text to Mary. He was worried about earlier, and just wanted to make sure everything was OK. A reply came back even before he had reached the supermarket. Mary had said that she was not contactable, and they could not talk as she was going out to lunch with Bob. He was taking her to a carvery. Michael felt an immediate jealously. He knew he shouldn't but he couldn't help it. He was sure that Mary would much rather be with him. At least he hoped she would. Why then did he have nagging doubts? He had to tell Mary of the sacrifices he was prepared to make, and of what he would do just so that they could be together.

Michael purchased the papers and immediately understood why paper boys seemed to be a thing of the past. Judging by their weight it would take a muscled man to carry a bag of them. Michael trudged back feeling lonely. It was a lonely business and he wanted to sit down with Mary to explain it all to her. He needed both her help and approval. He had to have it. The responsibility was simply too much. After all he was doing it for them. He was doing it for a better life for both of them.

Michael looked back towards the casino where he had his bad luck last night, but felt certain that his luck in life would change. He turned around and continued walking. He realised he would have to face Sharon when he got back, but he would not have to suffer her for much longer. No he was resolute. She would get what she deserved.

FOURTEEN

Sharon had taken her paper and its supplements back to bed. She was feeling decidedly the worse for wear. Once again she vowed not to drink too much when they went out. She never used to be this bad. Certainly in the past she had not drunk that much, and certainly in the past she did not feel that bad the day after. Was it because she was trying to block out Michael or was it because she was getting older? Surely the older you got the more you got used to drink? It certainly did not feel that way.

Earlier when she had looked in the ornate mirror in the hall she had almost frightened herself. She had to admit that she did look rough. Some women could carry a look without make-up. She looked like she should be carried off. She certainly never wanted anybody to see her without her war paint on. Not even any of her friends. Especially her friends. She wondered briefly what both Julie and Mary looked like without theirs on as both relied on it almost as much as she did. Well certainly Mary. Of course Michael did not matter. She did not mind if he saw her when she was not made up. Not anymore anyway. He did not count anymore. She did not care what he thought any longer. Her mind drifted to a certain man that she had recently met. A man who was obviously attracted to an older woman. An older married woman. Surely he was more used to girls of his own age. Many girls nearer his own age, she thought, did not wear make-up, and appeared to rely much more on the natural look. They also seemed to her, to wear quite often much more sensible shoes. She had never worn a pair of DM's. Sharon had read recently that Dr Martens had nearly gone bust in 2002, but had just been sold for millions and were now selling over five million pairs a year. She could see why they were popular, and they did now have some very attractive designs. They also looked very comfortable. However, they were just not her and she could never see herself owning a pair, and thought she probably never would. But wasn't it her generation that were asking for problems later in life as complexion, foot and leg problems meant they would definitely suffer for their vanity.

Was it vanity, she wondered? Was it not expected of her and her contemporaries? Was that not how she had grown up? Was that not what all her teenage magazines had been about just boys and beauty? Obviously, there was music as well. But that was more often than not also about love, which in turn was about boys and men. Had there been much more to life then, when she was a teenager? In all honesty was there much more to life now?

Further, was it not then, and now, a mask from the world? All these years wasn't she hiding from the world and not wanting to reveal her real self? Surely, this had started in the sixties before her time, and continued for over half a century. Was she not any different to any other women her age or was there something more? Did she not actually like herself? Did she not want to present this face to the world? A face that she felt comfortable with.

Sharon doubted that she would ever feel comfortable again. She couldn't believe how bad she felt. She pulled the sheet snugly around herself. She did not want to get out of bed. For some reason she had a pain in her lower back and she felt very weak. She wanted to close her eyes and go back to sleep. Yes she did like to lie in on a Sunday sometimes, but she had certainly never wanted to spend the day in bed.

Michael knocked on the door and then opened it. It was strange, she thought, that now, after they had been married all these years, he had taken to knocking on the door, as if she were a complete stranger. It was as if there were some invisible wall between them. At times it was a respectful barrier. Two people who shared the same space, and breathed the same air, but no longer had much in common. It was hard to believe that they had once been intimate.

Michael had a cup of coffee for her. 'Are you going to stay in bed all day,' he asked, as he placed it on the bedside table.

'I don't feel that good,' Sharon said softly.

Michael made a face and said sarcastically, 'I can't believe that. I wonder why? Might it have something to do with how much you had to drink last night?'

Sharon shook her head and realised that hurt. 'I did.........I didn't have that much.'

Michael laughed. 'I've seen an alcoholic get by on less. If you cut yourself now it is red wine that would pour out. Not blood.'

'Well I promise that next time we go out I won't drink.
Michael laughed again.

'No I mean it,' Sharon said. 'The way I feel at the moment

I don't think I ever want to drink again.'

Am I really that bad, Sharon thought to herself? Did I really drink that much? She knew that she did like a glass or two in the evening either with her meal or sitting outside looking out to sea. She remembered dropping her glass the other evening and how it shattered on the decking; but that wasn't because she was drunk that night. Though now she had to admit she did feel poorly. She did not want to feel like this again.

'Seeing is believing,' Michael said strongly. 'Still it's up to you. It's your liver. It's your life.'

It really annoyed Sharon when Michael took the higher ground. He had always spoken down to her at times as if he always knew best. 'Anyway, thank you for the coffee. Let me be for a little while. I'm going to read the papers then I might have a little snooze. After that I'll probably get up. You didn't want to do anything today did you?'

'Oh no. I had no plans for us to do anything. I've got loads of things to get on with. Get up when you like.'

Sharon was grateful when Michael had left the room and gone. The last thing she needed was a lecture. She wanted to return to peace and quiet. She wanted to return to the papers. She rested her head back against the pillow and she considered shouting out to Michael to get her a couple of paracetamols for her headache and back pain. Perhaps shouting was not such a good idea. She wondered if she should ask him for a little bell. She definitely did not want to get out of bed and walk to the kitchen, and she did not want to shout. Suddenly she had an idea. She reached down to her handbag which was by the side of the bed, and rummaged in it for her mobile. Michael was one of her 'Favourites'.

Well according to the memory of her phone anyway, and she pressed his name on the screen. Strange, she thought, as she waited for it to connect. She actually had no idea what his number was. In fact she could not really recall the phone numbers of any of her friends. Strangely the number was engaged. She carried on reading her paper and tried again after she had finished the next article. It was still engaged. Third time lucky, Sharon thought. She carried on reading, and then called him again. This time she managed to get through and Michael dutifully brought her the tablets, and a glass of water.

Sharon felt very tired and weak. Perhaps age was taking its toll. She picked up the two tablets and took a sip of her water, even swallowing was painful.

Sharon put down the paper, picked up the Sunday supplement, and flicked though it. An article immediately caught her eye, 'Is Monogamy for Mugs?' It immediately set Sharon thinking as she continued reading. Its main structure reasoned that when a man has an affair he often gets caught, but when a woman has an affair she often leaves her husband. Sharon found herself nodding in agreement. She could recall several women that she had known who had found out that their husband was having an affair, but they had forgiven them. The men had stayed in the family home. Perhaps the men were not that unhappy? Perhaps they might still have continued seeing someone on the outside that gave their ego a boost or perhaps it was purely sex? Nevertheless, to give up the comfort of their own home where all their meals were probably still being cooked, and most probably all their clothes were still being washed and ironed, would be a big wrench. Therefore, was it any wonder that the odds were on them staying? Men were quite often cowards, but they weren't stupid.

Women it appeared were different animals. Basically they weren't animals. Well not like men. For men it could be purely about sex. An animal instinct to mate. It was also the novelty of being with someone different. A novelty that would often wear off. Women, it said, wanted more. For most women it was not about sex. It might be a little bit about missing the intimacy of sex, but they were not driven by sexual desire. It was much more emotional.

Often though with woman, it said, a woman also had the kids to care about. Fitting an affair around the children's routines could be very difficult. Most women realised that if they were discovered then there was a great danger that their husband would not be forgiving, and not only might they be forced to go with their new partner, but that they would also have the kids in tow. Not an easy thing to take into consideration. For women with children in that situation an affair was not an easy way out. Very few women would leave both their husband and children to go off with a new man. An affair was really a big sign that her marriage was in trouble, if not finished. Nevertheless, the woman was also probably not in a financial situation that allowed her to be completely self-supporting, and that might well depend on the man she had met. It was not the only uncertain factor, because although the man might definitely want her, would he really want to take her on, and also have the responsibility of her kids. An instant Dad with an instant family. It was enough to make most men run for the hills. It was all of these things that a woman needed to take into consideration before embarking on an affair, and the conclusion was that not unless she could be fairly certain that the guy was after long term commitment, and not just a quick fling, then it was best not even thought about let alone started.

Sharon folded over the magazine. She could relate to a lot of what she had read. However, the one thing she did not have was children.

Sharon put her hand to her head. The tablets had still not kicked in. Was the article applicable to her she wondered? She too was in her forties, and obviously not in a happy marriage. Well certainly not a conventional marriage. Was it possible to have a marriage without sex? Was it really as basic as that? Would an affair do her any good? Would it actually put her marriage right or at least make her marriage bearable? Would an affair be fun or would it end in tears? Did it matter if it ended? Wasn't it ended already? Sharon wasn't sure. She was not sure of anything.

She rested her head against the pillow and closed her eyes. The image of the Muscles from Brussels came into her head. He was certainly attractive. Of that there was no doubt, but was he a man that was after long time commitment? A long time commitment with an older woman that would age quicker than him. An older woman that had already aged quicker than him. Was that not a recipe for disaster? If not now, certainly in the future. Having said that, she argued should she not live for now? Did she not deserve to have some fun?

FIFTEEN

Michael remained in the lounge with his notebook computer in front of him. On the coffee table was a new book that he had just acquired on the *Titanic*. He had purchased it from one of his favourite bookshops in the North Laines area. Michael had always loved everything about the sea. He loved living near it, and he loved reading about it. He was also extremely interested in the tragedy of the *Titanic*.

The story had always fascinated him ever since he was a small boy, but with its one hundred year anniversary just passed, even more facts and new angles emerged. This was one such book that not only told of the sinking, but also told about the complete aftermath. Michael always found there were so many interesting stories that were not really well known such as the band members who became legends because they played, without lifejackets, up until they ship went down. However, it was also little known that they actually had their pay deducted from the time the ship went down because they did not work the full passage. Some of their relatives even received a bill for the loss of the uniform they were wearing when the boat went down. Even when the family of one of the band members, whose body was recovered, asked if he could be brought back home, they were informed that, 'normal cargo rates would apply'. Therefore, the body was not repatriated, and the twenty one year old violinist was buried with 120 other passengers and crew in the Fairlawn Cemetery in Halifax, Nova Scotia.

Perhaps more astounding was that the *White Star Line* had, arguably and purposefully, enrolled the Band Member's as Second Class passengers. This meant they were on a lower rate, and also meant that after their death they, or their families, were not even entitled to any Workmen's Compensation. Michael already knew that in keeping with Maritime Law, a sailor was officially shipwrecked the minute the ship went down, and therefore unemployed and that was the point in time when their pay stopped. Nevertheless, the *Titanic* Shipping Line owners did seem to be particularly brutal and heartless. Even in death the First Class passengers were afforded all the respect expected as their bodies were recovered from the sea. Unfortunately for those that looked like steerage class, and for those who were certainly crew, they were often simply put back into the sea. There were so many stories about injustices and Michael really looked forward to reading them later.

He sat back on the sofa and thought how times had changed. How Health and Safety had taken over the world and now wanted it all wrapped in cotton wool. The rights of the common man had certainly changed in the last hundred years. They certainly wouldn't get away with treating their workers like that nowadays. Workers were extremely powerful and protected in industry today. They had a minimum rate of pay, and could only work specified hours, and they were paid for their holidays.

That was how it should be.

Michael picked up his coffee and smiled to himself. Of course, there was one industry where the workers were still not protected. One industry where at times the workers were perhaps little more than smiling slaves. One industry that appeared to break all the rules, and be driven by only one motive, and that was to keep the costs as low as possible. An industry that was staff heavy. The cruise industry.

Michael knew that he was typical of many others. He, like probably the vast majority of cruisers the world over, wanted more for less. He enjoyed the product and gave little thought as to how such good value could be achieved with the money he paid. Or perhaps, if he or others did think about it, they chose to put it to the back of their minds. Was he any different to Sharon, or any of her friends, who delighted in the bargains they could get in some of the large department fashion shops? Basically, they did not question how clothes could be made so cheaply or by whom they were made, or in what conditions. No, they put that from their minds as they purchased fashion items at silly prices.

Cruise line ships often sailed under flags of convenience. Michael knew from his naval books that flags of convenience went right back to early naval warfare. These flags of convenience, as they flew the flag of a neutral country, made the ship neutral, and it would stop them from being attacked. But cruise ships were not at war. At least not with the passengers. Nevertheless, they still found these flags extremely useful. If the ship was registered with a country that had strict employment laws and union membership then it could make the hiring of crew that much more restricting and expensive. No it was much more convenient to register with another country so that third world labour could be taken on without the worry of nationality, and only cost.

Michael remembered reading an article about it when he had been carrying out some research last week as he tried to learn as much as he could about the industry and the workings of a ship. He had been appalled at how the staff were often treated. They worked long hours for very little pay, and were often housed in very cramped conditions. It was not unusual for some of the crew to work over one hundred hours per week which could mean that their actual pay averaged out to less than one pound or even less than one dollar an hour.

What astounded Michael was how the cruise industry defended themselves and almost stated that they were doing the crew a favour. They knew that often these people were from desperate conditions in third world countries, and wanted to escape the poverty from which they had been born into. The cruise industry spokesmen were well known for saying that they did not put a gun to their heads and force them to work for them. They came willing and able, and there was always another willing person to take their place.

Therefore, if the industry was not bothered, why should the customer be concerned? It did not appear that they were. They were happy to receive five star treatment at budget prices, whilst the people who served them so wonderfully lived up to ten to a cabin, and ate far inferior food to what the passengers dined on.

It appeared that nobody was on their side. The crew had no rights and no one cared. They could be sacked for joining a union. Well, unofficially anyway, and probably best of all, they were not protected by proper rules or laws. Often in keeping with Maritime Law and tradition, it is the Captain who has absolute power, and that can include fining the crew or demoting ones that rely on tips to jobs which don't pay tips. Even the mortuary might, although perhaps rarely, appear in the ship's plan in the brochure, but you could bet that the brig or jail that would contain crewmen who had fallen foul of the powers, would not be shown.

Michael looked down at his mobile. He had still not received a text from Mary. It was starting to worry him and he began to fidget. Why he wasn't sure. He knew where she was. She was out with her husband. She was probably having a wonderful time as her husband could not resist treating her to anything that she asked for. It appeared he enjoyed spoiling her, and Michael could not help thinking what she might do in return as a way of saying thank you. His hand moved towards the mobile. He could feel the tension. He wanted to contact her. He knew he could not stand it much longer. He knew that if he got this right he would not have to stand it much longer. How he wished Bob was out of the way.

Michael sat back and smiled to himself. It was as if a light bulb had come on in his head. This could be more fun than he thought. Wouldn't it be a good idea if Bob and Mary joined them on the cruise rather than just he and Sharon. He had no idea how they might feel about all going on holiday together let alone all going on a cruise together, but it could work. Michael began to warm to the idea and then briefly thought that it would be great if he could get rid of Sharon, and that he could get rid of Bob at the same time. He did have to admit that perhaps it was not very realistic, but it did have some legs. Bye-bye Bob as he pushed him overboard. A sort of 'two birds with one stone' scenario or a very good 'buy one get one free' type transaction. It would then be plain sailing for Mary and him to sail off into the sunset.

It was certainly something that he thought he should consider seriously. It was obvious from the cruise websites he had read that in the vast majority of cases where there was some question regarding whether the tragedy was completely accidental or there was something a little more sinister behind it. These couples were travelling on their own. In other words just the two of them. Which is why it might be easier to think that the surviving partner might have been planning something. Would there be safety in numbers if the four of them travelled together. Everybody would be able to see what a wonderful time they were all having together, and everybody would be so shocked about the accident.

Michael went into the kitchen and got himself another cup of coffee. He began considering the option. The end result would be the same, but it might well work better with the four of them. It might also be more fun. Fun was probably not what he meant. Nevertheless, there would be Mary nearby to steady his nerves, and Mary would also be there to comfort him with his distress of losing Sharon. In fact it would be so emotional that it could provide the actual cover story for the distant future of how through his grief, Mary had comforted him, and then they had fallen for each other.

Michael went to reach for his book when his mobile phone started to ring and he automatically went to ignore it. It was probably Her Highness wanting something. She would just have to want. Normally he would respond without question. She was used to him responding. This time if she wanted something she would have to get out of bed. She would have to put one foot in front of the other and walk all the way from the bedroom. It was hardly an epic trip. She did not need the spirit of Scott, and he did not need to put down base stations along the way to aid her.

Michael glanced briefly at the screen and then realised that it was not her number. In fact, it was not a number that he recognised at all, and he thought he had better answer it.

'Hello,' he said gingerly.

'Is that Michael?'

'Yes,' he answered to the female voice. 'It is. Who is it?'

'Michael of Sparks?'

'Yes,' he said, wondering who could be calling him on a Sunday.

'It's Mrs Giles of Queens Park. You were due to come to our place tomorrow.'

Michael's heart appeared to miss a beat. It was the rewire that he had planned for next week and beyond. It was a large house and he had been recommended to her by Mary. He had already purchased all the materials. He was ready to go. He needed this job. His business needed the profit. It was the only big job that he had planned.

'Well I am sorry to say that I am afraid we will have to cancel the job, and stop the rewire.' Michael was about to protest, but then she continued. 'Unfortunately my husband lost his father earlier today, and obviously you realise that it would not be a good time. He has to sort out the Will and everything. I am sure you understand.'

Michael nodded. What could he say? He sunk into the settee after he finished the call. It looked like his business could be finished. He had very little work without this job.

He went to his case and took out a paper notebook and pen, and began scribbling down a few figures. There was no doubt that he was in trouble. None of it added up. He would certainly need the benefit of a high pay out from the insurance policies, and the other thing he had not considered was the Will, as the call had reminded him. It was always something he was going to do. He had never made a Will, and he was sure that Sharon had not made one either. If she had would it make it easier or would everything automatically go to him in any case?

Perhaps if he did one, it would encourage Sharon to do hers. Perhaps, though, he needed to pick his moment. There were so many things now he needed from her. He picked up the pen and wrote down a couple of notes. Michael had no idea what went into a Will. Did you need to employ the expensive services of a solicitor or could you simply do your own? He had heard of companies that were not solicitors who visited your home and helped you draw one up. What happened then? Did you have to lodge the Will with them or your bank?

Michael turned on his notebook computer and waited for it to boot up. It would certainly be much easier if they could do their own. He did not want to discuss his business with a complete stranger. Surely, a person with average intelligence could draw up their own. He picked up his coffee, which was cold, then put it down again. It was a bit of a predicament. He knew that they had not done Wills, but would he be better off if they left it. Yes, it was certainly something they both should have done years ago, but had never got round to it. If they did do them now would questions be asked as to how they had only just made a Will before the cruise?

Michael decided it might raise eyebrows. Was it worth the risk or should he leave it?

He decided to go online and do some research. Michael was completely caught up in it all as he went through site after site, and considered all the options and looked at some templates, and became engrossed. So engrossed that he did not hear Sharon come in the room and walk up behind him.

'What are you doing?' she asked innocently then studied the screen. 'How to do your own Will.'

Michael found himself flustered. He had not heard her coming. He did not have time to switch the screen. 'Yes......... yes,' he stammered. 'I was just thinking that I have never done one, and it is about time I did. If anything happened to me then it would make it easier for you.'

Sharon smiled thinly. 'The way I am feeling today I think it is me that should be doing a Will.'

Michael looked up at her and thought, 'Often a word spoken in jest.'

SIXTEEN

Sharon ran her hands through Claire's hair, and then stood back. 'What do you think?'

'It's coming on. Just a little bit shorter please.'

Sharon nodded and picked up her scissors as Claire smiled. Sharon smiled back ever the professional. She was still not feeling that great, and her back was aching a little bit. It was part of the price of being a hairdresser she guessed. She knew that it was well known that standing all day could take its toll, and many of her friends and colleagues from the past had suffered later in life from being on their feet, all day every day. It was certainly not good for the back or the legs.

Sharon was not sure if she was happy cutting people's hair in the comfort of their own home or if she missed the days when she had her own salon. Certainly both worlds had their own advantages. Her own salon had been fun, but it was mainly driven by Michael. He had helped her get it, and he had taken over the legal responsibility of running it so that Sharon did not have to worry. He even did the books for her, and he did not want to let it go. The finances had dictated otherwise, and eventually Michael had seen that the overheads could not be covered. The rent was far too expensive along with all the other costs associated with keeping a business running. It was also difficult to compete against all the new, one price does all, barber/hairdressing shops that appeared to keep springing up.

Sharon then decided that she would use her existing client base, and offer a cut at home service. At first Michael had not been happy. Sharon had guessed that it might be because he did not know where she was for a lot of the time. With the shop he knew exactly where she was. Michael had always liked to know where she was, at least in the beginning. Eventually he had seen sense, and as the business had started to lose money, they then mutually decided that it had to go.

Hairdressing was really all that Sharon knew. At least that was what she had qualified for, and it was honest work. She came up with the idea of travelling to her clients. She already had the clients. Some of them had been with her for years, even decades. It would be just a different way of working, and with the benefit that the only expense, apart from the products, was petrol. At least this way she was still able to earn her own money. Michael had not been that keen, and he had even suggested that she worked in a shop. At first he said that she should work for somebody else in their salon, and when she protested, he even suggested that she might want to quit hairdressing altogether and just work in a clothes shop or department store. He said it was more secure and regular, and she would not have to worry about where the next cut was coming from. Also, he pointed out that she would know where she stood, especially with the hours. With her visiting her clients at home to cut their hair it would have to be at their convenience. It would mean unsocial hours.

Sharon did not relent, and in the end she got her own way. It wasn't great money, but it was her money. Money that she had earned for herself. Michael, she knew, would have been happy for her not to work. He would have been happy to provide for both of them, if he was able. It was not what Sharon had wanted. She needed that bit of independence. She needed her own money, even if at times it was little more than pocket money. She could not, and would not, be completely beholden to Michael.

'Are you going away this year?' Claire asked.

Sharon thought for a moment. 'Yes,' she said hesitantly. 'Well I think I am. I was going away for a short trip with my girlfriends, but now I think that Michael wants to take me on a cruise. Both are on my Birthday. I'm not sure what to do.'

Claire laughed. 'My you are a lucky girl. Spoilt for choice.'

'Yes, but I'm not sure what to do. Either way I have to let somebody down.' Sharon thought for a moment. She had not spoken since to Mary or Julie. She had been too preoccupied by other things. She did not want to tell Claire what those other things were. She was also dreading telling Mary and Julie that they might have to postpone it. She was sure that Mary would give her some stick. Mary always gave her stick. It seemed that Mary would always delight in showing off how she had her husband under her thumb. Mary liked everybody to believe she was a free spirit. A spirit that could not be controlled; and she liked to show how much she had Bob in tow.

Sharon glanced down at her watch and noted the time. She did not want to be late for her appointment. She would have to rush. She found herself feeling a little nervous. That was only natural really, she told herself. She was walking into the unknown. What woman wouldn't be nervous?

'If you don't mind me saying,' Claire continued. 'How many years have I known you? More than I care to remember.'

'More than I care to remember too,' Sharon agreed. 'Yes I think it was even before Michael.'

'Yes. I think it was,' Claire nodded. 'I have always thought you were lucky. Perhaps you are still lucky. All these years, and your husband still wants to take you on a cruise. I wish my husband was as thoughtful and attentive.'

Sharon smiled or at least she tried to. That was exactly the trouble with all her friends and relatives they had all always thought Michael was Mr Wonderful. Wonderful with a capital W. There were one or two other words beginning with W that Sharon thought gave a better description, but knew her friends would not agree. Her friends had always delighted in telling her how charming Michael was, and how he could not do enough for her. It was her, they said, that made him grumpy as she drove him to distraction sometimes. She simply had to try harder to please him. He certainly tried his hardest to please her. Even her mother had agreed. She was lucky to have found a man such as Michael, and Sharon needed to work at her marriage like Michael did. It had been the same in her mother's day, her mother reminded her. People did not work at anything anymore including marriage.

Sharon looked at her watch again. She really was not feeling that great, but she needed to rush. She needed to get to her appointment. She began cutting quicker. The rhythmic snipping of the scissors seemed to be speaking to her as she cut. Michael or Mary they seemed to say. Which one should she please? Which one should she let down? Michael or Mary she repeated to herself. It had a kind of natural ring to it. It could have been the name of a children's programme. It seemed to go together, but which one did she want to go with. Perhaps she knew that she did not have a choice. When had she ever defied Michael to that extent? When had he not got his own way with something like this? As usual she did not have a choice. Michael would win. Michael always won. She would have to let Mary down. She would speak to Michael when she got home, and then she would have to call Mary and Julie. She continued cutting.

~

Sharon looked down at the dashboard clock, grateful that she had finally got away. She needed to get a move on. Doing Claire's hair had taken longer than she thought. She wished she could put her foot down, but it was impossible in this city. The Green Party had seen to that. Firstly, in their hate of cars they had reduced the speed limit to twenty miles per hour. Then they had introduced cycle and bus lanes throughout the city, but because of the congestion and the amount of time every driver now had to stay stationary, journey times were much much longer. It must have actually increased the pollution threefold and not reduced it. All the residents were very angry with the council and the green party, apart from the very few bike riders who just went through the red lights, and ran around at night without any lights.

Sharon had memorised the address that she had been given. She had not written it down, preferring to commit it to memory. She could feel herself becoming more nervous as she got nearer. She likened it to when she had gone on dates many years before, when she was a nervous teenager. But now it was different. Now her body had changed. Even her hands started to feel a bit sticky on the wheel. She pressed a button to let the window down a little just as a dog ran out in front of her. At first she thought she was going to hit it, but she managed to stop a few feet short. She waited and braced herself for the car behind to hit her. This was not what she needed. How would Michael react? He would surely blame her for risking the car just to avoid a dog. She heard the screech of tyres. Her arms straightened and stiffened on the wheel ready to help absorb the impact. It seemed an eternity. Didn't they say that if a person drowns all their past life seems to go by before their eyes? How did they know? She glanced up in her rear view mirror. It was one of the few times she used it other than to check on her make-up. The car behind had stopped. It wasn't going to hit her. She wasn't going to have to face Michael. At least over the car. The dog instantly disappeared not caring about the chaos it had nearly caused.

Sharon took a deep breath and then continued. As if to make matters purposefully worse it started to rain. That was all she needed. She did not have an umbrella with her. She did not want to turn up looking like a drowned rat. She wondered how close she would be able to park. Parking was another problem in the city. It was a subject that you did not want to get Michael started on. The council did not seem to care, car or van, they were all easy targets for the council controlled wardens who were employed to get results. They were certainly not employed for their sense of fairness and common sense, as their only concern seemed to be to fleece the motorist for the obscene amount of money they made each year for the council.

Sharon reached down for her bottle of water and took a quick swig as she waited for the lights to turn to green. She had trouble swallowing and wondered if that might be down to nerves. She tried to put any thought of the future to the back of her mind. It was now that mattered. It was now that she had to live for.

Sharon looked up at the sky. It appeared to have stopped raining. The sky was beginning to clear. Maybe her luck was beginning to change. Maybe things would work out for the best. She noticed a road name, and knew that she was getting near to where he told her to go. She needed to turn into the next road, and was delighted to notice there were several parking spaces. She was right her luck was changing. She parked the car in one of the empty spaces, and turned off the engine. She reached into her handbag and took out a lipstick, and using the rear view mirror, applied it. She wanted to look her best. She needed to look her best. Yes she was nervous, but she needed to get over that. It was now or never. She pressed her back into the seat. No she had to do this. She needed to do this. She had to know. She reached for the door handle. She was not going to be a coward. She got out of the car and began walking. There was no turning back.

SEVENTEEN

Michael had time on his hands now he was not working. He had time to kill. He had time to plan how to kill. Sharon was out again and he could see no reason for rushing out of their home. If she did come back he could pretend that he was between jobs and just popped home. He knew that he had to be careful. He could not be careless again. He shuddered when he thought of how Sharon had caught him looking at making a Will on the Internet. He had not heard her coming. He had been miles away. Normally he could have switched screens seamlessly to something like a news site or even pretended that he was playing poker. Playing poker was always a good one as she left him alone. He was sure that men the world over did it as they looked at sites that they knew their wife would not approve of. They were probably looking at porn sites, and ready to switch the second their other-half came into the room. Michael knew that he had got away with it this time. It could have been so much worse. He knew that he must not alert her in any way.

Michael switched on his notebook computer. He could relax now. He could research at will. He was still worried about the insurance policies. He was sure that the ones they already had in place would not pay out nearly enough. If he took out another specialist insurance policy would they all pay out? Was it like winning the lottery when all your numbers came up at once? Could you even take out two or three travel insurances or were you only allowed to have one? Obviously, having more than one was too obvious, but if you picked the one with a big pay out you could be on to a winner. He guessed that the travel policy together with the one that covered the mortgage and the one that covered your partner's life added to it would make a nice nest egg. It would certainly provide enough to sell up and start a new nest.

He had been searching online and looking at various travel insurance offers. It seemed that people nowadays were not interested in value for money. They seemed more interested in what particular furry toy they might receive if they took out a policy. It certainly did make it easy to compare the market, and the furry toy seemed to have taken over the industry. The world's most famous meerkat had recently introduced all his friends as well. Was it any wonder, Michael thought? He had read somewhere that the fictionalised biography of Aleksandr Orlov had actually out sold the biography of the former Prime Minister, Tony Blair. The meerkat's book was written in his own simple style and it was called, *A Simples Life*, and Michael had to question how simple some of the readers were.

Michael had to admit that the policies looked simple. In fact, they were actually too simple. The life insurance element was not immediately evident from the large number of quotes that came up. It seemed they preferred to focus on the medical and baggage cover. Then something else caught his eye in the top corner of the screen. Apparently one of the Meerkats, who went by the name of Yakov, had not stitched enough toys, and therefore anyone visiting the site for travel insurance was going to be bitterly disappointed that they would not be getting a new furry friend.

Michael also did not find it very informative, and wanted to switch to sites that only promoted travel insurance. The first site that he clicked on offered a bronze, silver, and gold. The more you paid for the policy the more they paid out. The highest appeared to be black. How they came to the label black he was not sure, but he supposed it might be a black day for the claimant. That appeared to pay out over seventy five thousand for a Personal Accident, but what did that mean? Did that mean it paid out on death? You could not exactly call them up to ask them. Well I suppose you could, but he was back to the same old problem of not wanting to flag his intentions. It was difficult. He would have to think about it.

He decided to switch sites and went back to the Cruise Ships Deaths site that he had bookmarked. He began reading the small précis of each case on the home page and one case caught his eye. It concerned a young woman who was a freelance writer who had travelled not only with her husband, but with her mother as well. All three had shared a mini suite. It seemed to Michael to be a cosy arrangement and he was sure that if he had been forced to share accommodation with both his wife and his mother-in-law then one of them would be guaranteed to be going overboard.

The first lesson that Michael learned was not to draw attention to yourself or your partner. Certainly do not do or say anything flippant or make a remark that might come back to bite you or even put you under the spotlight. The couple had taken part in an onboard game show that had been called, 'The Not So Newly Weds.' It was obviously like the Mr and Mrs Show that cluttered up the English television and something which Michael would never had watched, although he had seen it briefly once. It was obviously a little more spiced up for the benefit of the cruisers, and one of the questions had been related to the most unusual place that the couple had been 'familiar'.

Interestingly the couple had only been married for about a year, but their answer had been, 'Well, where haven't we done it. We've done it on cruise ship balconies. We've done it in cruise ship bathrooms. We've done it all over cruise ships. All over. We are cruisers, and we do it all over cruise ships.'

Michael wondered if the husband was not actually advertising what they did and where they did it so it would not appear as shocking if his wife had an accident. Was her husband that clever? Had he planned that far in advance, and perhaps more importantly how could her husband have known that they would get a question such as that? Perhaps he was just an opportunist. If he had been it certainly worked because the couple were definitely remembered by one passenger who was a retired state trooper, who described them as being loud and wild. So much so that when he heard a woman had gone overboard he had immediately thought of the contestant in the 'Not So Newlywed' game.

Michael also thought how a careless comment could come back to haunt you, as one passenger said that after Jennifer had disappeared and the search had begun, he actually bumped into her husband who said that he was going to go down to the casino to see if could change his luck. Michael made a mental note not to skip down to the casino with his chips after Sharon had had hers.

Certainly the disappearance did look a little strange. The couple at first appeared very 'together'. They obviously had their own problems as they both suffered from weight problems, which was what had brought them together in the first place. They also did not appear to be the experienced cruisers that her husband claimed, although Jennifer's first husband had proposed to her on a cruise some years earlier. What caught Michael's eye was that her husband, Raymond Seitz, had been arrested last April for domestic violence and been accused of head butting his wife. He had then been admitted to a correction programme, and Jennifer had asked the prosecutor not to pursue the case. Therefore was it not obvious to all that perhaps there might have been something amiss here. Michael wanted to find out more, but the article did not give a conclusion, and it appeared that she had just been listed as missing.

Michael knew that he had to find out more. It had happened in 2008 and perhaps there had been more developments or even a closure. He switched to Google but just as he began to type, a text message came through on his mobile. He glanced down and read it.

'Is Mr Grey coming out to play? He is summoned to be here by twelve sharp. Failure to do so will render further punishment. Do not disappoint me.'

Michael laughed and then looked at Google, but it was

Mary that had got his attention. He looked at the clock in the bottom right hand of the screen. If he was to get there on time then he certainly had to hurry or perhaps would it be more fun if he were late. He wasn't sure. He wasn't sure about any of this. He had never done anything like this before.

It had all been Mary's idea. She, like millions of other women, had obviously read the Shades of Grey trilogy, and Michael remembered reading how successful it had been, and how women up and down the country were shocking their husbands with their new found ideas. Michael had certainly been shocked. All he had done is mentioned how he had lost the rewire, and had been left with all the materials such as cable, cable ties, and tape, etc.

Mary had immediately leapt on the idea. Apparently, she told him, that the Fifty Shades story had begun when Christian had walked into the hardware store that the heroine had been working in and purchased such items. Therefore, he was under strict orders to bring his tape and ties and visit her. Michael could only imagine what she had in mind. This was out of his league. It was not really his bag, nor had he and Sharon ever done anything like that. Sharon, he was sure, would have preferred a cup of Earl Grey to the attention of Mr Christian Grey. He was really not sure what to expect, but he knew that he could not disappoint Mary. She was not a woman to disappoint.

Michael accelerated away from the Marina up towards Mary's home ignoring the city's 20 mph speed limit. It would be tight if he was to arrive there before the appointed time, but it was nice to know that the coast was clear. Clear, meaning that Mary was certain Bob would not be home, and they had the afternoon to themselves. Michael considered saving time and pulling into their driveway or parking on the road outside, but then he had second thoughts, as he remembered last time he was parked there and Bob came home early. Now he could look back on it and laugh, but at the time he had not found it funny. It made sense to park around the corner and walk. If anybody did clock his van he could always have been at the job he had lost. It paid to be one step in front. Michael was learning quickly. He parked up some distance away from her house, grabbed the materials he was told to bring, and made his way to her house.

Michael certainly felt nervous as he rang the doorbell, and it seemed an eternity until the door opened, as if by magic, and a feminine voice from within said strongly, 'Come in.'

Michael obeyed. He stepped into the hall and caught his first sight of Mary. It was not the Mary that he recognised. Mary was in a black skin-tight cat suit complete with mask. Michael felt his pulse race as he bent towards her to kiss her.

'Don't touch,' she demanded sternly. 'Don't even look at me unless you are invited to do so. Look at the floor. Did you bring the stuff that I asked you to?'

Michael nodded obediently. Bess, their Labrador looked up from her bed in the hall as if she was disgusted by their behaviour, and then went back to sleep.

'Good boy. Now get upstairs take all your clothes off, and I mean everything. Nicely fold them. Then lay down on the bed on your back and wait for me. Do not take long. Do everything I say. Do not disobey me, and do not disappoint me. Do you understand?'

Michael nodded meekly and did as he was told. He wasn't

sure if he was nervous or excited, but he was certainly out of his comfort zone, and he was sure that Mary was not about to offer comfort. He wasn't even sure how it happened, but he found himself secured to her brass bedstead. Mary then produced a silk scarf that she used as a gag. Michael opened his mouth as she applied it. He could now only communicate by his eyes. He wondered what was coming next. He did not have long to wonder as Mary brought a feather duster into play.

Suddenly his phone went off in his pocket of his trousers that were neatly folded on the chair by the side of the bed. He could tell from the ringtone that it was Sharon. She had her own sound so he instantly knew when it was her calling. The track Michael had chosen for her personal ringtone was, 'The Bitch Is Back.' Of course, Sharon did not know as she was never there when she called him.

Mary went over to his phone and took it out of his pocket. For several seconds he thought Mary was going to answer it, and just hold it to his ear so he could speak to Sharon. It was the sort of thing that Mary would do. She would certainly get a kick out of it. She would have to undo the gag first. Instead, to his surprise Mary just terminated the call. Michael breathed a sigh of relief. The phone beeped again. Obviously, Sharon had left a message. Michael could feel his excitement diminishing.

Mary shook her head. 'You are such a naughty boy, but you disappoint me. Aren't you excited anymore? I hope you are. Do you know what I do to naughty boys?'

Without the power of speech Michael could only shake his head. Mary laughed. She went over to her drawer and took something out. Something that Michael could not name. He wasn't exactly sure what you did with it, but he did have an idea. Mary walked towards him just as her mobile, which was sitting on her dressing table, went off. Mary glanced at it, and then said casually, 'It's Sharon. Shall I answer it?'

Michael shook his head violently. Mary laughed. 'Where is your sense of humour? It might be fun.'

Mary picked up the phone. She could see the fear in Michael's eyes. She laughed again, and pressed the button, 'Hi Sharon,' she said brightly.

Michael made a face.

'Oh what am I doing? Oh just a little bit of light dusting. Yes. Yes I've got the feather duster in my hand as I speak.' Mary laughed. She was obviously pleased with her clever answer. She glanced at Michael and then her expression changed. 'Oh you want to call in. Well where are you? Only I was just about to go out afterwards.'

Michael looked anxiously towards Mary. It was obvious she was having trouble putting Sharon off. He wondered what Sharon wanted and why she was so keen. Mary put down the phone. 'She'll be here in a couple of minutes. Apparently she was just going past and wanted to pop in to see me. I couldn't put her off. Especially as she knew I was in. Oh shit.' She reached down and undid Michael's gag.

'What are you playing at?' he said angrily. 'Quick untie me.'

Mary started taking off her gear. Well peeling it off to be precise. Mary was really struggling. 'Give me a minute. I can't go down to her dressed like this can I?'

'What am I going to do?' Michael asked.

Mary laughed. 'Well there's not much you can do. You'll

just have to keep quiet.'

'What? At least untie me.'

The doorbell rang. Mary struggled with the ties. 'Sorry. I can't do them. I'll have to cut them off later.'

The doorbell sounded again. Mary managed to struggle out of her outfit and threw it on the floor. She reached in the wardrobe and grabbed the first dress she came to. 'Sorry lover,' she said. 'Just hang about. I'll be back when I can.'

EIGHTEEN

Sharon stood on the doorstep resisting the urge to press the doorbell again. She had already pressed it twice. The heavy wooden Victorian door also had a large brass door knocker shaped as a lion's head. Obviously, it was only ornamental as, because of the size of the house, they still needed a doorbell; but it was in keeping with the property. She also realised that their dog, Bess, had not barked. Perhaps it was asleep or it might have been out with Bob. Maybe, like all of us, Sharon thought, it was just getting old and could not be bothered.

Finally the door was opened by a dishevelled Mary. She certainly looked a bit out of sorts, and not her normal assured self. Sharon smiled warmly and Mary smiled thinly back. Sharon immediately thought she had called at a bad time. Why, she didn't know. Mary had only said that she was dusting.

'Come in Sharon,' Mary said. 'It's an unexpected pleasure.'

Sharon detected a little bit of sarcasm in her voice. It was certainly not the welcome that she had wanted or expected. It immediately put her on edge. Perhaps it had been a mistake to come here. She could have talked to Mary over the phone. That would have been easier, but Sharon had thought that face to face was better. Now she was not so sure.

'What can I do for you anyway?'

Sharon hesitated and then followed Mary down the hall and into the kitchen which was three to four times the size of hers, complete with a large expensive range cooker. 'Well originally I was going to give you a call tonight, but I was just passing and thought I would drop in for a coffee.'

Mary walked to the machine and switched it on. 'What would you like?' Mary's tone remained monotone.

Sharon tried to smile and lighten the mood. 'See, it's just like Starbucks. I'll have a Cappuccino, please.'

'Would Madam like chocolate sprinkled on it?'

Sharon nodded pleased that the mood seemed to be getting lighter. 'Oh I do like your dress,' she giggled. 'How long have you had that?'

Mary smirked. 'Yes it is a bit crass isn't it? It was literally the first thing I put my hands on in the wardrobe. We all don't want to look like a princess when we are cleaning. But I guess I should throw it out. I'll never wear it out again.'

Sharon looked at the feather duster with its long stick handle that was on the kitchen table. It looked almost too good to use for cleaning. 'I hope Bob appreciates your efforts,' she said as she nodded towards the duster.

Mary laughed, picked up the duster, and waved it at Sharon. 'Oh yes. You would be surprised how such efforts can be appreciated. In fact, I might even get to do more. You should try it on Michael.'

Sharon looked quizzical as she spoke, 'Well to be honest

I was trying to get hold of Michael, but I can't seem to.' She took her mobile phone out of her handbag.

'I expect he's tied up,' Mary volunteered. 'Probably tied up and can't answer the phone.'

Yes I think he's around here somewhere on a new job. Well at least he is supposed to be. Do you mind if I go out in the hall to call him. See if he answers this time.' Sharon went to stand up.

'Don't worry,' Mary said quickly. 'Stay here and call him, I've just got to nip upstairs.

When Mary had left the room Sharon tried Michael again. She got down from the kitchen stool and paced the room as she waited for the call to connect. Strangely, for only a few seconds she thought she heard a phone ring with an Elton John ringtone, and then her call went straight to answer machine. She put the phone back in her bag not bothering to leave a message again.

'Any luck?' Mary said as she walked back into the room. 'Did you get hold of him?'

Sharon shook her head. It was a shame she just wanted to confirm with Michael about the cruise that he had surprised her with. Was it actually booked? Could it be moved? Did she have to cancel the holiday with the girls? Now Sharon was not so sure. She had wanted to tell Mary face to face, but now did not seem to be a good time. She also wanted to tell Mary where she had been and what had happened. She needed to tell someone. Mary was her friend, and if you could not confide in your friends, who else could you confide in? She just had to tell someone.

'Well you'll see him tonight? Won't you? I think we might even be seeing you later in the week.'

'Really?' Sharon answered. 'I don't know anything about that. Michael never mentioned it.'

'Oh. Must have been something Michael mentioned to Bob.'

Sharon raised her plucked eyebrows. She always seemed to be the last person in the know. It was always like that. Sometimes she resented Mary for it. She knew she shouldn't as Mary was her friend. But Mary always liked to revel in being the one in the know and in charge of everything. She was like the leader of the gang. Sometimes she was great. There was no better person to have around in a crisis, and she would literally do anything for you if she could. Nevertheless at other times she could be quite cruel and spiteful like she derived some sadistic pleasure from the discomfort of others. It seemed to depend on her mood. Today she did not seem to be in a good one.

Sharon realised that she felt like a small child again and she suddenly needed the bathroom. 'Can I just pop upstairs and use your toilet?'

Mary appeared to stiffen. 'Err. Why don't you use the one downstairs?'

Sharon wasn't sure. She had never really used the one downstairs before. It was very small. She wondered why Mary was so jumpy. 'I don't mind,' Sharon said lightly. 'Whichever.'

'Just that I was cleaning the one upstairs. Was actually in the middle of it.'

Sharon stood up and made her way to the lower one. She decided that now was certainly not a good time to discuss the holiday or the cancellation of it. It was also not a good time to confide in Mary where she had just been and what had happened. It would have to wait. She would make her excuses and leave.

Sharon drove down to the shopping centre called Churchill Square. Some years ago it had been refurbished from an outside one into a modernised indoor one, and the architects had cleverly managed to get in two floors. It was basically just like any other Mall within the country with the usual range of shops. It was also a bit claustrophobic, and at times the noise from the shoppers reverberated in the tight enclosure. Sharon had decided that she needed some retail therapy to make her happier after her visit to Mary. She decided to treat herself to a new outfit. What woman did not feel better after a bit of shopping for themselves? Sharon parked her car in the NCP car park aware of the high hourly charges, and walked up one flight of steps straight into the shopping centre.

She was immediately greeted by the noisy buzz of the centre. She started to feel better already. She glanced at her watch and briefly wondered where Michael was, and immediately wished she hadn't. Michael often made her feel guilty especially if she had been shopping and he was at home when she returned with her bags. Michael could be the most generous of men and often used to treat her to something like an expensive handbag, especially if he had a good win at the casino. In later years when he played more prudently, the generosity had been less evident. There were other times though when he would have given Scrooge a run for his money. It might even have been something small like Sharon throwing out the tomato sauce bottle when there was a small amount left to use if it had been stood on its top.

Sharon, like other women, she was sure, had developed

a number of stock answers to diffuse questioning. These included such classics if he noticed a new top or outfit as, 'Oh had this years just not worn it for a long time,' or 'Oh yes I got it in a sale.' Of course, she always remembered to remove the price tags and kept any receipts in her purse.

Today, though, she would not be brow beaten. She deserved it and she was going to treat herself. She looked at her watch again. She had a few hours until the shops shut.

When Sharon returned home Michael was in the lounge wearing a towelling bath robe. The robe she knew had been a complimentary one from one of their cruises with the cruise lines name monogrammed on it. Perhaps it was really intended for their use whilst aboard, and not actually theirs to keep, but like most cruisers they had packed it away at the end of the voyage. Michael saw her immediately as she came through the front door so there was no time to hide the bags. He glanced down at them and although it was obvious that they did not come from a cheap shop he didn't say anything.

'Hi,' Sharon said. 'Did you have a good day? I did try to get hold of you a couple of times, but you didn't answer your mobile.'

Michael held up his hand as if in a peace gesture, and the cuff on his robe fell further down his arm. 'You wouldn't believe how bad it was.'

Sharon immediately noticed that he had a reddish mark around his wrist. 'What happened to your wrist? Is it painful?'

'Oh that. No. It's nothing,' Michael said quickly. 'Just a burn when I was pulling cables through.'

Sharon nodded without really wondering how that could cause such a mark. It appeared she was winning. Michael certainly did not appear to be himself. Never before could she ever remember her coming home with some shopping and Michael not questioning her on what she had bought. Especially today, she reasoned, by the type of packaging, it was obvious they were not from one of the more well-known large cheap as chips shops. But no he had said nothing. Was the man ill? Sharon decided that she did not want to hang around and find out. She did appear to be winning, and as her father had always said to her when she was a little girl, 'Quit when you're ahead.' Sharon knew that she was never really that much ahead of Michael, and any victory would always be short lived. It had been so, up until now.

She walked into the bedroom ready to put away her new clothes quickly, but then she thought better of it. No she would enjoy trying them on again. Why should she bow to pressure from Michael? If he was hungry then he would just have to wait for his dinner or simply do something for himself.

She had become tired of worrying what Michael wanted. She had become tired of being beholden to him. What did she have to be scared of anymore? Why did she need to be scared of Michael? Did they not say that, 'An Englishman's home is his castle?' That had certainly been true of their home. It had certainly been Michael's castle. His little castle in the clouds, but to her it had been a prison. Sharon often felt shackled and restricted. It often felt like a prison with a fantastic view, but then again that was probably what the inmates of Alcatraz thought as they looked out towards the bay. Now it was time for her to break free. Time to let down her hair and escape.

Firstly, she decided, she would clear out her wardrobe

and get rid of all the clothes that she would never wear again. Mary had given her the idea with the old dress she had been wearing and was going to throw out. Sharon decided she would do the same. She had to let go. She could give them to one of the many charity shops that now occupied the town. Someone else would benefit from them, and the charity would benefit from the money. She immediately felt pleased with herself.

Sharon pushed shut the bedroom door and picked up her mobile. She then drilled down all her contacts until she came to the one listed as MFB. MFB, she laughed to herself. She had listed it as such so that if it was seen it did not look like anything or anyone. It looked kind of innocent and reminded her of that cheap furniture chain that had now gone to the wall and no longer traded. What did they used to be called? MFI, or as Michael used to joke to her, Made for Idiots. Anyway, anyone picking up her phone would have no idea that MFB stood for the Muscles from Brussels. Then again it could have stood for My Fuck Buddy. Now there was a thought. That was her secret. A secret that she still wanted to share, but that would have to wait for now.

Sharon looked towards the bedroom door and then started texting.

NINETEEN

Michael could not remember ever feeling so humiliated, nor could he remember feeling so embarrassed. He went red just thinking about what had happened. He had certainly not become a fan of Fifty Shades of Grey, and although he was sure that Mary would not tell anyone, he did wish she had signed a Non-Disclosure Agreement (NDA). That would not only have kept it true to the story, but it would have made him feel a bit better. He would certainly never tell a living soul. He was sure that he went fifty shades of red when he recalled the events. If it had not been so embarrassing it would have almost been funny. However, he was not laughing, and he was hoping that Mary was not still laughing at him. Honestly, you couldn't make it up.

Michael pictured himself again being tied to the bed. He knew that he was a man that liked to be in control. He was always in control so perhaps the thought of Mary taking that control and turning it into fun had actually been appealing. Mary's outfit, and the concept had been very exciting. Mary did not do things by halves, and as always she pulled out all the stops. It was Sharon that had spoilt it.

He could have happily strangled Sharon with the ties. Of course, she did not know what she had done. She never would, but he still resented her for it. Every minute had seemed like an hour as he had struggled with the ties. He had felt so helpless and at first he had flapped like a fish out of water. Then he realised that he needed to empty his bladder. Oh the shame, and then worse. He thought he was going to soil the bed. Bob's bed. How would he have ever got over that embarrassment? Perhaps more importantly how would Mary have been able to explain any evidence of it to Bob? It did not bear thinking about. His phone going off that was the other thing. Mary stopping Sharon coming upstairs to use the toilet. By powers that he did not know he had, he held himself together, but it had been a close run thing. It was certainly not an experience that he was in a hurry to repeat again.

Worse was that Mary had laughed about it afterwards until he had become angry. Mary had never seen him as angry as that before. He had seen the shock on her face. Perhaps he had gone too far, and he wondered if it might have damaged their relationship. He glanced down at his phone. There was still not a new message from Mary. Anyway, he decided nothing should deter him from his mission. Sharon was in the bedroom doing what she did best: trying on clothes and sorting them out.

He switched on his computer. Now he thought would be a good time to find out what happened to the missing overweight female freelance writer he had researched earlier. He typed her name into Google and was immediately rewarded with several sites all offering further information. He began to read intently.

It seemed that many of the passengers had been shocked how the incident was handled. There had been no ship's announcement or photo posted, and none of the passengers had been asked if they could shed any light on it. The ship carried on as normal, and the news really only spread by word of mouth. Certainly the cruise line did not seem keen to gather any information about the incident. One family, in a cabin below, even reported that they had heard someone shouting, 'Stop hitting me.' This was on Christmas Day and they called security who did not even respond. They also found out that her husband did not report her missing for six hours. Six hours. Michael found that interesting because even the strongest swimmer would have succumbed by then.

Michael reached for the television remote control, and began to surf the channels. He settled on a news programme. He did not really take in what the news reader was saying. What he was reading was news to him. It was probably news to most people. Even people that went on many cruises. Yes, so this single case might well have been on one of the many American channels as a news item, but it was as he had thought previously, here now and gone tomorrow, and people were both too busy or too lazy to connect all the incidents like this that happened at sea. It was an outrage that didn't outrage, basically because nobody knew. Certainly the many millions of cruisers who kept coming back for more were seemingly oblivious to the dark side of the industry, and here was the evidence to prove that the cruise companies wanted to keep it this way.

Michael went back to his computer, and read a report of how one of the passengers had overheard an FBI Agent giving a report to his superiors. It was either very basic poor investigating or they could simply not be bothered to do it properly. In short there was no investigative drive. The blogger, who claimed to work in a high security field said it was highly unusual to give an open report in an unsecured area. The Agent had not even mentioned all the persons involved, and had also failed to properly secure and seal the cabins as a crime site.

It was obvious to Michael that absolutely nothing should spoil the enjoyment of the cruisers. They were a protected species. Well those that survived were. If they lost one or two on the way round then no matter. Let the cruise line close the ranks and as long as the ship sailed on time, all was well and ship shape.

It certainly was a Christmas to remember on the ship that had a Nordic name, and it was also rumoured that the ship had video of a woman wearing a white robe going overboard on Boxing Day. Michael wasn't really sure what to think. It was obvious that many of the passengers did know something had occurred and were shocked at how it had been handled. Some said they actually found out on CNN. All seemed to agree that no comprehensive search had been carried out.

What was perhaps unusual about this case was that the couple had become almost high profile by their appearance in the game show. They stood out from all the other passengers. However, when the incident happened even the ship's security were quoted as saying, 'No comment,' if they were asked any questions about it or how someone had fallen off.

What astounded Michael was that even reading between the lines it seemed that because of the very history of the couple, and especially the behaviour of the husband, both before and on the cruise, it should have surely rung alarm bells. Not to the cruise line. All that seemed to matter was as long as they could still ring their ship's bell to carry on as normal, all was well in their world.

Michael was still interested in the aftermath. How did it conclude? Was there any closure? He needed to dig deeper and find it. It did not take him long. In fact, it took him a lot less time to find out than it did for Mary to untie him or at least cut off the ties. He looked at his mobile again and hoped that Mary had not severed her ties with him now after his angry outburst. There was still no message.

Michael then found another site that told him what he wanted to know. The article was written two years after the woman, who was named Jennifer, had first been reported missing. It confirmed that unfortunately her body had never been found despite a search by the US Coast Guard. The FBI had concluded that she was either pushed or she jumped. They had decided on the second conclusion. The family had issued a statement four days after she disappeared stating that Jennifer had emotional problems, and it was likely that she had taken her life. No suicide note was ever found.

That was it, Michael thought. Case over. No foul play. That was the official verdict from the authorities. Her husband had never been available for comment afterwards. Michael would have loved to have asked him if she had been insured and how much had he cashed in. He even wondered if the husbands luck had improved in the Casino. This was definitely one of the most interesting cases that Michael had read so far. To him there were so many holes in the case, but it still ended up without any criminal trial or conviction. Having said that, this was not the only one. There were many, many others. It appeared the law of the land did not extend to the law of the seas. Michael knew that he would have to be careful. He would certainly not be so obvious, and he would certainly not be as stupid as some of the husbands and partners that he read about. Nevertheless, even they had got off scot-free or perhaps they were only guilty of being stupid.

Michael sat back on the sofa feeling very pleased with himself when suddenly there was a loud crashing noise from the bedroom. Quickly, he jumped up and ran into the bedroom. He didn't bother knocking and just opened the door. Sharon was lying on the ground surrounded by clothes an upturned chair was next to her. If he had not known that she had been in there he would have thought that they had been burgled. Clothes were strewn everywhere.

Sharon looked up and half smiled and half grimaced, as she laid on the floor.

'What happened?' Michael asked. 'Have you hurt yourself?'

Sharon shook her head. 'No I don't think so. I was just up on the chair trying to get that box, and had a sharp pain in my leg. Then I just toppled over. Lucky I had a soft landing and landed on all these clothes.

Michael extended his hand and Sharon took it. Slowly he helped pull her up. She sat on the edge of the bed. 'Are you OK?'

Sharon looked shaken although she tried to smile it off. 'Can you get me some bin liners, please? I need to bag all this lot up.'

Michael nodded. 'What the hell are you doing? Why are all these lot out? What are you doing with them?'

Sharon rubbed her leg. 'Well it was Mary that gave me the idea really.'

'Mary?' Michael did not want Mary giving any ideas to Sharon. Her ideas to him were enough. What was the woman playing at? 'Mary. What do you mean?'

'Well when I visited her she was wearing this horrible old dress. Not like her at all. Anyway, she said she had only put it on to do the cleaning. Said she wasn't going to wear it out ever again.'

Michael shuddered. He did not really want to be reminded of that occasion.

'Well I thought I would do the same,' Sharon continued. 'I have so many clothes. Now I know that I will never wear this lot again. They are just taking up space. Someone else might get some enjoyment out of wearing them, and I can raise some money for a charity.'

'Can't you sell them on eBay?' Michael asked. 'You could get some money back.

'What?' Sharon said incredulously. 'Are things really that bad? I thought your business was doing well. Surely we don't need the money that badly. Besides, I can't be bothered with photographing them all, uploading, and then if I do get a buyer I have to package and post. No it's just not worth it. As I said I want to do some good with them. I want them to help a charity, and someone else can enjoy them. I will never wear them again. Anyway, you were forever moaning about how many clothes I've got, and how much room they all take up. I thought you would've been pleased.'

Michael decided not to argue. He certainly did not want her to question how his business was doing, besides he had other things to consider. So if Sharon was considering downsizing her wardrobe what did it matter to him? If he took the long term view it would probably make his life easier in the future as there would certainly be less to sort out. He would just leave Sharon to get on with it.

'Anyway,' Sharon said defensively. 'What are you doing at the moment in the other room? Are you still thinking about doing a Will?'

Michael was not sure what to answer. What was the right answer? Sharon knew what he had told her before. He could not deny it, but he did not want to labour the point. It was a loose end that perhaps needed to be tidied up. He just wasn't sure how. 'I'll get you those bin liners,' Michael said trying to buy time.' He went into the kitchen and when he returned Sharon was already beginning to fold the clothes.

She looked up. 'Well if you are doing a Will I think I should do one too.'

Michael tried not to show his surprise. In the past Sharon had never ever wanted to discuss the future, and certainly never the inevitability of death. She had an almost childlike attitude to life as if she were going to stay young and live forever. God knows she spent enough on creams and potions trying to keep ageing at bay. She had certainly bought into all the hype regarding the advertising in many of her women's magazines. What, he wondered, had made her have a change of mind? Was it something he had said or done? He would have to be careful. Now he had a problem.

Michael went back into the lounge. Originally that had been exactly what he wanted. Originally he was wondering how he was going to get Sharon to make a Will. Now he was not sure if it was such a good idea. He looked up to the heavens as if looking for inspiration, not that he really believed in any great super power. He never had. No, he thought, Wills and insurance policies were often the overlooked items of the living, and often ignored. Was it because the living were too busy living or too lazy? It was always something that they would get round to, but often never did. Perhaps it was because the living did not want to be reminded that perhaps the only certain thing in life was that we were all going to die. It was just a question of when and how? Anyway, Michael considered that if there were ever an investigation after the demise of Sharon then surely all of these pieces of paper would come into play. It might then look strange if they had only both just made a Will before the cruise? Would that not raise a few eyebrows as being rather convenient? Might he be better off if Sharon had not made one? He paced the lounge. Would Sharon be suspicious if he put her off doing one? Should he put her off doing one, and not do one himself either. He would have to give it some thought. He realised that he still had some way to go. He still had a lot of things to do and a lot of things to think about and to take into consideration. There seemed so many hidden traps that could trip him up at a later date after the event.

Michael looked down at his mobile and noticed that he had received a text. He picked up the phone and punched in the code. The text was from Mary.

'Hi lover. Are we still friends? If so would you like to drop by for a blowjob with a difference? I have hot chocolate and toothpaste ready. R.S.V.P.'

Michael reached for his mobile. There was a God.

TWENTY

Sharon drove towards the city centre. All the bin bags stuffed with her clothes were in the back of the car, and she was feeling very pleased with herself. She had found it very therapeutic sorting them all out. It was almost like New Year's Eve and out with the old, but she was determined not to go mad with the new. Perhaps she would buy one or two outfits, but nothing like the number that she was now giving away.

She reached the traffic lights at the bottom of Lower Rock Gardens, and they immediately turned red. She automatically stopped. It was time to stop in her life. Time to reflect. Time to move on. She had new things she wanted to try. She now had to move on. The traffic lights turned to green. She turned right and then drove down towards the roundabout at the Pier. That was another one of Michael's gripes, as she glanced towards the large neon sign that said, 'Brighton Pier'. To him it would never be *the* 'Brighton Pier'. To him and thousands of other residents of his generation they would always call it by what is used to be known, 'The

Palace Pier'. Brighton had always had two piers until the West Pier had been burnt to the sea. The West Pier was now just a metal skeleton and home to thousands of starlings, but nevertheless it seemed obscene and unkind to refer to the remaining open pier as if the West Pier had gone altogether. The West Pier's rusting outline almost serves as a monument that would remind both residents and visitors of what had once been there. It was a reminder that nothing lasts forever, but Sharon was sure that in its present form it would still be there long after she was gone. Sharon had always agreed with Michael about the naming of the surviving pier, but then at times she wondered if she did have her own opinion or was it just Michael's influence that she had.

Did it mean that the longer couples stayed together the less individual they became? Had she really, all those years ago, stood and said, 'To honour and obey?' Had she actually said those words? She realised that nowadays they had been dropped from the marriage ceremony. Well at least the 'Obey' one had. Women nowadays were not so stupid and naive. Although when she married she had been happy with her lot. Michael had always been the main breadwinner. It was not a role that she questioned or challenged. She had been happy to rely on him. That was the way of the world then.

The world had changed so much, and she had seen so many changes. She knew that she would not see that many changes in the future. It was almost impossible to appreciate how the world had changed since she was a little girl. From party line telephones and black and white television. Now nothing was black and white anymore. Nothing appeared that simple. Life then had been slow but sure.

Sharon slowed the car, not that you could drive fast

within the city anyway. She looked through the passenger window towards the sea. It was calm and she knew she too needed to remain calm. She looked down at her mobile sitting on the passenger's seat. She knew she should turn it on. Michael might be trying to get hold of her, but that was the very reason why she had turned it off.

Obviously she did not want him to know where she had been or why. Her body was still tingling from her earlier meeting. Sharon took one hand off the wheel and put it to her face. She felt a little hot and flustered. She turned the car's temperature dial down. She now knew that her life would never be the same. It could never be the same. She played back in her mind what he had said and how reassuring his words were. How kind and thoughtful he had been. Not at all like Michael. He had spoken to her softly. His touch had been gentle. It was obvious that he was experienced, but he had made her feel special as if she was the only one. She had not even been embarrassed about her nudity. She had soon got over that. He had not rushed. He had taken his time. It was all about her. It was as if she was the centre of his world and he did not want her to worry. She realised he was quite a few years younger than her, but that did not seem to matter either. He was experienced and he knew what he was doing. That was all that mattered. Now it was over. Now it was behind her. Now she knew. She would never be the same person again. She wanted to call him. She wanted to see him again, but she knew she would have to wait. She would have to wait until next week.

She reached over and turned on her mobile. It immediately beeped to inform her that she had at least one message waiting for her. She was tempted to pick it up but she did not have hands free. She never had. She was not like Michael. All that seemed to come naturally to him. He could answer his phone when he was driving. She had to risk three points, and a fine, or risk his wrath and questioning. On this stretch from The Pier to West Street she could not even pull the car over. There was no place to stop. She would have to keep moving, and if it was Michael he could keep moaning.

She parked the car in the West Street Car Park determined to keep within the two hour price range band. That was all she needed. The first message was from Michael. She started to listen to it and then by impulse she just deleted it. It was actually the first time ever she had not listened to a message from him all the way through, but she thought she got the gist, and now she had more important things to think about than him ranting on. The second message was from Julie. She too had just arrived and was waiting for Sharon in their favourite coffee shop. It was time for a natter.

~

Julie returned from the counter with two coffees and Sharon thanked her. For a moment there appeared to be an awkward silence, and then Julie spoke. 'So what have you been up to then? Is he good? Tell me all.'

Sharon twiddled with the long spoon that went to the bottom of her coffee cup, as she debated her answer. Julie waited patiently, but Sharon was in no hurry to answer. Once the three of them had never seemed to have any secrets. It was a kind of girl Musketeers thing, 'All for one and one for all' or 'The Pink Ladies'. Now as they got older it was different. It wasn't Julie that she did not trust, but at times Julie could often forget things and then blurt them out in her excitement. Mary was behaving strangely sometimes.

Sharon certainly thought she had been lately. That was why Sharon had still not told her about not going away with the girls. Would she be brave enough to tell Julie, who in turn would probably go straight home and tell Mary?

Finally Sharon spoke, and she said demurely, 'Sorry, I don't know what you mean.'

'Oh I think you do. I think you know only too well. It's written all over your face. I know you have something to tell me. I have known you too long. I can read you like a book.'

Sharon nodded. Julie was right. She was dying to tell someone. She had to tell someone. She had to share it with somebody. But could she trust Julie? What damage could it do if it got out? Surely she was best off not telling anybody. She should keep it to herself. Yes that was best. It was best kept to herself, but it would be difficult if not impossible. She knew that. She made a promise to herself that she would not reveal anything. Not at the moment. She would keep it to herself for the moment. She would wait and see how everything panned out. It was too early to say. She should learn from past mistakes. She should, but she never seemed to. This time it had to be different, there was too much to lose.

'So when are you seeing him again?'

Sharon wanted to say, 'Next week, but it's not like you think.' Instead she just smiled. Her mother would have said, 'Has the cat got your tongue?'

Julie was more patient. That was one thing that Sharon liked about her. She was not pushy. Excitable, but not too pushy. She knew Julie was waiting. She had to say something. Sharon smiled. 'Trust me, Julie. I don't want to large it all up or worry you. I don't really want to involve anyone else or draw anyone else in. This is about me. It is something that I have to do for me at the moment. I might need help. I might need your help, but please be patient with me. I will tell you when I need to or when the time is right. Besides, I really don't want Mary to find out anything. I really don't.' Sharon settled back in her chair.

Julie picked up her coffee cup and took a sip. She had left a little bit of froth on her lip, and Sharon laughed and pointed to it. Julie laughed as well, and wiped it off.

'Mary?' Julie looked startled. 'Yes she does seem to be a bit different these days.'

Sharon sighed. 'I thought I was the only one that noticed. She has certainly changed.'

The two women sat there silently for a moment. It was what they didn't say, not what they said. It was as if a confidence had been extended between them. It was obvious that neither one wanted to directly betray Mary. After all, they were all friends, but maybe they both had enough of her overbearing ways. She had certainly become more controlling lately, and there was something altogether different about her. Sharon was glad that Julie had also noticed.

Sharon seized on the moment. Maybe Julie would not mind if she cancelled their trip. However, she had still not confirmed with Michael. She did need to speak to him about it. She really needed to speak to him about a lot of things.

She would have to measure her words carefully and consider what she was going to say. Michael could get angry quite quickly and then he would twist her words and confuse her. It would all come out wrong, and it would sound wrong even to her. Michael would then know that he was winning the argument, and she would feel deflated. It could not be like this any longer, she decided. She had to be strong. Really if she were honest Michael could be a bully. Perhaps though it was her fault, as he often said she had driven him to be angry. He only wanted what was best for her. He was only trying to look after her. Perhaps she was being unfair.

Sharon looked at her watch. 'I can't be too long. I've got to get to the Charity Shop.'

Julie raised her eyebrows. 'Fallen on hard times? Shopping for second hand now are we? Trying to save a penny or two? That's not like you.'

Sharon smiled. She had never been against these shops. There were more and more charity shops springing up every day in Brighton. They hopefully did some good, but memories of second hand clothes brought back her childhood. That was really all Sharon had known as she was growing up. Hand me downs and Jumble Sales. She shuddered at the thought. Admittedly many of her friends had been in the same position, but she had still felt poor and ashamed. She had longed to grow up and earn her own money so that she could buy new things for herself. She always dreaded going back to being poor. It was something that she knew she would never get over.

Her mobile started to ring. She glanced down it was Michael. She immediately pressed the red button. She knew that Michael would probably be annoyed at being cut off. He would almost certainly question her as to why, and ask her where she was? Normally she would have panicked. Now though she felt surprisingly calm.

'Take it,' Julie said. 'It might be your friend.'

Sharon shook her head. 'Michael.'

Julie look disappointed, but Sharon did not want to

enlighten her. Julie probably had a good idea what Michael was like, but Sharon certainly did not want to take Julie into her confidence regarding what else was happening in her life. She had to do this on her own. She had to be strong.

Her mobile started to ring again. It was Michael. This time she decided to answer. 'Hi,' she said coolly.

'Where are you?' he asked.

'In town,' she answered. There was no need to tell him that she was with Julie. He would probably offer some smart remark about him working hard while she was a lady of leisure, and how lucky she was. She decided to turn the tables. 'Have you finished work early? Are you home?'

It worked. Michael took a second or two to answer. He did not sound angry. In fact far from it. 'I just wondered what time will you be home?'

Sharon looked at her watch. 'In an hour or so. Why?'

'Well I am sure that you won't want to cook tonight. Thought we might go out for something to eat.'

Sharon sucked in her breath. 'Just the two of us?' She was sure that she sounded shocked. It was not really what they did. Not just the two of them. She wanted to ask to what she owed this consideration.

'No,' Michael continued. 'Well to be honest we have been invited out with Bob and Mary. Yes, sort of last minute thing. Thought it would save you cooking. Don't worry about rushing back. We haven't got to meet them until eight thirty.'

Sharon put down her mobile and looked at Julie. There was so much she wanted to say. Michael had sounded so different. So considerate. He had been so even and thoughtful.

Why she wondered? What did he know? What had he

found out? What had come over him and why? That was the question.

TWENTY ONE

Michael put down his mobile and smiled at Mary. 'That's settled then. It's all arranged.'

Mary snuggled a little bit closer to Michael on her sofa. She rested her head on his shoulder. Michael sighed. He felt like the cat that had just had the cream. Well he had of sorts. He had just had one of the most amazing experiences thanks to Mary. The toothpaste that had been used in between the warm hot chocolate, as she used her mouth so expertly on him, had sent him to places that he never had been before.

Mary was by far the most skilful and experimental lover he had ever had. Her text said it all, and she had delivered. In fact she had exceeded herself, and coming from Michael that was praise indeed. How could he not be with this woman? She was his Helen. His Helen of Troy. OK, he wasn't her husband building his wooden horse to get her back, and he would not launch a thousand ships, but Michael would launch somebody from a ship for her. He would actually commit murder to be with her. He would then build her their own Troy so that they could be together forever.

'Won't Sharon be a bit suspicious about us all going out tonight? Won't she think it odd?'

Michael thought for a moment. 'No, I don't think so. Why should she?' He was pleased he had spoken nicely to Sharon for two reasons. Firstly he was sure that it would make Sharon less suspicious and secondly it showed Mary how kind and thoughtful he could be.

'Well if we are all there tonight and I bring up the subject of a holiday nobody can really object, can they? How are they both to know? How can they possibly realise what we have chatted about and planned?" Michael took hold of Mary's hand and held it between his two hands. 'I do so want to be with you. I would do anything for you. You do know that don't you?'

Mary laughed. 'Yes. Yes I do. You are like most men. I know that the way to your heart is not through your stomach. It's not hard to keep you happy. Speaking of hard, did you enjoy that?'

Michael nodded enthusiastically. 'I should say so. That was the best. The very best.'

Mary smiled a knowing smile. She was obviously very pleased with herself. Michael wondered what she was planning next. He did not have long to wait. She leaned a little closer to him and in a hushed tone whispered, 'I tell you what I am going to do tonight. I'm not going to wear any underwear under my clothes. Just some high heels with some hold ups. Oh and it will be quite a short skirt so I'll have to be careful won't I? Will that turn you on? Will that do it for you, my lover? Just think all you have to do is bend down below the table and have a little look and I can give you a flash. For your eyes only. Is the thought making you excited?'

'Yes. Yes,' Michael stammered. 'But won't Bob notice?'

Mary laughed. 'I could stand in front of Bob either completely naked or with my finest underwear on while he was watching Match of the Day, and all he would do would be to ask me to move out of the way.' She took her hand from his and placed it on his crotch. 'Are you getting excited again?'

Michel knew that he was, but he looked at his watch. He needed to rush home and be ready before Sharon, and now he had less than an hour. Besides, it had not been that long since the last time, but he felt like a teenager again. He knew his expression gave him away. He was putty in her hands. Well perhaps putty was not the best example. Well not in its softened state.

Mary reached down into her handbag and produced a packet of extra strong mints. She held them up and smiled. 'See,' she said. 'You don't necessarily need toothpaste. I have read that you can get much the same sensation with extra strong mints.'

'Really? Where did you read that?' Michael asked.

'Mary laughed. 'Well I don't think it was in a Trebor advertisement. Anyway, shall we see?'

Michael looked at his watch again. Mary virtually undressed the packet with the same delicacy as if she might have been appearing in a Cadbury's Flake advert. She took out a mint and then rolled it around her mouth with her tongue looking straight at Michael. 'Don't worry,' she said. 'If you don't have time. But I think it would be a shame to waste it. Don't you?'

Michael nodded sheepishly. He felt like a schoolboy. How could he refuse? Already he found himself rising to the occasion.

Michael returned home feeling both smug and satisfied. In over five decades on this planet he could not remember having a more exciting afternoon. Mary brought both experience and excitement to the table. When he thought about what she had said about him looking under the table he could feel himself becoming aroused once again. Though, what she would be like to live with full time, he wondered? Would she be a short wonder or would the excitement continue? Could it continue as it had done? He heard of couples who worked at having very successful marriages, and still behaving like love sick teenagers right up to their old age. She certainly made him feel young. Never, had he thought about sex so much since his teens. There certainly seemed to be no end to her tricks. She was always coming up with something new. She never ceased to amaze him. He had to have her. She had to be his.

Michael stripped off all his clothes. It was time to wash her scent from his body. He checked his clothes to see if he could find any of her black hairs. They would certainly stand out from Sharon's blonde hairs. Michael had always liked Rod Stewart, but he certainly could have disagreed with him about blondes having more fun. Obviously, Rod had never met Mary.

Michael found himself singing, 'Da ya think I'm sexy?' as he stepped in to the shower. He felt like a new man. He wanted to wash away all his problems. Mary seemed to make him forget them all. He remembered a time when he would have almost been suicidal if Sharon had left him, as she had threatened after some of their arguments. He had said to Sharon that if she had have gone then his business would have gone down. How could he have carried on and concentrated without her? Now his business was nearly gone, but Sharon had not. How strange it was now that he wished she had gone, and he wished now to help her on her way. How quickly it had all changed. It had all changed because of Mary. Mary was becoming an obsession. She was occupying all his waking thoughts. There was nothing that he would not do to have her. The end certainly justified the means to him, and he certainly meant to carry out what he had so carefully planned.

Michael settled down on the sofa. He had a glass of beer in front of him. The evening could start early. Sharon was still not home, but he was sure that she would be back soon. She knew that they had arranged to go out with Bob and Mary. He had briefly thought of doing some research and then thought better of it. He did not really have time. He would relax until Sharon came home.

Michael leaned forward and picked up his Titanic book that he had left on their coffee table, and began flicking through it. He settled on a story about the silent movie actress, Dorothy Gibson, who had actually been on the Titanic and managed to get on Lifeboat 7, which was the first one launched. She then reached New York aboard the rescue ship Carpathia. Dorothy then went on to star in the first film made about the sinking which was made within months of the disaster and was called, *Saved from the Titanic*. In it Dorothy wore the actual white silk evening dress that she had worn on that famous and fateful night.

Michael marveled at how this woman had taken maximum advantage of her plight, as she had even part written the script for the film. He glanced at his watch and then continued to read. Suddenly he stopped as he took in the meaning of what he was reading. It was something that he had overlooked or not really thought about with regard to all the souls that were lost. When the news broke that the ship had sunk panic and confusion reigned. Women fainted in theatres and even in the street. Crowds gathered at the offices of the White Star Line in New York as news was released that only just over seven hundred souls had been saved. It was obvious that the chances of survival for First and Second Class women and children was much greater, with no children from either of those classes lost. In fact it even emerged that there were at least two, if not three dogs that survived from First Class. What was shocking was that over double the number of survivors saved were actually lost, which was over fifteen hundred souls. It was a lot to sort out, and it needed to be done quickly amongst the tales of heroism and cowardice.

Therefore the authorities almost immediately declared that all the passengers and crew who had not been rescued by the Carpathia were legally dead. Legally dead. Legally dead within days of the disaster. Michael took in the words. He had remembered reading about this sort of thing before, but he had simply forgotten about it.

It had been the same with the September 11 attacks on the Twin Towers. The authorities were within days issuing death certificates. Of course, for both disasters the number of bodies did not match the missing list. There was not the actual proof that all those people died, but just an association from them being there and then missing. He had read that some, it was believed, had actually gone to Ground Zero and thrown their wallets into the rubble. When the wallets were found they would be presumed dead in the disaster, and then they were free to start a new life with a new identity.

Michael was not sure if this was true, but it certainly was a possibility, but perhaps more importantly for him both disasters proved one thing and that was that there had to be special dispensation to issue a death certificate without a body. The bigger the disaster, the easier it was.

Michael picked up his tablet. This was something that he had really overlooked. Would the insurance companies actually pay out if there was not a body? Would that person be automatically presumed dead or just missing? If it was missing then how long did they have to be missing for before they could be declared legally dead? What would happen to their estate in the meantime?

He looked towards the door, grateful that Sharon was not back yet. Within a few key strokes he had found out that the official title seemed to be: 'Declared Dead in Absentia' or 'Legal Presumption of Death'. It appeared that the length of time varied from country to country. For England and Wales it was 7 years. How could he carry on for that amount of time? He would struggle if it was for 7 months. Michael did manage a small laugh, grateful that he was not Italian, as in Italy it took 20 years to declare a missing person dead. Then came the bit that really worried him and almost sent him into a blind panic. If the death had occurred in international waters, or if that country did not have a reliable police force, then other laws could actually come into play.

The more that Michael read the more that he became confused. It did not seem to be clear. It was not clear at all. He then discovered that the Law had changed in March 2013 and a Presumption of Death Act was passed to simplify the process.

It seemed more than confusing than ever. All he really

needed to know was would the insurance company pay out if there was not a body or would he have to wait seven years or longer. Again it was all unclear.

Michael carried on researching, and found out that the insurance company had to satisfy themselves on several levels if the person really was dead, and if there was a likelihood, however small, of them coming back. Apparently there had been a case some years ago regarding a canoeist whom the coastguard had failed to find. It was believed that the insurance company had paid out, only for the gentleman to return some years later.

Therefore in any case where the person had returned to life, what would happen? Was it then a criminal case? Did that person owe the money to the insurance company even though they were perhaps not a direct beneficiary? If so, what chance was there of getting the money back? Apparently, only in clear cut cases of foul play would the insurance company look to get their money back, and even then it was only down to the discretion of each individual insurance company. Often it was just written off.

Michael found a quote from someone within the Association of British Insurers that said a person would be declared dead seven years after being declared missing. There it was in black and white. It was not what he had wanted to see. It continued that where there was compelling circumstantial evidence of suspected death it could possibly be paid out earlier, even without a body. However, an application would have to be made and the insurance assessors would look at all criteria including the actions of the disappeared and if those actions were inconsistent with their normal behaviour, as well as if the insured was in high danger.

Michael stood up and began pacing the flat. He could not believe there were so many things to think about, the Wills, the insurance premiums, and now paying out without a body. Did he need a body? He could not wait seven years. Did he have to hope that they recovered the body, otherwise he was in trouble or was he likely to be in more trouble if they did not recover the body?

A body or not a body? That was the question. It was a question that he was still pondering when the living breathing body of Sharon walked through the door.

TWENTY TWO

'What are you doing?' Sharon said irritably to Michael. 'That's about the third thing that you have dropped this evening. I'll get the waitress to get you a new fork.'

Michael retrieved the fork from the floor, and held up the offending article as he returned to an upright position. He smiled sheepishly at Sharon.

Mary laughed, and Bob smiled. The four of them were in a Brighton seafront restaurant named Little Bay. Little Bay was a restaurant with a difference as diners were often treated to an opera singer. The singer would wander between tables as he or she sang some of the more well know popular classic operatic songs. Sometimes the singer would actually climb up to a box and surprise the eaters. It was perhaps not as serious as those that might have attended Covent Garden Opera House, but it was a fun place and the food was great.

The restaurant was divided into many little opera boxes that housed parties of two, four, eight, or more. Michael, Sharon, Bob and Mary were seated in a box for four that was painted cream and framed with red curtains with gold tassels. Conveniently Michael sat opposite Mary and Sharon sat next to him, but opposite Bob. It was not the first time that any of them had dined there so it was a favourite of them all. The only one that had any knowledge of opera was Bob, although the others at least knew most of the songs that were sung, even if they couldn't name them.

'Don't worry,' Michael answered. 'I can just wipe it.'

Sharon shook her head. Michael was one of the fussiest men she had ever met. Everything had to be just so. Sometimes though he seemed to drop his guard or was that what he was really like? If it was, she preferred it. He certainly seemed more normal. He looked quite hurt, as if he were a naughty schoolboy, and had been caught out. What he had done wrong though, she had no idea. Dropping a fork was hardly a capital offence. Sometimes perhaps she was too jumpy. Maybe she was too hard on him. Bad habits were hard to get out of. God knew though, most of the time he deserved it, she thought. She did not want to spoil the evening. They should keep their petty squabbles to themselves. Sharon sensed the atmosphere had changed.

'Did you enjoy your starter?' Mary said, as if trying to change the conversation as she looked at Bob.

He nodded. 'Yes. It was very nice.'

'What was it?'

'Well basically a goats cheese croquette or as it said on the menu, red onion and fig Tarte Tatin. It was very good.'

'Don't you get fed up with always having the vegetarian option?' Sharon asked.

Bob thought for a moment. He was the only one of the group that did not eat meat or fish. Bob even looked like a vegetarian. He looked like a man that should have been a lecturer at the Open University, and even his dress sense or lack of it, would have added to that illusion. Bob had wild white hair and a beard and he did not care for dressing up or fashion. He preferred chinos and trainers. 'No. Guess I'm used to it by now. It comes automatically.'

'What are you doing for a holiday this year?' Mary looked at Michael.

Michael thought for moment. 'Well I was thinking about taking Sharon away for her birthday. Was thinking of taking her on a cruise?'

Mary looked disappointed. 'Really. Oh that's a shame.'

'Why?' Michael asked.

'Only the girls were thinking of going away at the same time. Julie, Sharon and me. Just a short break so that we could all celebrate with Sharon. After all it is the big one.'

Sharon looked at Mary and then at Michael. Sharon was not sure how Mary would take the news or if there might be a bit of a debate. Mary, she knew, liked to get her own way. Michael did also. She looked up and the waitress was standing there, and Sharon requested another fork for Michael.

Mary looked a little disappointed, but Michael continued. 'Well sorry, but I have planned it for some time. I was going to try to keep it as a surprise for Sharon. Although I did mention it to her once. Perhaps I'll keep the surprise for her for when we are on the boat.'

'You do like cruising don't you?' Bob joined in. 'Don't think I would.'

'Oh you would,' Michael continued. 'Everybody says that until they try it. Once they try it they are hooked. That's why it's the fastest growing holiday sector.'

'Too formal for me with all that dressing up and then being led around like sheep. No. Not for me.'

Michael glanced at Mary. 'But I'm sure Mary would love it. If not for her sake. Besides, it does not have to be that formal. Do you remember our first cruise, Sharon?'

Sharon nodded. Mary she noticed had kept silent and not passed comment. 'Yes wasn't it on that boat *The Island Escape*? The one with the small salt water pool. Yes, it was quite an experience and remarkable value for money. It was quite low key compared to some of the bigger boats, with only about fifteen hundred passengers, but an ideal introduction.'

'What a thought,' Bob exclaimed. 'I don't think I can imagine anything worse than being stuck on a boat with that many other people. My worst nightmare. It must be Butlins on Sea. I'd start an escape committee.'

Everyone laughed.

'That's nothing nowadays,' Michael said knowledgeably. 'When you think about it, that number were lost on the *Titanic*. Now some of the larger ships have nearly six thousand passengers, not counting crew, but you would be surprised how easily you can find your own space. You can even go for a walk in the park.'

'A park. They have a park on board?' Mary questioned, as she raised her plucked eyebrows.

'Oh yes with real bushes and trees on some of the cruise flagships. Ice rinks, rock climbing walls, zip wires, even a street with shops. But the one that Sharon was talking about was not that big.' Michael stopped for a breath and then continued. 'That was an ideal first cruise. It was what they call a Freestyle cruise. It means no formal dress code or assigned tables or even any set times for dinning. It is up to you. You do what you want. When you want. I know when we went, there was also another cruise line called the *Ocean Village* who offered the same. I'm not sure what has happened to them, but I think there are still some other cruise lines that offer Freestyle.'

Sharon added. 'Well, anyway, it was the first one we went on. It was some years ago. We couldn't believe the Captain could we? Do you remember?'

Michael nodded. 'Yes he was tall and blond if I remember right with a great big grin. Everything was a photo opportunity. One night they had a Blues Brothers night, and everybody wore shades and those hats and that included him. Kids could even be pictured in his chair on the bridge with him, and wearing his cap. They must have made so much money selling photographs with him in them to everyone. Mind you, that's when we learnt about the Jesus bill isn't it?'

'The Jesus bill. What's that?' Mary asked.

'Well when you board they take your photograph and then they give you a credit card size plastic card. It's all you really need. You use it when you get off and when you get back on the boat as they then use it to identify you rather than your passport. More importantly you use it on the boat instead of cash. Every time you buy a drink you just give the card to the waiter or waitress and you sign a chit which they give you a copy of. You use the card to purchase everything from duty free perfume and cigarettes to photographs, services, and gifts. No money ever changes hands.'

'So why do they call it the Jesus bill then?' Mary asked again.

Michael continued. 'Well they are very good at selling you all sorts of things and extras. Even upselling you to eat in another restaurant or an excursion. So realistically by the end of the week you really have no idea as to how many drinks you have had or what else you have bought or done. So generally on the last night of the cruise you are presented with an electronic print out of your bill with all the items listed. It's almost like holding up a toilet roll and then when you scroll down to the very bottom you at last see the amount that you owe. You can guess it: that's when most people say, 'Jesus'. It can be quite a shock, but as they have taken details of your credit card you will find it automatically deducted. I do believe that nowadays you can keep an eye on it as you go through the week by viewing your account on the television set within your cabin.'

Everybody laughed. Sharon smiled. She did remember that cruise fondly. It had been enjoyable. It had certainly given them the taste for cruising. The ship itself had been quite small, and compared to some of the other lines had been limited on entertainment. Nevertheless, the officers and crew had all gone out of their way to ensure that all the passengers had an enjoyable voyage. Nothing had been too much trouble.

Sharon remembered how Michael had wanted to save money and not go on any of the excursions. He had insisted that they would do their own thing. They had walked up Vesuvius, after sharing a taxi there with another couple, and haggling with the driver over the fare. She remembered getting a bus to Pisa. It had only cost a couple of Euros. They had shopped and gone on the beach at Toulon. They had even spotted a garage named the 'Brighton Garage', when they had been on Malta. It was funny looking back at it. Perhaps she had been too harsh. Maybe she had a better time than she thought. Maybe they both had a better time than they thought. Maybe they both had many happier times than they thought.

The waitress appeared again with the main course. 'Butternut squash?'

Bob nodded.

'Apricot stuffed pork belly?'

Mary nodded, and the waitress went to retrieve the outstanding two remaining meals.

'So can you dress up if you want?' Mary asked.

'Of course. But on the *Island Escape* it was not compulsory,' Michael cut in. 'There was no actual formal nights that you might get on other lines, but those can be fun. Black tie ones. What woman doesn't enjoy dressing up?'

'Do you think I would enjoy it?' Mary asked.

'I'm sure you would,' Michael said quickly. 'I am sure both of you would love it. In fact,' Michael stopped to make sure that he had everyone's attention, and then continued. 'In fact I've just had an idea. Why don't you both come with us? Why not? That way we can all be with Sharon on her birthday, and the girls get to go away together.' Michael sat back looking pleased with himself, and the waitress returned with the other two meals.

The music began and the group stopped talking as the opera singer began to sing. His voice filled the restaurant, and they all tucked into their meals. Afterwards Mary excused herself, and a couple of minutes later Michael did the same leaving Sharon and Bob alone at the table.

'Do you really think I would enjoy it?' Bob asked. 'I can get seasick in a rowing boat on a large duck pond.'

Sharon laughed. 'They all have stabilisers on them nowadays. Seasickness is very rare. Michael will even tell you that Nelson used to get seasick. He often used that one at the dining table.'

'I'm sure Mary would love it. It's much more her cup of tea, but I know it's not mine. No. I think we will have to decline Michael's kind offer, but Mary may have other ideas.' Bob looked at his watch. 'They have both been gone a bit of time haven't they?'

Sharon looked at her watch. 'I don't know. No idea really. Mind you, you do have to use the toilets in the hotel next door. It's a bit of a trek.'

'Well the time they've taken they'll probably come back with the morning papers,' Bob suggested.

Bob and Sharon continued making small talk, and the wanderers returned. Sharon glanced up at Mary and just for a second as she caught Mary in a certain light, as she was about to sit down, she was sure that Mary was not wearing a bra, but quickly dismissed the thought. What Mary did or did not wear was up to her, but it did seem a bit odd. She never noticed her not wearing one before.

When they were all seated Michael asked, 'Everybody for coffee?'

The other two agreed except for Mary. 'No, you know what, I'll think I'll ask them if they will do me a hot chocolate. I just fancy one.' Mary reached into her handbag and pulled out a packet of sweets and offered them around. 'Extra strong mint anyone?'

TWENTY THREE

Michael sat in his van and shook his head as he thought about Mary. Mary what a woman she was. Boy did she like sailing close to the wind. Oh how he wished they were sailing with him and Sharon. He thought that he had cleverly engineered the conversation around to Mary and Bob joining them, and how if they did it would help his plans. He was still waiting to hear if they might. Mary was doubtful if Bob would relent, but she told him she was trying to talk Bob in to it. She would try to persuade him.

One thing was certain it would not require much for her to talk him into anything. He would not need too much persuading. She was a woman who liked to live dangerously. She liked the excitement. She was almost so brash that nobody suspected a thing. At least he hoped that they did not. He thought back to the toilets in Little Bay. Well the toilets weren't actually in the restaurant, but were in the hotel next door which had adjoining doors. She had actually followed him into the Gents after he had told her the coast was clear. There she had proved beyond any reasonable doubt, that she wasn't wearing any underwear. Not that there was doubt. It had been clear from him peering under the table. He shuddered when he recalled Sharon scolding him for dropping the cutlery, but he was sure she had not clocked what he was up to. Anyway, within the cubicle they had what he would have called the quickie of quickies. He wasn't sure if he had been so quick through excitement or fear. He had tried to read the others when he returned to the table. He felt as though there was a big neon sign on his forehead that said, 'We have just had a shag.' Of course, he knew there wasn't, but he wondered if his reddish colour had been from exertion or guilt.

Mary, of course, was not happy just to leave it there. At the end of the meal she had to ask for a hot chocolate followed by offering everyone an extra strong mint. He knew that would not actually mean anything to the others, but that was not the point. She had looked directly at him when she said it and drawn pleasure from his discomfort. Then she had very quickly dived under the table and given him a very quick tug. Realistically it had been so quick that he was sure none of the others had noticed, but nevertheless it had got his pulse going in more ways than one.

Michael glanced out the window of his van and thought he had better brave it. No he was not talking about the weather. It was the woman in the house where he was due to do his next job. When he had been a young electrical apprentice he had dreamed of an older woman seducing him while he worked. Alas it had never happened. Not one woman had ever asked him to check the wiring in her bedroom without meaning exactly that. That was until now, and now that he was older, a lot older, the older woman was no longer that attractive. How, long ago he had yearned for someone older to make him experienced, but it was not to be. He'd had a couple of giggles along the way. Once he pulled a couples bed out to get underneath it to lift the floor boards; he discovered some naked photographs of the wife, and he and his mate had a good laugh. Another time he discovered a box of sex toys and aids under a bed when they had been doing a rewire. His sexual knowledge, he had to admit, was limited. Very limited. That was until now. Now he had Mary.

Michael got out of the van and retrieved his toolbox and a large box of accessories, then rang the doorbell sheepishly. Within seconds the door was opened by an older lady draped in silk. Michael immediately sensed a non-professional atmosphere. He needed to get in and out. Well in an electrically safe way. The problem at the moment was that work was work. He could not really afford to be choosy. He had lost work and it was getting harder and harder to get more. It wasn't just the economic climate, because he was aware that most people would not take a chance on their electrics. It was probably the one trade that people would not risk. Nevertheless, he had found foreign competition hard to compete with.

'Can I get you anything?' The lady asked. 'I mean anything.'

'Oh, yes. A cup of tea would be nice please with milk, but no sugar.'

'Is that all?' She sounded disappointed.

Michael smiled. 'Yes sorry. I am pushed to get this done before my next job.' Michael lied. He did not have another job for the rest of the day. He wanted to go into town and get some brochures and then get home.

The woman retreated to the kitchen and Michael breathed a sigh of relief.

Michael returned to the flat with the brochures. He wondered where Sharon was. He had tried calling her, but the call went straight to voicemail. Michael washed, showered and then began his research. At least this way if Sharon did catch him looking up anything about cruise ships she would not suspect anything. Michael thought back to their first cruise on the *Island Escape*. It had been great. It was a little boat, and now he wanted a much larger one. Preferably one with a higher balcony. Michael had already worked out that nowadays the security cameras covered most of the decks, and the balconies were sometimes the only unmonitored open areas.

Michael opened up the lid on his notebook computer, and went to the Cruise Ship Deaths website because he remembered one of the entries mentioned a woman who had gone missing whilst travelling on the *Island Escape*. She had been on the ship back in 2006. Michael remembered then that he had questioned if that was the year and even the month when they had been on it, but he couldn't recall the exact date and had thought no more about it. Now it seemed to matter. His eyes ran down the columns until he came to it and was shocked to see in red capitals: UPDATED MURDER ARREST.

Michael began reading. In short, the 55 year old lady was travelling with her husband when she had gone missing. Her husband originally claimed that she had left their cabin in the early hours of the morning to get a cup of tea. He then said that he reported her missing after he had woken up and could not find her. Michael liked that bit. It was obvious that her lawyer husband had tried to buy time from the time of her disappearance until he had reported her missing. That was clever. So what had gone wrong?

Michael could not believe his eyes. Her husband had been arrested seven years later. Seven years. He must have smashed a bloody big mirror, Michael thought. The number seven had always been Michael's lucky number. It certainly was not anymore. This poor bastard thought he had got away with it. He had for seven years. How bizarre that the law said you had to wait seven years also to be presumed dead. He was back to that one. Seven years without a body. However, with this case there had been a body. That was why he was caught. It seemed the husband had been a fool to himself, and for a lawyer he seemed to have had a dodgy past, because back in 2000 he had been arrested on a charge of sexual conduct with a minor. Obviously his lawyer training had then come into play, because the couple divorced to protect their assets from civil litigation. Who said romance was dead? It was reported that they continued to live together, but that their relationship had deteriorated. Where had he heard that one before?

In May 2006 they had sailed on the *Island Escape* and the wife had gone missing as the ship sailed between Sicily and Naples. That was the same route they had taken, Michael remembered. Her body had been washed up the next day, and an Italian doctor concluded that she had been strangled before she went overboard.

Michael found that a very sobering thought indeed. If the body was recovered then that would solve the insurance seven year thing and all its complications. But if there were any bruises or marks on the body that would only spell trouble. So why had they taken seven years to charge him? Reading between the lines it appeared he was transferring over a million dollars from his ex-wife's account into his new wife's account.

Michael could still not understand why it had taken them seven years to arrest Mr Kocontes. What did make Michael smile was that an Italian newspaper had published an article titled, 'The Perfect Murder'. It reminded him about what he had already thought about the perfect murder, but one thing was for sure that this was not it. Michael searched for the actual article and found it, but it was all in Italian. He briefly thought about dropping it into the Google translator, but from past experience although it tried its best, he would be better off trying to decipher Martian. Then again he supposed he could take it down to his local Italian restaurant and they would probably translate it between courses. 'Signore, we can translate 'The Perfect Murder' article. May we ask why Sir is so interested in it?'

As he always thought, there was a perfect murder and perhaps some of these cruise cases were proof of that. In fact some were far from perfect, but even then the perpetrators would have still got away with it, had they had not been so stupid. Many seemed to have very dubious circumstances, but appeared not to have been investigated as the boat and the world moved on. He felt confident that his original Eureka moment had been correct. This was the answer. This was the solution. He had not been wrong. He just had to be careful. He just had to plan everything and examine each minute detail.

Michael was not a man who made lists. It was Sharon who loved her lists. She had a list for everything from shopping to paying bills. She even kept a list of things that she needed to take on holiday that she produced each time she went away.

Michael always relied on his memory, and he did keep a diary on his phone. However, if he missed Sharon's birthday or their wedding anniversary it was not the end of the world. If he made a mistake on this one it could be the end of his world. Well his world as he knew it. He could end up inside. He could take no chances. He needed to document what he had learned so far, and put it into some kind of order. He could not afford to forget something or slip up.

Michael opened a new Word document and began typing a list:

1. Need a body, but it must have no marks on it.
2. Higher the balcony the better.
3. Only take out one insurance policy, but would also help if my automatically included bank account travel insurance pays out. The bank only covers for travel in Europe.
4. Forget the wills. Too late now.
5. Do not draw attention to yourselves on the boat.
6. Never argue or shout at your partner on the boat.
7. Show you are a solid loving couple.
8. The bigger the ship the better. The more passengers on board the less they will want to hold them all up.
9. Probably the best time is within two days of the end of the cruise, as not only does the cruise line not want to hold up all the passengers on the boat, but they will always want to avoid the nightmare of thousands of passengers waiting to embark at port on a boat that won't be there as it is held as a crime scene elsewhere.
10. Always remember, even with the above, that investigations can or will happen so no foul play

must be suspected.

Michael sat back. He was pleased with himself. The list was by no means the definitive one, and he would no doubt add to it. Nevertheless, it was a start. Perhaps he could even produce his own eBook afterwards, he jokingly thought to himself. How many men would pay a fortune to buy it? It would probably be a best seller.

He wiped the smile from his face when he heard Sharon come in. He flicked to a site of a company that offered cheap cruises. He pretended that he had not heard her, and then looked up. 'Where have you been?' he asked. 'I tried to call you a couple of times and it just went straight to voicemail.'

Sharon looked shocked. 'Oh. I. I forgot to charge my phone last night. It ran out of battery. What are you doing?'

Michael looked back at the screen, and then up at Sharon. She looked distressed. He decided not to question her further. Obviously she wanted to change the subject. He smiled. 'Well to be honest I'm looking at cruises on here.' He pointed to the stack of brochures on the coffee table that he had picked up earlier. 'I also got these. I thought we could have a look through them together tonight. The top one looks good. The *Eureka Cruises* one. They have a fantastically large flagship with literally everything on it you could possibly want. Yes I thought I would treat you. You know how the higher the cabin the more expensive it is? Well the best suites on this one are near the top. What fantastic views. Yes I thought as it is for your birthday we would get one of those luxury suites at the top complete with their own private balcony.'

Michael looked up at Sharon and then up at the heavens. He knew now that his Eureka moment would come to fruition. All he had to do was persuade Sharon that a nice high suite on the *Eureka Cruises* ship would be a holiday of a lifetime. Her lifetime. The Eureka coincidence was too much. It was written in the stars.

TWENTY FOUR

Sharon had put her dress back on and said goodbye. She knew that she would not see him again. She did not need to see him again. She had come to a decision. It was a decision she had already reached this morning, but nevertheless she had gone through with it one more time just to be certain. Now she knew she was certain. Sad but certain.

Sharon got into her car and drove away. She had a tear in her eye, but she did not look back. She did not need to look back. She had done too much of that. All her past had been spent looking back. Now she had to look forward. Look forward to the future. She kept her eyes straight on the road ahead as she drove to meet Julie. There were so many thoughts shooting through her mind. It was hard to concentrate on the road ahead. But she had to concentrate on what was ahead now. The past did not matter. What had happened in the past was gone. She entered the car park and looked for an empty space. It was time to park the past. It was time to forgive and forget.

Gingerly she entered the coffee shop and spotted Julie. She tried to gauge Julie's mood as she approached and wondered how long she had been there. Julie was not a friend that was upset easily. She was generally very easy going and Sharon wondered how she had taken the news when they had spoken on the phone earlier. Sharon had so desperately wanted to see her face to face.

'Hi,' Sharon smiled. She looked down at Julie's cup that was nearly empty. Obviously, she had been there some time. 'Sorry I'm a bit late. Would you like another one?'

Julie nodded, and Sharon thought Julie looked glum. Although it was not very surprising really. It was understandable in the circumstances.

Sharon returned to the table with two Cappuccino's.

'Thank you,' Julie said, as she reached out and placed her right hand on top of Sharon's. 'You don't have to say anything. You don't need to explain. I understand. I totally understand.'

For what seemed an eternity both women just sat there, and Sharon knew the true meaning of friendship. Sharon smiled. She could feel herself becoming emotional. She did not want to cry. It had been a long time since she had cried. In fact she thought she had forgotten how to cry. She had built up her own defence system. She had built it up for so long now that she was not sure how emotionless she was. Had she always been this hard? Had she been this hard when she was a little girl? Perhaps, it had even started then. Her father had always made her promises. She knew she was his Princess, he had told her enough times. He told her she was the most important woman in his world. However, she was not very old when she had learned that it was easy to make promises, and it was even easier to break them.

Parents made up lies. Perhaps they did not do it on purpose to hurt the child. Obviously, they did it just for fun, but did they know the damage that they did? It always started when the child was young. Why? She had stopped believing. She had stopped believing so early in her life. Maybe at first it was harmless or was it? Father Christmas, the Tooth Fairy, the Sandman. Wasn't it really a form of control and bribery? If the child was good then there was a reward. Of course, if the child was naughty then Father Christmas or the Tooth Fairy would not come to see them, but the Sandman always would.

Her father had said that if she did not eat her crusts she would not get curly hair. She had eaten them and ended up in adulthood with straight hair. There were many more things that he had said that were either based on folklore or old wives' tales. Her face had managed to change and had not stayed in the same position despite the wind changing, and she had always had an apple a day. Her father had told her so many things and made so many promises. All though her childhood her father had promised her this and promised her that. He had rarely delivered.

Meanwhile her mother had preached to her about God ever since Sharon was a small girl and she was brainwashed into believing. Her mother's faith was so strong. It had to be true. How could her mother live her life by something that was not true? Her mother had lived her life by it, and if she found out it was not true it would certainly be too late to complain or do anything about it.

Now Sharon felt she had been betrayed. Obviously when she was young she had questioned the world, but not as much, or with as much confidence as others. Young people questioned the world. It was what they did. It was what they had always done. In her day and before. Now she was settling into middle age. She was soon to be 50. Was it now normal to question everything again as one tried to look forward, but studied the past, and wondered if things could have been done better or differently?

She did not have time to run through all the usual menopausal excuses or reasons for her sex. Maybe that would explain a lot. Perhaps, though, it was simpler than that? Was it not the same reason for the opposite sex when men, as they approached middle age, then suddenly felt the need to get a motor bike or an open top sports car? Were they all now realising their own mortality? Time was ticking down. They now knew they would not last forever. One last fling before the rot set in. Age was not kind. Age was cruel, but ageing was certain. However, even that was not assured as statistics clearly showed that many horrible things often appeared to be waiting for a person when they got over fifty. It was often payback time with diseases and ailments for the past life that they had led. Although, of course, sometimes people were just plain unlucky, and through no fault of their own developed or got nasty things. Life, Sharon knew, was a lottery. Most of it was down to luck. It was a cliché, but true, and sitting here with Julie she did not feel lucky. She felt sad. It was perhaps time to make amends.

Sharon reached across with her other hand and placed it on top of Julie's hand and smiled, and for a little while her fast world appeared to stand still. Years ago she remembered reading about how men and women came from different planets. It was exactly right. Sitting here she knew Julie would listen and just be sympathetic. Men she had found, especially Michael, always wanted to offer a solution. Always wanted to butt in and solve the problem. Even if he could not. He always thought he could. Even if all that was needed was a sympathetic ear.

Julie smiled and Sharon withdrew her hands. 'I feel so foolish,' she said to Julie. 'Do you think I have been stupid? Is it too late?'

Julie shook her head sympathetically and raised her plucked eyebrows. 'It is never too late. We all have regrets. All of us would do something differently if we could turn back the clock. Hindsight is a wonderful thing.'

Michael used to say to me that the only qualification I had was a degree in hindsight. He used to say that whenever I said anything after the event.'

'I think every woman is a bit like that,' Julie volunteered. 'It is always easy to know better afterwards.'

'Yes, poor Michael.' Sharon said as she wiped a tear from her eye. She had not really had any feelings towards Michael for more years than she cared to remember. When was the last time that they had sex? She shuddered. Not because the idea repulsed her, but because they had gone past that. It would be so awkward now. Almost embarrassing, as if they had gone past that stage. It was like thinking of your parents having sex. Of course, they didn't. Didn't most children think like that? They never wanted to imagine their mum and dad grinding away. They never wanted to hear them. Besides, they had had their children so why would they want to do it anymore, their own children would think? Some people Sharon knew, or at least read about, had sex right up into their eighties and probably later. Then perhaps they stopped, but she and Michael were so much younger. How had it come to this?

'What do you think is the best thing to do?' Julie asked.

'Do you think you should tell Michael?'

'Oh no. Definitely not.' Sharon shook her head violently. 'I don't feel that guilty. It would not serve a purpose him knowing. No he most definitely must not know or find out. He would not understand.'

'Oh I'm sure Michael can be understanding and even be forgiving. But, well it doesn't take too much understanding does it?'

Sharon held up her hand and said emphatically. 'No. He must not know. Promise me you will never tell him or let on that you know or knew.'

'What do you think I am?' Julie said in a hurt tone. 'I would not be much of a friend would I?'

'Well perhaps not on purpose, but you might let it slip.'

'Of course I won't.'

'And,' Sharon said, 'you must not tell anybody else. Not even in confidence.'

Julie frowned.

'No I mean it,' Sharon said strongly. She tried to think of the right way to say it. It would sound like a betrayal. She would sound really mean, but she had to say it. There was no other way. 'What I meant was don't tell Mary.' There. She had said it. She sat back and picked up her cup. She watched Julie as she took a sip.

'Mary? Do you think I will tell Mary, especially if you have told me not to? What sort of friend do you think I am?'

'Well I know what a great and valued friend that you are. What I am worried about is that you might let it slip to Mary or even confirm her suspicions. Perhaps even tell her in confidence.' Sharon put down her cup. 'No. I know we are all friends. I know that we have all been for a long time.

Perhaps there was a time when we did not have secrets, but I can't explain it. There is just something different now. Something that I can't put my finger on, but things have changed. Perhaps we all have changed. Mary certainly seems to be a bit different these days.'

Julie nodded. 'Yes, I had also noticed, but I didn't want to say anything. She does seem to have changed. Anyway, you don't need to worry my lips are sealed.'

~

Sharon felt relieved as she drove along the seafront towards her home. Their home. Yes, she had reached a crossroads now. The battles between Michael and her had been going on for so long now it was almost the norm. Sometimes they seemed to have a truce, but then they would have a skirmish, then a small battle, which could occasionally turn into a full scale war. Mostly though they both just plodded along in a no man's land and just sniped at each other. It was surprising how hard it was to remember any other way of living. They were both in their own little trenches that each had dug. It had become a way of life for years. Both had their heads buried, only occasionally raising a periscope to see what was out there, but neither one daring to venture away. Instead they stayed together in circumstances where neither was particularly happy. Sharon decided that it was now time to run up the white flag. It was time to talk. She would not surrender, but there had to be a way to find peace.

Sharon looked down at the fuel gauge. She had nearly half a tank. Half full or half empty. It was the old conundrum. In the past perhaps half empty, but now she had to turn that to half full. Sharon continued along the seafront. The traffic was becoming heavy. The commuters were leaving the town and heading along the coast road, and she was thankful that she only had to go to the Marina, and not through Rottingdean or further, and get held up by the ridiculous bus lane that the council had put in. She did not want to get stuck in traffic. She had reached a decision and she did not want to change her mind as she stopped and started in a traffic jam.

She looked in the rear view mirror. There was no going back. Perhaps she was being a little silly and sentimental, but it would be better for both of them. Besides, it was not just her. Michael had changed as well. Yes, there were quite a few things that Sharon had noticed lately. Even when he had dropped his fork he had not wanted to get another one and make a scene. He certainly was not so overbearing or controlling. He had even spoken nicely to her on the phone. He had not questioned her in the way that he so often used to do. Perhaps his change of heart had been when he had offered her his hand when she had fallen off the chair in the bedroom and he came rushing in. Perhaps that was it. Perhaps he had been offering her his hand in peace. Now it was her turn.

Michael had already showered and was in his towelling robe when Sharon walked in. He looked up from his computer and smiled.

Sharon smiled back and asked Michael if he would like a cup of tea. He nodded. Sharon went into the kitchen and then returned to their lounge with the cups. She placed them on the table, and unusually settled on the sofa beside Michael. He looked a little nervous as he picked up his cup and then closed his computer lid down.

'Oh I feel so tired,' Sharon said. 'It has been one hell of

a day. I feel bushed.'

Michael looked quizzical, but unusually did not say anything or pass comment.

Perhaps she was right, Sharon thought. Maybe Michael was changing. It was now or never. It was time to make her peace. Perhaps in the only way she knew how. She rested her hand on his bare thigh just inside the gown and looked straight at him, and then said seductively, something that she had not said for absolutely years, 'Shall we have an early night?'

TWENTY FIVE

Michael had decided to go out for a run. He needed to clear his head. He needed to think, and perhaps most importantly he did not want to be alone in the same room as Sharon. It was a light pleasant clear evening and he was not alone. Walkers, dog walkers, and other runners all occupied the seafront's top road as he ran down from the Marina towards The Brighton Pier.

Another runner younger than him, and female, with an athletic body was running towards him from the opposite direction. She smiled and nodded as she passed. Michael smiled back. It was like an unwritten code between runners as they acknowledged each other. It reminded Michael of when he was a small boy and the RAC patrolman used to salute as they passed you in your badged car on the road. How the world had changed since then. Running still seemed to be a civilised thing to do. There was a code between runners, as was always plainly obvious, when a Marathon was televised. They helped each other. It had come a long way since it was called jogging, and Michael often thought it ironic that the man who made jogging the phenomenon it became, had had a heart attack and died after his daily run. He recalled that the author of the best-selling book, The Complete Book of Running, Jim Fixx, joined a long list of persons that had been killed or died from their own inventions or interests. Yes jogging had fixed Jim Fixx, and Michael laughed to himself about others that he knew about, such as the man who demonstrated his own parachute suit by leaping off the Eifel Tower and plummeting straight to his death in 1912. Indeed hadn't Thomas Andrews, the ship builder and naval architect in charge of the plans for the Titanic gone down with the ship in the same year? Yes there were other examples Michael mused such as Marie Curie who died of exposure to radiation. Death, he thought, came in many strange ways and often connected to strange coincidences.

Michael looked down at his watch and noted the time. Today was not about times or distances. He did not have his headphones on or the app that told him how he was doing, his time, and the distance, although his phone was nestled snuggly in his armband. No this run was clearly only to clear his head. He needed to think. He needed to plan. It had been all going so well. He had his list. He knew what he was doing, and then Sharon had shocked him.

Michael wiped his brow with the sleeve of his shirt. Why was he sweating, he wondered? Was it because he was actually pushing himself or simply nerves. Sharon had really surprised him last night. She had shocked him to the core so that he began to question it all. They had led separate lives for longer than he cared to remember. It had become a way of life. He had got used to it. She had got used to it. So where did this sudden rush from Sharon come from? What was the meaning behind it? Why? What had she done? Was she trying to cover up something? What was she guilty of? The whole thing made Michael feel uneasy. He took a sharp intake of breath and sucked in the sea air, then quickly sidestepped two men walking a small dog.

Michael stopped for a moment, bent over and placed both his hands on his knees. He tried taking deep breaths. He almost felt dizzy. Surely he was not that much out of condition. Normally he could run for miles without stopping. He looked around and then decided to sit in the Victorian shelter that was on the top road just below Lower Rock Gardens. There was only a couple sitting in there and two young men.

In the evening Michael had often driven past it when he was on his way into town. It was where they gave out soup and bread to the people who waited there. Michael had never really given them any thought. He had wondered why Brighton seemed to attract the down and outs and the druggies from far afield, but then he supposed that if you were down on your luck, and lived on the streets, then you might as well pick a nice place with a warm climate on the south coast to stay.

Michael sat on the wooden bench and recalled how Sharon had sat next to him on the sofa and rested her hand on his thigh. He had felt his body stiffen. Not perhaps the bit that would be expected to stiffen, but his whole body. He had gone rigid, but probably not as Sharon had anticipated. His whole body had frozen. Her actions had completely taken him by surprise. He wasn't sure how he was supposed to react. Was he supposed to be grateful? She had not actually moved her hand, but just placed it there. Nevertheless, he was certain that the action could not be misconstrued.

He had just smiled or tried to. It had been so long since he and Sharon had had any intimacy. That part of their relationship had long since gone. Why would Sharon want to rekindle it? Was there a reason behind her actions? There had to be and that was what worried him. It had made him feel uneasy. Sharon had just smiled and then walked out of the room, but her invitation had been clear. He just had to take her up on her offer. That was if he wanted to. That was if he could.

It had worried him all evening. He had dreaded bedtime as he sat looking at his computer. It was a complication he could do without. It was complicated enough really without it. His mind had been made up long before. He had Mary now. Mary was who he wanted to be with now. Sharon could never bring the excitement to his life in the same way Mary did.

He stayed in the lounge and Sharon had gone to the bedroom. He was not sure what she had been doing, and he had not wanted to go in there to find out. Instead Michael remained on the sofa with his computer trying to think it all through. At first he had thought that if he did have any kind of sexual relationship with Sharon that he was not being fair to Mary and was being unfaithful. That was mad because he was married to Sharon. He also wondered if Mary still had sex with Bob. It was something he always put out of his mind. It was something he did not want to think about. He suspected that they did or perhaps Mary just did it to please Bob and keep him happy. Perhaps that was how she always managed to get Bob to change his mind. She was a very persuasive woman especially when it came to men.

Michael tried to take his mind off what happened and

buried his head in his computer. He had just received an email from one of the cruise companies that offered advice, but was really a thinly veiled advertisement to sell cruises. The feature had been about all the things that could be done on a balcony when on a cruise, and a list had been provided. Michael read it with interest as he considered that at present falling from the balcony seem to be the favoured option, with the higher the balcony on the ship the better. It could also help him persuade Sharon why he had splashed out on a balcony, as normally the most they ran to was an outside cabin. Michael could see the merit of an outside cabin, and the complete freedom of a balcony. They had never liked inside cabins. Of course, you did not actually spend much time in an inside cabin. Some only used them for washing, changing, and sleeping. The reason might have been that the occupants were not actually aware of the time of day or indeed what the weather outside was like. Perhaps you could always look at the web cam view that they showed on the television set, but that was not the same and the television had to be on and tuned to that channel. No the article was right. A balcony was well worth the extra money or at least it was this time. The email was very comprehensive and Michael tried to memorise it so when he had to explain it to Sharon, he did not want it to sound as if he was reading from a script. Some of the bigger boats with the very expensive suites enabled their occupants to fine dine on the balcony with their very own butler. Sometimes they could even watch a show below in the Aqua Theatre. They would also provide the cruisers with large balconies with cocktails and canapés so the occupants could party with other guests who they had met or travelled with. These suites did not come cheap.

Michael decided that he did not need such luxury for his purpose and a simple balcony would do. He looked at other ideas that would sell it to Sharon. They did not need to dine on fine lobster and champagne on their balcony. In fact, that might actually be counterproductive. If it was on their balcony nobody except the butler would see them. It needed to be more public than that. They needed to be seen dining together in public. They had to be seen as a couple who were obviously happy together. Michael had made a mental note that he would take Sharon to one of the upgrade restaurants that offered, for a cover charge, more exotic cuisine than their normal dining room, with the cost added to their bill at the end of the cruise. It would also mean that they would be seen together in one more restaurant and Michael wanted witnesses as to their happiness and closeness.

A balcony had many advantages especially for a celebrating couple. He was certain he could justify the extra cost. Sharon would love taking her morning coffee in her dressing gown looking out at the sea, and equally they could share a drink under the stars before they dined or even after they had eaten.

Some couples liked to be towards the stern so that they could be mesmerised by the wake of the ship. Michael had even found a feature on this called, 'Show Me Your Aft'. It told how popular these cabins were, and Michael had thought that someone launched from the stern had even less chance of being spotted than anywhere else on the ship. Michael worked out that it was all about angles and if he insisted on having an aft cabin it might go against him later.

No. Michael decided that cost would obviously be a factor, but in some ways he had to be demonstrative towards

Sharon. He had to show her and the ship that he cared. He had gone to all this trouble so that they could celebrate her Birthday and then tragedy had struck. He would be the crestfallen distraught husband. He had laughed to himself when he had thought it might even have twinges of *Romeo and Juliet*. Had she not been on a balcony? Of course, their deaths were a pact. But the thought had amused him that in this new version, Romeo would survive.

There were other advantages as to having a balcony, although as neither of them smoked, that reason would not be a valid one, although he was aware that some lines had now banned that. What he and Sharon would enjoy was reading and relaxing in their own peace and quiet with the sound of the waves. Michael could picture himself with his chair pulled close to the railings and his feet up. His eyelids getting heavier as he took in the ocean breeze. His head would get heavy and he would not fight it as he drifted off. He just hoped that Sharon would not fight him when the time came.

The article finished with the obvious benefit of having your own balcony. The obvious one benefit that no one talks about or advertises. Basically, bonking on the balcony. Yes amorous alfresco activity did not actually bear thinking about when you took into consideration some of the ages of the cruisers. However, this article had admitted that it did go on, but it was rumoured that a couple in their twenties were on a cruise in the Gulf of Mexico and had been doing it when they toppled over into the sea. Michael was not surprised to find out that they were not wearing life jackets. However, apparently, both had trod water for four hours and then been rescued. Of course, this was a happy smiley story, a little bit tongue in cheek, which probably still sold more balconies than it put people off. It was really saying: You can be naughty, but be careful, and if you do, do not forget your protection. Your life jacket. Michael had certainly not been shocked that they did not use the example of the newlywed game show couple who had boasted that they had done it on cruise ship balconies.

It had confirmed to Michael that the balcony was the best bet with probably bonking being the excuse as to why one of them went over. However, there did appear to be one problem and that was how long after the event should the alarm be raised. Immediately, and he could not be faulted, but as the article had proved there was a chance that a person could tread water and survive. The longer it was left to report there would be far less chance of that, but if he was found to be lying with regard to the timing, it could lead to many more awkward questions. Therefore, if the event took place at around Midnight he thought that he could afford to leave it two or three hours, or maybe more. That was the definite timing that he decided on. It would ideally be between eleven and midnight, and say two days before the end of the cruise.

Michael suddenly felt pleased with himself. He looked around. The two young men had gone. The other couple were too engrossed in each other to notice him. He took a sip from his water bottle. It was time to run on. He still had some way to go. He stood up and started running again. He did not want to run towards the Pier anymore. He turned towards home. It was no good running away from it. He had to face the situation. He had to face Sharon.

He picked up the pace and started to breathe easier.

The thought suddenly struck him that Sharon was actually helping him. She was actually playing into his hands, or to be precise he would actually put himself in her hands. Yes that was the answer. In fact it might not just be in her hands it might actually be her body.

Michael increased his pace as he warmed to what he was thinking. Originally he had been worried if the body was recovered. He had then found out that a body would really be needed so that death could easily be declared, and to guarantee an immediate insurance pay out. Obviously, if the body was marked like the one on the *Island Escape* where the wife was found to have been strangled before she hit the water that would be his undoing. However, Michael was now sure that if her body was discovered it would prove that he was telling the truth. He would stick to the story that they were making love and she had slipped over, and he had raised the alarm immediately. Therefore should they later pick up the body then they would run their forensic tests and what would be the one thing that would prove his story. The answer was simple. Semen.

Michael laughed out loud as he remembered the old myth from his youth about all the characters who were supposed to have been in *Captain Pugwash*, such as Roger the Cabin Boy, Master Bates, and Seaman Staines. He knew that these were all fictitious, but somehow everybody seemed to believe that they were actually in the programme.

Michael was sure that he had the answer. Semen was the solution. He had originally considered playing with himself so that if there was any forensic test on the balcony there would be some proof that sex had taken place. Now there would be no need to do that. Not now that Sharon had demonstrated that they might resume a sexual relationship. It was ideal. It would also mean that when they found her she would only be partly dressed. It would make it all add up. All he had to do now was bring himself to make Sharon believe that he wanted her again. He would have to find an excuse as to why he rebuffed her. He wondered if he was up to the task.

TWENTY SIX

'I think you are so lucky,' Mary said eagerly. 'I so wish we were coming with you. I really do.'

Sharon smiled, and sat back on her sofa in her lounge. 'Well you could have done. Michael did offer.'

Mary shook her head. 'Yes I know, but you know what Bob is like. He said that wild horses could not drag him to see the white horses. He seemed quite pleased with himself with that. Turned it into a bit of a joke. Don't think he even considered it seriously to be honest.'

Sharon made a sympathetic face. She was actually starting to believe that she was lucky. Others, if they knew the truth, might not have agreed. Nevertheless, Sharon had been brought up to believe that it was never too late. Her father always said all the time there was still breath in your body it was never too late. You always had a chance. She never really gave up on her father, even when it was obvious that he would not change. Now in his case she knew it was too late, but it was not too late to make peace with Michael. She still had time. They had wasted so much time. They had wasted so many years. It had been going on for so long it was difficult to remember how it had all started. It was impossible to recall whose fault it was. Both of them had stood their own ground in their own way. She knew Michael could be a bit of a bully, but he had always been insecure. She was sure that she had added to that insecurity. He wanted reassurance. She had almost gone out of her way to make him feel insecure. She had stayed out too long. She had wanted to go out with her friends when all he wanted was to be with her.

She thought about the cruise. Now they were to be together. Look at all the trouble he had gone to. All the trouble for her. Just for her Birthday. It was time to show she was grateful. It would be just the two of them. It would be like it should have been a long time ago. Nothing was forever her father had always told her. She knew that. She would make up for lost time. You could live a lifetime in six months. She had to try. She owed it to herself. She owed it to Michael.

Sharon picked up a brochure and turned to Mary. 'Yes, it is such a shame. I think it could have been a lot of fun with the four of us. I'm sure Bob would have actually enjoyed it once we sailed. It's just not like he thinks it is. Mind you Michael's not booked anything yet. It's not too late.'

Mary took the brochure and flicked though it. 'Yes, my Bob can be a bit of a stick in the mud. In fact, I don't know how I have stuck him for so long, but when his mind is made up, it's made up. He likes to think it is, but there are some ways and little things that I can do to persuade him otherwise. Poor man does not know his own mind sometimes. Having said all that, though, his mind is made up on this one. He is such a geek. A Mr Gadget Man. He would probably have married a computer if he could. That is maybe why he won't go on the cruise as he won't want to leave it behind. That and the dog. They both get more attention than me. No. You two go.'

Sharon smiled sympathetically. 'Oh well. What will be will be? I'm not even sure where to go. Michael did seem keen to stay in Europe for some reason. Not a problem really as there are still a lot of nice stop offs.'

'How long will you be going for?'

'Just the week, I think. Michael has a lot of work on, so I think he wants to take as little time as possible out. Still. You can get to go to lots of nice places. Strange though Michael was trying to explain to me the other night that cruising is probably the only holiday choice that is not made solely on the destination. Of course, if you want to go to one place to see it then you need to book a cruise that stops at that port. I think Michael seems to have done a fair amount of homework. Apparently he read that the size of the boat, the line, the entertainment, the facilities, the length of the cruise, the date of the sailing, and obviously the price, are all things that people consider before they notice where it is going. Can't think of booking any other holiday like that.'

Mary was a bit bored, but Sharon did not notice. She took the brochure from her and began flicking through. It was certainly a different way of choosing a cruise. It normally worked that Michael would receive emails from cruise or travel companies discounting their current offers. Some might have included upgrades such as from an inside cabin to an outside one with a window. Some might include all the tips prepaid or an allowance to spend on board. Some a cheap all inclusive drinks offer. They even offered free on land stays. Then the eye catcher was the special price. Some of them might be late notice, and only a few weeks or even days away. But whatever the offer, or offers, the price sold the ship, and off you sailed. Of course, it might not have been the exact locations that you wanted or even been on the exact date, but the bargains gained more than made up for that.

This time though it was different. Michael wanted to take her away for her birthday. They had to go on a specific date. No doubt Michael could have trawled through his emails, and found something suitable. But no. This time Michael would do it all properly. This time she had the brochures and she could choose. Sharon found it quite a humbling process, and she also found herself feeling guilty about how she had sometimes treated Michael.

Her eyes settled on one seven night western Mediterranean cruise that started from Barcelona. It would mean that they would have to fly from the UK, but as it was only a week that did not matter too much as she could pack light. Well, relatively light for her. It was one other thing that Michael and Sharon had often argued over when he lifted her packed case, and his hand scales measured it against the airlines baggage allowance.

'But I need it all. Formal outfits, informal, and leisure. You do want me to look my best, don't you?'

That had always been Sharon's standard response. Sometimes Michael had agreed to pay the excess if they were challenged, but only rarely, or he would pack his lightly to compensate for hers. Otherwise it became a third degree grilling on each item as he almost demanded an explanation for its inclusion. Of course, if the cruise sailed from an English Port such as Southampton or

Dover then there was no restriction on the amount of bags or luggage that passengers could take. His scales became redundant. The car could be loaded and short of hiring Sherpas, off they went.

Sharon loved Barcelona. They had been there before and she loved strolling and relaxing in Las Ramblas. The other ports also looked interesting and included Naples and Florence which was where they had stopped when they had been on the Island Escape. She remembered when they had arrived at Livorno she had wanted to go to Florence, but Michael had wanted to see the Leaning Tower of Pisa, and that is what they had done. Michael said it was a bit too difficult to do on their own to reach Florence, and the excursion was too expensive. So the local bus to Pisa had won. He had said the same when they went to Civitavecchia which was the port for Rome. Then when they went to Naples they had the choice of going to Vesuvius or Pompeii. They had ended up getting a taxi to the mountain as it was nearer. Sharon hoped this time it would be different. This was her Birthday treat and she wanted to see the Eternal City which was probably proof that some things do last forever. She also hoped that Michael would take her to The Gates of Paradise in Florence. She had certainly been to The Gates of Hell with him at times. Now it would be different. It was time to make peace and make amends.

'What do you think of this one?' Sharon pointed to a ship in the brochure.

Mary nodded and then looked away disinterestedly.

Sharon frowned and put down the brochure. Perhaps she was being a little thoughtless. She did not want to rub Mary's nose in it. She was sure that Mary would have loved to have gone, but boring Bob had said no.

Suddenly Mary's expression changed as she spotted a pink and black bag down by the glass topped coffee table. Sharon had meant to put it away earlier, but had forgotten to do so. Mary pointed to an Ann Summers bag. Ann Summers was a long established high street sex shop that was well known for its lingerie and sex toys. 'What have you been buying in there? Have you got a lover?' Mary waited for her to answer, but Sharon said nothing, and then Mary continued. 'Surely it can't be for Michael can it? I thought you and Michael were through with all that messy stuff. A celibate marriage. Have you been telling me porky pies? Have you got a lover? Do I know who he is? I think I might. Or is Michael the lucky man? Are we shopping for the cruise early?'

Mary got up and reached down and picked up the Ann Summers bag. She peeped inside at the black and green Basque, but did not take it out. 'Very nice,' she said. 'I love the lacy bits on it. I bet that will look great with stockings and heels. Mary put the bag back down on the floor.

Sharon sat back. Her face blank. She did not want to say anything. She did not want to argue with Mary, but she could not believe Mary's cheek in daring to look in the bag without even asking her first, then questioning her if she had a lover. Yes, the green and black Basque was very eye catching, but she had not bought it for the eyes of Mary. Sharon briefly wondered if Julie might have said something to Mary, but dismissed that instantly. No, it was her own stupid fault for leaving the bag out. She did not want other people knowing her business, and for some strange reason that included Mary. Why was she unsure? Perhaps it was a woman's intuition. There was a time when she would have willingly confided in Mary. But not anymore. Something had changed.

Sharon's mobile in her bag began to ring. Sharon pretended that she had not heard it.

'Aren't you going to answer it? It might be important. It might be Michael. Then again it might be somebody that you are not telling me about,' Mary said teasingly.

Sharon reached into her bag. The number was either from a business or it had been withheld. 'Hello.' Sharon looked towards Mary, then stood up and walked out of the room with the phone pressed against her ear. She returned a few minutes later. 'Sorry,' she said to Mary. 'It was a lovely Irish nurse named Megan from the Royal Sussex County hospital. The result of a test.'

'Oh. Yes.' Mary answered. 'Of course it was. Is everything alright?'

Sharon nodded. 'Oh yes. Just a routine test. Nothing to worry about. Nothing at all.'

Mary's expression was one of disbelief. Sharon sensed an atmosphere as she glanced at her watch. She had hoped to have put Mary off the scent but it did not appear that it had worked. Mary had not bought it. Maybe she should have been a bit more forthcoming with Mary. Nevertheless, she had also sensed coldness and aloofness in her lately. Maybe they both had secrets. Mary, she knew, did not want to share hers with her any more than she wanted to share hers with Mary.

Sharon undressed and put on her bath robe. She wanted to put this afternoon behind her. She knew that she probably had an hour before Michael came home. She was looking forward to a nice long soak. She needed to think. She would put her music on in the lounge and let it drift into the bathroom. She would let the soul soothe her soul. She picked up her mobile to carry it into the bathroom. Almost immediately it started to ring. Sharon did not recognise the number as she answered it, but she immediately recognised the voice. 'Bob? 'Bob had never called her before. She did not have his number, and she did not know that he had hers. 'Bob. Is everything alright. Mary was here until a few minutes ago.'

There was a brief silence at the other end and then Bob spoke again. 'Yes, I know. She just called me. She said she is on the way home. I've only got a few minutes, but I wanted to speak to you.'

'Why?' Sharon wondered what Bob could possibly want or what he wanted to tell her. 'What is it?' Sharon could feel her pulse rise and her breathing got faster. Perhaps she was being silly. Perhaps it was that Bob had reconsidered going on the cruise with them and he wanted to discuss it with her before it was booked. Something, though, told her that was not the reason for his call. 'Can you tell me what it's about?'

Again it went silent for a few seconds. Bob was obviously measuring his words. 'Do you think we could meet? I really need to speak to you. Speak face to face.'

'What is it? What's the urgency?' Sharon had absolutely no idea what Bob could want. What could it possibly be? It was a most unusual request from Bob. He had never called her before like this. Never. 'Is it about the holiday?'

'I would rather not say over the phone. I think we need to meet. I would like to see you face to face without Michael. Can I come over to your place when Michael is at work?'

'Can't we meet elsewhere if you really think that we need

to? What is wrong with that?'

'No. To be honest. It is best that I come to your place when Michael is not around. What about tomorrow?'

'Well I've got to be somewhere in the morning,' Sharon said quickly.

'OK. Will he be at work tomorrow afternoon?'

'Yes. I expect so,' Sharon found herself answering.

'Great. I can leave work early. I can be with you at three. Is that OK?'

Sharon nodded automatically. 'Yes. Yes. Can't you tell me a bit now about what it is about? I shan't sleep tonight. I shall be worried sick.'

'No sorry. We can discuss it tomorrow afternoon. I must go, Mary will be home any minute.'

The line went dead, and Sharon realised that Bob had terminated the call.

TWENTY SEVEN

Michael sat staring at his fried bread. What was he doing? It had been a long time since he had tasted fried bread. He had forgotten how good it tasted. Since he had started running he had given up all sorts of things, and that included fried breakfasts. Today, though, he was treating himself. Today he felt decadent and almost defiant, and the fried egg virtually smiled back at him. Yes, it was a sunny side up day.

Why he was in this mood he was not sure. He had not been in this particular cafe for some time. It had once been a favourite of his, and he had eaten there most days. These days he did not stop for breakfast if he was busy and working. Instead he chose to nibble a few breakfast biscuits that were supposed to provide the required energy levels. Today, though, he had nothing to do, and was just hanging about waiting. Although he was not sure exactly what he was waiting for. At first he thought it had been the upgrade fairy, but he put her out of his mind as he thought about Sharon.

He had noticed that Sharon had been behaving strangely these days. It was all sorts of little things that had got his attention. Sharon was not herself, and it worried him. Maybe his mind was working overtime, but Michael did not want to take any chances. To him life was no different than a game of chess. Whilst he was busy planning many moves ahead, he still had to be wary of what his opponent was also planning. He never wanted to be taken by surprise. Perhaps he was guilty of thinking too much, but he knew something was afoot.

Michael recalled some of the things she had done, and not done lately. Often he found that she turned off her mobile as he could not get through. She blamed not getting a good signal, but he knew it was probably not that. It was obviously off for a reason. Sometimes she would be on the phone when he came in and then she would terminate the call quickly so she did not need to speak in his presence. She was often vague about where she was going when she went out, and just as vague about where she had been when she came in. In fact, Michael knew damn well she had not been where she said on more than a couple of occasions.

Mary had also noticed, but even she had told him she thought Sharon was hiding something; she had been unable to prise out of her what it was. Even this morning Sharon asked him more than once what time he would be home. Sharon was not as subtle as she thought she was. Why did she want to know? Did she suspect that he did not have much work on and was trying to catch him out to see if he got home early? Well, he was wise to her. He would make sure that he stayed out for a bit longer than usual. She would have to try harder than that.

Perhaps Mary was right? Perhaps Sharon was seeing somebody? It was obviously a possibility. She was a good looking woman for her age. She had a good body. Just because he had lost interest, it did not mean that some other bloke might not fancy her. It was strange how he had no sense of jealousy. He had to admit there was a time when he would have been jealous. Insanely jealous, especially when they had first been together. He would have almost dreamt murder even to think another man was only looking at her. Now he was dreaming murder, but another way. Had he really changed that much over the years or had just his feelings changed? Was that what they called mellowing with age? He would not let the thought that she might have a lover get to him. He had to be honest with himself, and honestly he knew he did not want her. He wanted another woman. Why, then, should he let the thought get in the way. Michael smiled at his maturity. He was no longer a young buck that did not want someone, but would not let someone else have them purely because of silly male pride. No. Good luck to them. Let him enjoy her while he still could if that was the case. Besides their fun would be short lived. The time was getting close.

Perhaps she might not even have a lover, but even if she did, he did not care. Now he had Mary, and soon he would not have a wife. Soon he was to be a widower.

Michael decided to concentrate on his strategy. He knew that he must stick to his game plan. He had been planning it for so long now and that was why he was here. It was time to take it to the next level. He reached down into his bag and took out the Eureka Cruises brochure. Michael smiled to himself. He was pleased with what Sharon had chosen. In truth, as usual, he had guided her to what he wanted. He was always able to do that, but Sharon would always think that it was her idea, and that she was in control. Admittedly, on this occasion she might have chosen the specific destinations, but that was fine. He was thankful she had kept to Europe as he had suggested. He could now purchase a decent travel insurance policy to cover them for all specific eventualities and no one could accuse him of being anything other than a sensible caring partner as he protected them both. Of course, he would then conveniently forget about the travel insurance that was automatically included with his bank account. That was until the time came, and then he could claim both in a 'double bubble'.

Michael dipped his fried bread in the egg. Bliss. He flicked through the brochure and settled on the page of the cruise that Sharon had chosen. The dates were ideal. Although, perhaps what was not ideal was the price. This was certainly a different way of doing it. Normally Michael read the various emails that he received from cruise companies. Well, at least he glanced at them and only read further if something caught his eye. Sometimes they were cruise only which meant that the purchaser had to get their own flights. Michael had often considered doing a cruise this way as it could make it a very cheap holiday. Cruise Lines were reluctant to let the ship leave port with empty cabins. Even if they let the cabins go very cheaply at the last minute, at least the occupants would be spending on the ship. The only problem could be if the airline cancelled their flight then they had no redress with the cruise line.

Nevertheless, he knew he would be forced in a few minutes to go down to the travel agent and book it through them, and at their prices. When he first sat down he had thought about the upgrade fairy. She had been mentioned in one of the articles that he read about how to get an upgrade on a cruise. Upgrades were obviously well known on airlines and all travellers had dreamed of being upgraded to Business or even First Class. For the majority it would always be a dream. It was generally something that did not happen to the average flier.

Cruise ships were no different. In fact, Michael understood that you had even less control. Upgrades appeared to be pure luck and virtually a thing of the past. Sometimes, you might get a slightly better or bigger room than the one you had paid for, but generally only better in the eyes of the cruise company, such as a higher deck or a more convenient mid-ship location. Upsells and upgrades at a reduced cost were far more likely. Sometimes, he had read, if the cruise was not selling that well then the cruise company upgraded passengers so that it freed up the lower priced cabins for them to sell. All the experts appeared to agree that not only were upgrades rare, but they were really the luck of the draw.

Michael sat back. Everything had to be perfect. It was no good risking it in order to save a few quid. Imagine if they paid for an outside cabin in the hope of getting upgraded to one with a balcony and it did not happen. He couldn't exactly push her body out of a porthole could he? Mind you Michael did remember reading exactly that. He even recalled a girl, on a cruise, who was English, and only 21, had been killed by a member of the crew. Her name, he remembered, had been Eileen and her body had been pushed out of the porthole.

Michael knew that he needed to pay the full price. Why was he so reluctant he wondered? He was obviously astute enough to realise what a few pounds or even several hundred pounds extra really matter in the great scheme of things. Not really one iota. Besides, he would be getting the insurance money. He guessed it was probably purely pride. He always hated it when someone had tried to get one over on him. However small he did not like it. It always made him angry. In short he hated being done or conned. It was his nature. It always had been. He would not be outsmarted. Why should he pay more when he knew perfectly well that he could get it for less? He hated being taken for a mug.

Michael finished his breakfast. This time he would have to swallow his pride. He looked down at the brochure and even he seemed to be seduced by its glossy pictures and sensational statements. The *Eureka Cruise Line* evoked wonderful images of days gone by. A life of luxury of the old fused with the new and a Greek theme. Each boat was named after a Greek God and the one Sharon had chosen was the flagship named *Apollo*. It was even bigger than Zeus which would have been Michael's preferred choice. Michael had to admit he was almost looking forward to it. In other circumstances he certainly would have enjoyed it. Still there would be plenty of other opportunities, and he hoped to enjoy cruises with Mary. The thought really did seem to make it all worthwhile to put his hand deep in his pocket.

Almost certainly he and Sharon would enjoy a drink in the Acropolis Bar which topped the ship with its spectacular views and sloped glass sides, but he knew the nectar would have been sweeter if he was with Mary. Still, he could enjoy a show in the Delphi Theatre, and he knew Sharon would love being pampered and spoiled in the Olympic Pool and Spa. That was all part of his plan. She had to be seen enjoying herself, and he the loving husband would see to it that she did. Yes. It would also be good if they could be seen enjoying an ice cream together in the dedicated ice cream parlour named The Icarus.

The Travel Agent smiled at Michael. 'Well Sir that's the exact booking that you want secured.'

Michael smiled back. The girl, who was young enough to be his daughter, or even possibly his granddaughter, had long blonde hair, and was immaculately turned out in her uniform. The name badge said that her name was 'Katie', and that she was the 'Assistant Manager'. She was obviously well trained. She had already tried to upsell him many other unnecessary extras. Unnecessary extras which all added up together cost a lot extra.

'What about excursions,' she asked. 'It would be such a shame to go on such a lovely boat, and when you checked in to find that all the places on the excursions have gone. Such a shame, and they all are very popular destinations. I am sure that you don't want to take that risk. Imagine your wife's disappointment. Can I book them for you now? Then you can be certain they are all guaranteed.'

Michael smiled thinly. He doubted in the history of cruising that places had ever sold out. They would always find places. It was the oldest trick in the book. Did she think he was a complete idiot? All she wanted was her commission, and his money, before he had a chance to change his mind. Of course, there was always the danger that when he went home he might do a bit of research and find just how easy and much cheaper it was to arrange their own, and he might well find out that they did not need to be escorted and shepherded around like sheep. He knew that excursions were a big money spinner for the cruise lines, and sometimes a headache, as they fought to control the local operators that they hired. Italy was actually well known as being a country where operators also like to make a buck or two on the side by making an unscheduled stop at a bogus factory so they pocket a commission on each item a passenger purchases.

Just at that moment, Michael's mobile pinged, and he received a text. He ignored it. 'Yes'. Michael heard himself answering. 'That would be nice. Pompeii, Naples, and Rome please. You are right. You see it is my wife's birthday treat. She will be fifty. We can't risk her being disappointed can we? It is going to be the holiday of her lifetime.'

The girl smiled and immediately began tapping her keyboard eagerly. It could almost have been the sound of the keys on a cash register. Michael took his mobile out of his pocket whilst she was engrossed reading the screen. He looked down at his mobile. It was a text from Mary.

'Can you call in on your way home? Bob said he will be late home. I have something to tell you and I have also been shopping in Ann Summers. I've got a new green Basque, my lover'

TWENTY EIGHT

Sharon tried to busy herself in the flat as she waited for Bob's arrival. It reminded her of when she was a child, and how she had tried to keep herself busy so she would not have to think about the time and the up and coming event. Normally, it had been a happy event she was looking forward to such as Christmas Day. Sometimes, of course, when the time came, she had been disappointed, especially if she was looking forward to something that her father had promised her like a particular present. Nevertheless, she would soldier on and even now all these years later she still adopted exactly the same approach. This time though she had a feeling that Bob was not visiting her with good news. In reality she did not have any idea why he had called. She did not even know that he had her number. It was all very mysterious. However, she was sure that it was not good news whatever it was.

She wondered if perhaps he had news about Mary that he did not want to share over the phone. Maybe, that was why Mary had been a bit erratic lately? Perhaps she had something on her mind. Something that she also could not share. Could it be that Bob wanted to warn her so that she could make an allowance? Could it even be that Bob and Mary might be splitting up? She had always thought that their marriage was one that had not exactly been made in heaven. Although who was she to judge? Look at her marriage. She had no right to talk. What was wrong with the modern world today? Did nobody stay together anymore? Nevertheless, whatever it was she would know soon enough. Soon it would all make sense. Although Sharon suspected that very little would ever make much sense again. At least she had the peace of mind that Michael would not come home when Bob was here. Michael had assured her that he was working when she had casually asked him, although she had sensed Michael being a little bit prickly when answering. He too had seemed like a man with a lot on his mind, but in truth Sharon did not have the energy to take on other people's troubles. She had enough of her own. They were both adults or at least should be. Her own life was complicated enough, and now, she thought, was Bob about to add to her worries, or at least give her something else to worry or think about? She was also mystified as to why he wanted to come to their flat? Why did he not want to meet on a more neutral ground? He had to have had his reasons. He was very insistent. Well soon she would know. Soon the wait would be over.

~

'She said what?' Bob laughed haughtily. 'Wild horses and white horses. That's a good one. In fact, I think I would have been proud to have come up with that one. I can't believe that Mary came up with that one on her own. That's not her style. I think Michael is the one that loves looking at white horses or at least loves staring at a wild sea albeit in a picture or even from your window.'

Sharon look perplexed. 'Well that's what Mary told me. She said she had done everything to persuade you to go on the cruise, but your mind was made up.' Sharon reached across and topped up her wine glass. It was definitely early in the day for a drink, but she felt nervous. Bob had already been there some time, but it had all been small talk up until now. Was he about to drop a bombshell? She held up the bottle.

Bob shook his head and covered his glass with his hand. 'Well to be honest I can't think of anything worse than a cruise, personally. However, I am one to say, 'Never say never', and 'Don't judge it until you have tried it'. I have heard people say that they thought they would hate it, and then they absolutely loved it. I was actually prepared to give it a go. If not for my sake, but for the sake of Mary. Certainly, if she had her heart set on it. Besides, she can usually get me to change my mind. Our Mary can be very persuasive believe you me. You see I do have a habit of pleasing Mary. I mean look at us? You wouldn't really see a much more different couple than us, would you? You couldn't find two more different people if you tried?'

Bob looked straight at Sharon, but she did not answer. She did not want to say anything. How could she say anything? She could not answer. Yes. They were so totally different. The odd couple. Nevertheless, didn't that work sometimes? Did they not say that opposites attract? These two were poles apart, but what did she know? How could she say anything? Look at her own relationship. Or lack of it.

Bob smiled. 'You don't need to answer. I know what I am. I know what Mary is. She is a very attractive woman. A very sexual woman. I often thought I was lucky to have her. I often wondered what she saw in me. Although deep down I know I am her security. I knew she would always come back to me. I'm not stupid. Yes, I know other men find her attractive. Why shouldn't they? She is a very attractive woman. She is a very sexy woman. I might be many things but I am not stupid. I know she is sexy. I know other men find her sexy. I am also not blind. She's been having small dalliances for years. I know that. I've always known it. Perhaps I was weak, but I did not want to lose her. I did not want to take that chance. I did not challenge her. I ignored it all. I closed my eyes. I pretended nothing else was happening. Perhaps I was wrong? Perhaps I wasn't. You tell me?'

Sharon smiled sympathetically. She wondered if Bob had just come round to offload all his problems on her like it was some modern day confession. Her mother had always liked going to confession. It was as she remembered as a child with her mother. It brought those days back. It was like confession time all over again. It was good for the soul, but was it good for her soul? Why did she need to know this? Mary was her friend. What was she supposed to do? Who was she to judge others? She did not want to judge her friend. She did not want to take sides. Was it really any of her business? Wasn't she just as weak? Did not everybody have their own weakness?

'You still haven't realised why I am here have you?'

Sharon shook her head and stuttered. 'Well no. Not really. Not exactly.'

'Well this time I think she has gone too far. What is that saying about messing in your own nest?'

Sharon still did not understand, but Bob just sat there

looking at her as if he was waiting for the penny to drop. Sharon could not oblige. She shook her head. 'What do you mean gone too far?'

Bob continued. 'Well normally the men are faceless. I suppose I have always seen them as less of a threat, as if they were not real men. Well, real to me in any case. Not a face that I can picture or run into. It makes it easier to handle. This time it is completely different. Who knows where this one will go. This time it is a complete threat to you and me. A complete piss take. This time the other man is Michael.'

'Pardon?' Sharon heard herself say. Had she heard right. Surely Bob was making it up. It couldn't be true. Of course, it wasn't true. Bob was obviously mistaken. Michael was many things, but even he would not cheat on her with her best friend. Even he would not stoop that low. She smiled, and was surprised at how calm she felt. 'Sorry, Bob. I can't believe that. I can't believe that for one minute. How can you possibly think that? Michael is many things, and far from perfect. I know that more than anybody. Yes, perhaps, he might have slept with the odd woman if I think about it, and strangely I never have had. If he had perhaps I could not blame him. No. Not if I am being honest with myself. But he and Mary? You must be kidding? Sorry, I don't believe that? I can't believe it. I won't believe it.'

Bob smiled kindly. 'I knew you would say that. I could not believe it myself at first, but I have seen them with my own eyes. I just did not want to see. I thought I saw them together once some time ago when I was walking the dog over the Downs. Well to be honest I saw Michael's van, and then I saw Mary in our car in the car park. I was at a distance, but I knew that was his vehicle. It was much too much of a coincidence not to have been the two of them. After that there were other signs. I never actually caught them in the act, but I think I nearly did on more than one occasion. I hoped it would blow itself out. I did not want to worry you, but unfortunately it hasn't. It is still going on. It is still very much going on. I don't think Michael has much work on at the moment. I think he probably spends as much time as he can at our place.'

Sharon laughed. Now she knew that he was being silly. She knew for a fact that Michael had a lot of work on, and was doing well. In any case he had just booked an expensive cruise for her birthday. For the both of them. That was hardly the actions of a man that did not have much work on, and had money problems.

Bob looked straight at her. 'I can see that you still don't believe me, but I am deadly serious. Just think about it for a moment.'

Yes, Sharon admitted to herself that Michael had been behaving strangely, but this was something else. This was on a new level. With everything going on in her life had she missed the obvious? She had had her own temptation. But Michael with her best friend? She knew that she and Michael had their problems, and some of them she had caused. That was why she had hoped to make her peace with Michael and to a certain extent make it up. She had hoped to resume sexual relations, but that had been a bit strained. She had thought it was because of the length of time it had been since they had done it, but if Bob was right that could have explained Michael's reluctance. 'Still going on,' Sharon repeated. 'Do you have any actual proof?'

'Yes and no,' Bob said. 'That is why I wanted to come

here, and not meet you elsewhere. That is why I bought my computer and some accessories.'

'Here? Your computer? I don't understand? What do you want to do? What do you mean?' All of a sudden Sharon felt light headed, and her stomach began to churn. On top of everything else she did not need this.

Bob reached down into his laptop bag and took out an external hard drive. 'I thought you might let me have a quick look through Michael's computer. I don't suspect he has it with him does he?

'No, it is over there,' Sharon said. 'But I can't get into it. I don't know his password. Besides, what do you hope to see?'

'Well,' Bob said. 'I can see from your expression that you don't actually fully believe me. Perhaps I don't fully believe me. This can put it beyond doubt, and don't worry I can jolly soon get into it. Don't forget I'm in IT. Getting into someone's computer is so much easier than people think. Yes, even if you don't have any computer knowledge people are so careless with their passwords. Do you know that one of the favourite passwords is, 'password'? Alternatively they use simple ones like the name of one of their children or a name of a pet. You can actually guess them, but I don't think Michael is quite that silly. No he will have used something that combines letters and numbers. You can be sure of that. No matter. It is still quite simple. All you need is a computer, an external hard drive, and a blank CD. The software hacking tool that I use uses Rainbow Tables, and the programme I use is called Ophcrack. You do need to be in front of their machine. That is all. Then within a few minutes I can list all the usernames and passwords in the machine. We are not exactly cracking The Enigma Code.

Within a few minutes I will be in. Can I go ahead?'

Sharon found herself nodding in agreement. Was she being disloyal? She knew Michael had secrets. She had secrets. Wasn't it sometimes better left that way? Did she have to face the truth? Had she denied herself the truth for far too long?

Bob went to work. True to his word he was soon into Michael's computer, and then his emails. He did not take long to find what he wanted. Bob looked up and smiled. 'Look at this one. It is an email from Mary to Michael giving him a new number for a secret phone that she bought so they can keep in contact. Not just calls, but sexy texts. Do you want to read it?'

Sharon did not really want to read it, but she forced herself to do so, and felt more and more sick, as she continued to read. This was the proof. The proof beyond any doubt.

Bob took her hand gently. 'Sorry, but I just had to prove it to you. Let's look and see what else we can find.'

~

The next day Sharon stood in her favourite boutique in the famous Brighton Lanes. 'What do you think?' Sharon said, as she looked in the full length mirror. She pouted her lips and threw back her head in a way that she had not done for so long. She really did want to look her best. She really did want to be remembered in this dress.

'The lady in red,' Julie said laughing. 'Yes it suits you. It does look nice on you.'

'Oh that record,' Sharon replied quickly. 'I used to love it, but they overplayed it. You've put me off now.' Sharon looked down at the price tag. It was expensive. Very expensive. Possibly the dearest dress that she had ever contemplated buying.

Julie noticed and walked across and turned over the tag. 'Yes. Well it should be nice at that price. Mind you nothing is cheap in here. How many times will you wear it?'

Sharon looked thoughtful. That was the point. She would probably only wear it once, but she had to have it. It was stunning, and maybe it was in the red of the devil, because a little voice inside her was telling her that she deserved it. It was her treat to herself. Well Michael would ultimately pick up the bill. 'I think I had better take it off and pay for it before I change my mind.'

Julie laughed. 'It is a little daring for you.'

Sharon looked again in the mirror. Julie was right. It was. It was not her normal style, but it was exactly right for what she wanted it for. How many times had she tried something on and liked it then traipsed all around the shops only to return and buy it. She did not have the time. Time was running out.

It was a nice shade of red. She studied herself in the mirror and many old memories came flooding back, as her reflection gazed back at her, and she remembered when she was a small girl her father read to her at bedtimes. One of her favourite books which was fantastically illustrated had been *Alice Through the Looking Glass*. She had loved all the images, many of which had related to chess. She could still picture them now. Now standing here she thought of Michael and how much he liked chess. She had never made the comparison before. Now in this red dress she felt like Alice about to meet the Red Queen. The Queen was the most agile and powerful of pieces. Sharon let the imagery of that book float through her mind. The images seem to mix with some of her own. She had crossed many brooks and bridges with Michael, but soon the end would be coming. It would be checkmate. It would all be over between them. She had been shocked at what Michael had done. There could be no reconciliation now. Obviously the hope that she had for them had now gone.

Sharon now saw Michael as the Red Knight trying to capture her, and Bob as the White Night. Well maybe Michael wanted to take her away to celebrate her birthday, but in the book Humpty Dumpty was celebrating his unbirthday, and he went on to have a big fall. It was time to play Michael at his own game. Michael had always fancied himself as some kind of king. Well she might not have really fully understood the rules of chess other than in that book, but she knew that now they were in the endgame. They had lived in stalemate for far too long. She had already thought it through. She had it mapped out. Two squares forward, and then one at a time. She would no longer be his pawn. It was time to promote herself. She could still be the queen that her father had always promised her she would be.

Sharon pulled back her shoulders as she took in the image of herself in the mirror in the red dress. It was all coming together. Sharon now knew what she had to do.

TWENTY NINE

D-Day was finally here. It was the time that Michael had been waiting for. It was the time that Michael had been planning for. He remembered from watching all the programmes on the History Channel about the invasion of Normandy, and the code name for it was 'Operation Overlord'. Well now he had started his own operation, 'Operation Wife Overboard'.

Both Michael and Sharon stood on the Barcelona quayside looking up at the great ship. Soon it would be time to embark. All the months of planning would be put to the test. Yes, Michael laughed to himself, 'Operation Wife Overboard', said it all really. It was hard to believe that the time was nearly here. There were only days to go. In line with most military operations Michael had decided that D-Day would be the actual day of the sailing. The event itself would be well into the cruise. The exact day of the event was still to be determined. It was a seven night eight day cruise, and Michael realised the timing might also be based on opportunity so he had kept an open mind. It was just like planning a military operation really and Michael had it all planned right down to the last detail. All the research had been done. This was it. It was only a few days away. Michael had planned it to be around D-Day + 6. The authorities and the cruise line would certainly not want to hold the boat up, knowing that within a day or so there would be a quay full of new passengers wanting to embark, as well as all the ones on the boat who still wanted to enjoy what was left of their holiday, and would need to get off the boat so that they could return to their jobs and the mundane life from which they had used the cruise to escape.

Michael turned to Sharon. 'It's hard to believe how big she is, isn't it? When you think how they marvelled at the *Titanic*, but I believe that she is nearly three times as big as her. There are even some cruise ships nowadays that are nearly five times the size of the *Titanic*.'

Sharon nodded. 'Really? I always thought of the *Titanic* as the biggest ever. I loved that film. Such a good story. It was so sad when Jack died.'

'Oh yes,' Michael continued, ignoring Sharon's base reference. 'You measure a ship by its tonnage. Most people think that it is the weight, but it is actually the measurement of the internal volume, and as I said our ship is over three times bigger. Realistically there is no comparison on any level. The *Titanic* had about two thousand two hundred passengers and crew. This ship has over three thousand six hundred passengers and approximately thirteen hundred crew. They were so much more cramped on the *Titanic*, as well. Very little entertainment, and with the steerage class rammed in. There were over seven hundred of them, and believe it or not only two bathrooms between all of them.'

Michael stopped for a moment and took a deep breath. Michael knew the Titanic because of his interest in the tragedy and his love of the sea, but he also felt that he knew this ship. He had done his homework. He had to. Put like that it meant that there would be nearly five thousand potential witnesses on the ship.

'But is this ship really that much bigger?' Sharon asked.

'Yes if you put them side by side I doubt that the top of *Titanic's* funnels would even reach the top deck of this ship. I mean just look how high she is. Like a floating city. It's a wonder they stay afloat.'

Sharon smiled. 'Yes standing here just looking up at her is amazing. Where do you think our cabin is? Do you think we can see it from here? Are we on the left or right side of the boat?'

'Is that left or right when facing the bow or the stern?'

'Does it matter?'

Michael turned to look at Sharon. She seemed wide eyed. Was it in wonderment or did he sense a certain nervousness?

Michael laughed and put his hand on her arm. Was it his imagination or did she actually flinch a little? 'What you actually mean is, is it Port or Starboard? Port is actually to the left of the ship as you look forward, and yes, I think we are on the Port side which is lit by a red light at night. So yes, you probably can see our cabin from here. It is on the ninth deck.'

'It looks mighty high from down here. Goodness knows what it looks like when you are actually standing on the balcony looking down. You must get vertigo. Not sure if us having a balcony was a very good idea.'

'Oh believe you me,' Michael said quickly and evenly. 'It was a great idea. You will love it. Remember this is your birthday treat, and I want you to enjoy every minute of it.

You do not need to worry about a thing. Everything is taken care of down to the smallest detail. It is going to be the holiday of a lifetime.'

Sharon and Michael arrived at their cabin before their luggage. Sharon unlocked the cabin door with the plastic key card and used it to turn on the light. 'Wow,' she said as she stepped inside and took in the decor. The cabin was much roomier than they were used to. It was almost palatial. Michael had thought long and hard when booking it, and it had to be in line with his needs. It had been a toss-up between a Balcony Suite and a Balcony Stateroom. Both had the most important ingredient which was a private balcony. The cost differential was quite large, and apart from the size, as it was obviously bigger, the major differences seemed to be priority check-in and a priority departure. Michael had his eyes on a departure, but not one he had to pay more money for. The obvious major difference was the size, and he sure was not going to pay a sizeable difference for a room that was a bit bigger in size. The larger suites also had a complimentary concierge who would be able to organise breakfast, lunch, or a dinner service in the cabin. Not a service he wanted. In fact, quite the opposite as he wanted witnesses to recollect as to what a happy couple they were, if asked by the authorities, and how happy they had seemed at the dinner table.

Anyway, it did not appear to matter now. It appeared Sharon was very satisfied with his choice. He watched her as she ran her hand over the bedding and looked around, and she seemed genuinely excited.

'Oh how clever,' she exclaimed. 'I thought the Greek theme might be a bit much, but I think it works.'

The predominant colours within the cabin were black, white, and gold. The curtains depicted patterned Greek silhouette characters. Prints of Greek Myths adorned the walls, and there were even a couple of Greek urns as vases.

Sharon walked over to the sofa and then to the vanity unit which doubled as a desk, and then turned back to face him. At first he thought she was going to pass comment on the large king size bed. It was certainly, big enough for three or even four at a push. At least they would be able to sleep without their bodies touching which was certainly not something they were used to. Of course, he knew he could have asked for twin beds. That would not have been a problem. That is what they would have got, and he was sure that was what Sharon would have also wanted. The same that they had at home. Nevertheless, he had thought that if he had asked for twin beds then the request would have been recorded, and might it not look a little odd that such a happy couple had separate beds in their cabin?

Sharon did not seem to notice. She seemed to be in a very good mood which Michael wanted to take advantage of. He wanted to show her smiling to the world. He watched her open the patio type doors to the balcony and walk out and look down at the port below. Michael walked up behind her.

'My God it is high isn't it? Wonder what it will be like when we are out at sea? Wouldn't want to be out here if it were rough.'

Michael chose to ignore her comment. 'Come on,' he said. 'Let's explore the ship. We can start at the top and work our way down. It will be easier that way. We won't need to use the lifts. They are always so super slow on embarkation day with all the new passengers, and all the crew ferrying the luggage about. Drives you mad waiting. You wait for ages and when one arrives it is full and you can't get in.'

Michael had read several articles about how to start your cruise off in the right way, and how to make the most of your first day. Most passengers probably learned the hard way. Some probably never learnt at all, even seasoned travellers. People could generally not be bothered to do their homework and instead chose to just go along with it all only to find out quite often that they missed out after it was too late or that they had paid far more money than they needed to. One tip Michael picked up was to pack swimming costumes in the hand luggage so that all the pools and hot tubs could be used immediately and you did not have to wait for the luggage to be delivered first. It was also the time that they would be less used and less busy. However, Michael ignored that one as he thought it was really not their most important priority, but he was keen to get moving and make sure that he took advantage of any offers and discounts. 'Come on,' he said with a slight irritation in his voice. It was a habit hard to check.

'Hold on,' Sharon held up her hand then rummaged in her handbag for her mobile. 'I just want to take a couple of photos whilst the cabin looks brand new and spick and span. I want people....err.........our friends to see it how it should be in pristine condition.' She stopped speaking and turned to Michael as if she was thinking about what to say next. 'Yes, don't want the photos spoilt with your dirty underpants lying around as the cruise goes on.'

Michael did not laugh, and failed to connect any importance to the quip. He was feeling hungry. 'Come on. Let's also get something to eat.'

'What in the buffet?'

'No,' Michael said as he walked round the cabin turning things on and off and opening and closing doors.

'What are you doing?' Sharon asked.

Michael answered without looking at her as he turned on the hairdryer. 'Just trying everything out to make sure it all works and nothing is stuck before we get settled in.' He turned the television on and flicked through the channels. 'If it doesn't we can report it when we go down to the desk. We need to go down to the desk anyway, and purchase our 'All inclusive drinks package'. It is stupid to buy drinks or coffees in the meantime, and then buy the package later. If we buy it now we start saving straight away. I also want to check the seating for dinner.'

Michael turned towards Sharon. He thought she might accuse him of being tight. It wouldn't have been the first time. Instead she said nothing, and simply smiled. 'OK. That's a good idea. Then shall we go up to the buffet?'

A good idea. Michael was stunned. Was that praise? Surely Sharon had thought that he had not had a good idea in years. He felt confused. It was strange. It almost felt as if they were a couple. Of course, they were joined in matrimony, but they had not shared a joint interest or probably reached a joint agreement in years. He knew why he was on his best behaviour, but why was she on hers?

'This is your Captain, Tim Corbett.' The Captain's voice came over the ship's public address system welcoming them on board, and informing them that there would be a lifeboat drill later before they sailed.

Michael waited for the announcement to finish and then he continued.

'Well we know that the buffet is always the most crowded on embarkation day as everyone gets on hungry for lunch. I thought I might treat you to lunch in one of the other restaurants which will probably be empty.'

There was a knock on the door and Michael opened it. Their luggage had arrived. Michael realised that might buy him some more time so that he could explore on his own and get the feel of the ship.

'That would be nice. Thank you.'

'Tell you what,' Michael said quickly. 'Why don't you start the unpacking and I'll go down and get the drinks packages. Then when I get back we can have a tour and find some lunch. How does that sound?'

Sharon immediately agreed, and Michael left the cabin. Everything appeared to be going to plan. In fact, it was even better than he had anticipated. Sharon seemed to be genuinely enjoying it, and there appeared to be far less tension between them. Michael stared at the highly polished brass lift doors as he waited for the lift to arrive. His reflection looked slightly distorted as if he were in one of those hall of mirrors and he briefly wondered if he had not become a little distorted over the years. Was he actually thinking straight? The ping of the lift's arrival brought him back to the present and he squeezed into the lift amongst the other excited passengers. He pressed the top deck button. It was too late now to have second thoughts or to get cold feet.

As Michael walked out on the top deck. He needed moral support. He needed to hear Mary's voice. He had always planned to call her before they sailed. He knew that soon when they were out to sea he would not be able to get a signal. He did not want to have to pay sky high satellite roaming charges. He wanted to use his provider's European traveller's package.

Michael walked over to the railing and looked down at the sea below, then took out his mobile phone and unlocked it. He stared at the horizon as the tone changed and the ringing tone sounded. He did not want to look down. It seemed to take an age before Mary answered.

THIRTY

'Is that too hard?' Debbie said, as she pressed down on Sharon's back.

'No. That's great,' Sharon answered. 'Just right.'

Sharon closed her eyes and relaxed allowing her thoughts to drift in and out. This was her time, and she was determined to make the most of it. Michael had organised it as one of her birthday treats. She had been shocked at the trouble he had gone to so far. He was certainly trying to make it a trip to remember, and he was certainly trying to make it a birthday for her to remember. He had been so thoughtful this trip. It was not like him at all. Michael appeared to be a man of many faces. It depended on which one he cared to present to the world at any one time. The face that he presented to the outside world was not always the same one that he presented to her at home or when they were on their own. He really could be cruel at times, but he had always been reasonably generous with money although sometimes he would accuse her of being wasteful. Regardless whether he could afford it; and after all his business had done well, and was doing well. He would sometimes pick her up on little things, little things that cost little and that did not really seem to matter, but that did matter to him. He would save pennies, but waste pounds, and especially when it was on himself. Lately he appeared to be becoming tighter and tighter. He was now always looking at ways of saving money, and comparing the market to this and that. It was as if every penny counted.

Sharon sighed as the masseur's hands worked up and down her back. One thing she knew was that she could not accuse him of stinginess on this cruise. He had certainly pushed the boat out this time. Sharon laughed at her own pun. He had even thought of booking this massage for her in advance on the first day, because he was aware that many of the beauty and spa services booked up very quickly, and he did not want her to miss out.

'Are you enjoying the cruise?' the masseur asked.

'Oh, yes thank you Debbie,' Sharon said softly. 'What is there not to like? It is such a lovely ship.'

'Have you been on any of the excursions?'

'Well no, not yet. We did our own thing in Provence. Well really my husband's thing with the cable car and the military museum, and at Nice we just got off and walked around. We've not been there before. I thought Nice was nice. Completely different to the other places I have been to in the South of France. More like Paris by the sea. The old mixed with the new. My husband has booked three excursions I think. Florence, Rome and Naples. Well, for Naples we are going on the Pompeii trip. My husband loves history. Think he wants to see all those bodies there frozen in time.'

Sharon wondered if the lady was just trying to make conversation or was she even trying to push the trips ashore?

It was nice to be able to talk to another English lady. All the staff in the beauty department appeared to be European rather than the rest of the crew who were certainly from all parts of the world. She wanted to confide in her. She felt so relaxed. Tell her what was happening in her life. Tell her what she expected to happen in her life. How shocked she would be. She was sure that the masseur would be flabbergasted.

'So which one are you looking forward to the most?'

'Rome is the one place that I really want to see. Certainly one to tick off from my 'Top ten places to see before I die' list. Shame we don't get more time there. There is so much to see. Still I suppose a cruise is like that. Just a taster, and if you like a place you can always go back if you are lucky.'

'That's right,' Debbie said. 'Seems as if your husband has got it all worked out.'

'Yes, yes he has,' Sharon heard herself say, as she found her mind wandering. She wanted to say worked out in ways you would not believe. He has it so worked out that he is actually sleeping with my friend. Shagging her behind my back. Both of them are probably laughing at me. He thinks he can get away with it, and you would not believe what he thinks he can get away with. Basically he is a monster. A monster who is pretending to be Mr Nice Guy. He is actually being so nice to me at the moment that I don't recognise the man. I could actually like him if I did not know better. He is playing a game. A dangerous game with high stakes. He doesn't know I know about the two of them. Mary does not know I know either. I have never spoken to her about it. That does not mean I don't care. I did. Not now though. I am over it. But they are in for such a shock.

Shocks, Sharon realised, come in many many ways. It

was really when you were least expecting something. That was the best time to get the maximum impact. Before they had boarded the boat they had wandered around the Las Ramblas which was probably the most famous thoroughfare in Barcelona. The tree lined pedestrian avenue was filled with pavement cafés and souvenir kiosks, and has long been a favourite of tourists, and Michael and Sharon were no different. It had been hot and they had stood and admired the many human statues that entertain the tourists. Each one had on a different outfit, from a North American Indian to a businessman in a suit. Sometimes the human statues worked in pairs, such as a man and woman dressed in silver suits with silver faces, and on silver bikes. Nevertheless, whatever their disguise or outfit the result was always the same. To begin with they were frozen in time, inanimate, motionless, and devoid of any human emotion, and apparently unaffected by the heat. They would bide their time. Patience was the key, then when the time was right, normally when a small crowd had gathered, they would make their move, and surprise and shock the unsuspecting tourist. These were professionals and you could only learn from them. It was all about timing. Timing was king or in this case Sharon hoped queen.

Sharon closed her eyes and her mind began to drift as the massage overcame her. Debbie obviously sensed this and stopped talking. It was all so confusing really. Last night Michael had sat on the bed with a pen and piece of paper and actually tried to estimate how much the ship made from photographs every year. He had calculated that if each passenger only bought two photographs during the course of the week then the earnings from the photographic endeavour alone would be in excess of a quarter of a million pounds. That was only two photographs for each passenger and without all the upsizing and enhancements that kept pushing up the price of each shot.

Normally, Michael would not bother with purchasing the many photographs taken of them throughout the cruise. He always said it was blackmail. He was well aware of how the ship's photographer captured each moment for every couple or family, from boarding the ship, to outside the dining room when everybody was dressed in their finery. On this trip Michael had shocked Sharon. When they had been on the quay at Barcelona they had to go through an archway with the word Barcelona on it before they boarded. The background picture was the cruise ship, and as they were asked to stop, their photograph was taken. They were joined by a member of the crew who looked a little bit Spanish, and who was dressed as a matador. Sharon had to admit it was cheesy. A souvenir for the album nicely presented in its own folder. She could understand passengers buying the formal night one, the man in his black tie and the woman in her finest dress, stood against the ship at sunset backdrop, in a sort of a *Gone with the Wind* pose. Normally, Michael would have been gone like the wind when it came to buying any of them. Frankly he didn't give a damn. Not one thought. However, on this cruise he had actually bought the one of them boarding in Barcelona. He had returned from the photographers with it as if he was holding a prize trophy, and presented it to her.

Sharon's mind swirled as the masseur's hands worked in circles around her back. She didn't know what he was playing at. All these years he had never been like that. When she was a small girl she always had romantic dreams. *Gone with the Wind* had been one of her favourite films. It still was. She had lost count of the amount of times that she had seen it. She had even seen the musical some years earlier in London with Julie, in which Rhett had been portrayed by a rejected contestant from one of the old reality shows. It had been a lavish production that cost millions, and went on for nearly as long as the film. It had not been a hit and was pulled after just a few weeks as the critics had called it 'bum numbing'. Nevertheless, Sharon enjoyed it, and had wished that they had produced a soundtrack.

She had certainly never pretended that Michael was her Rhett although it had been his assured confidence that she had found attractive when they had first met. It certainly seemed as if he wanted to look after her and protect her in his cavalier way, and she wanted to be looked after. He was like the southern gentleman in the film and she wanted to be his belle. He appeared to be in complete control. Just how much he liked to be in control she would not find out until it was too late, and not until after they were married. They had then gone on to have their own battles. Their own civil war that had continued up until the present day. Their relationship had not been unlike that of the famous couple and she wished that she could have had the strength of Scarlett. Although perhaps she was also learning. Scarlett had to learn the hard way and drawn on reserves that she never knew she had. She would have to do the same. Michael, like Rhett, could be a charmer. He had even proved that on this cruise. Normally Michael would have ensured that they had a table for two in the dining room. It had always been the case up until now and Sharon was not sure why. It wasn't as if he wanted her all to himself or that they had great conversations. It was almost that he did not want others to observe them together. At least not at close quarters.

This cruise, though, they were at a large table and Sharon briefly ran through the names trying to count them. Sam, Lucy, Charlie, Camilla, Nevin, Erin, Steph, Niamh, Kane, and Heidi. She thought she had remembered them all. It was a table where conversation and laughter flowed, and Michael had very much ensured that they were part of it all. It made a change, and Sharon had to admit she liked it. It had made her realise how different life could have been. How different it could have been if they both had changed instead of shelling each other at every opportunity. If she actually listened to Michael, instead of switching off like she had trained herself to do, he could be quite entertaining. Earlier they had been enjoying an ice cream together when Jason, one of the entertainment staff that played a guitar in the bars and sometimes on the open deck, had stopped and asked them if they were enjoying it.

Michael had looked up from his tub of coconut ice cream that had been topped by desiccated coconut and laughed and said that he thought it ironic that the ice cream bar was named after a Greek mythological figure that had fallen into the sea and drowned. Jason did not know the story and he was sure that nobody on the boat did either. Michael then explained in an amusing way the story of how Icarus had been trying to escape from Crete but had flown too close to the sun and ignored warnings from his father. The sun had melted the wax on his wings and he had lost his feathers and fallen into the sea and drowned. Michael had then further explained after Jason had gone that it was an example of failed ambition.

Sharon closed her eyes. Failed ambition. She had many unfilled ambitions. One was that she had always wished that she had had a child, but it was never meant to be. Perhaps that had been the problem. Maybe, it was only the children that held a couple together. She thought of the dramatic scene in the film when Rhett had left after Bonnie died, and he told Scarlett that there was no chance of happiness for them. He even said that they had been at cross purposes, with each misunderstanding what the other wanted until it was too late. Sharon realised that they had a lot in common with the fictional couple, including the fact that Scarlett did not share a bed with her man. They had not shared a bed for years. Well not up until this cruise. Had Michael really thought that she had not realised? Sharon knew that she would make him realise many things including what he would be missing. She thought back to the end of the film when Scarlett thinks about going home, and promises that she will think of some way to get him back. Sharon had always presumed that Scarlett had wanted to win Rhett back romantically.

That had always been the interpretation. Not just hers, but generally. Scarlett would win Rhett back to be with him. She could not bear for them to be apart. Despite their differences they were meant to be together. However, could the words not be twisted? She would get him back could also be interpreted differently. Could it not mean that she wanted to get him back in a vengeful way? Could it be payback time?

Sharon found herself gripping the edge of the massage

table with both her hands, as she gritted her teeth, and thought the same words Scarlett had said in the closing scene. Silently in her head she vowed, 'I've thought of some way to get him back. After all .... tomorrow is another day.'

THIRTY ONE

Michael sat on the stool waiting for the dealer. It was his turn to cut the cards and he fiddled with the red plastic card, and waited to insert it into the combined decks. He was feeling lucky. He had a feeling that this was going to be his lucky night. Maybe the saying went that you could not be lucky in both cards and love, but he was not so sure. Perhaps he had not been so lucky with Sharon, but he certainly turned up trumps with Mary. He got a warm exciting feeling every time he thought about her. Maybe though it was not love. Maybe it was lust. Did that matter? Soon Sharon would be gone, and he and Mary could be together. Soon could not come soon enough.

Michael cut the cards and the dealer loaded the shoe. He was on a roll. He looked around at the other players. There were only two others. This was an early evening session that started as soon as the ship had left the port, as the tables were not allowed to be open when they were docked. Michael knew that it was often misconceived that the casino was the big money earner on the ship. In reality he had read that less than thirty percent of the passengers gambled, and the remainder just like to stand around and watch. This session was well suited for beginners because the minimum bet was lower than the one set for the later after-dinner session. Most passengers did not cruise to gamble so the cruise line would show a greater understanding to novices than a land based casino because of this. They were much more likely to refund a bet if the participant did not fully understand what they were doing or how to bet. As if to prove this point, the man on Michael's left, who was dressed in a loud Hawaiian shirt, took out some notes from his wallet and held them out towards the dealer.

She politely shook her head, and pointed to the table. 'Sorry, Sir. Please place them on the table. I am not allowed to take them directly from you.'

The game began. The man on Michael's right was in a different league to both of them. Michael noticed that the man always seemed to be playing the tables. He seemed to be always there when Michael was playing or when he was just walking past. The man always played with a number of stacked high value chips, three or four at a time and generally playing two or three circles at a time. Michael had already, on more than one occasion, seen him lose more in an hour than the cost of the cruise.

Michael looked towards him and studied this man who was probably twenty years or so younger than him. The man did not appear to be lucky in cards or in love. Michael had never seen him with a partner and his comb over, did little to disguise the fact that it was not just money that he was losing. Michael wondered what made him bet so recklessly. The casino staff made a fuss of him. To them he was probably a high roller, and he often tossed them the odd chip when he won a hand. Was the man that desperate for friends that he practically threw his money at them? He certainly did not appear to care if he won or lost.

Michael placed the single chip in front of him and waited for his cards. The first card he received was a picture. A face card. It was a Queen. Michael bided his time and waited until the dealer returned to him. He knew that it was all about biding his time. He could picture her face now. Mary would be back at home. She was his new queen. Would she be thinking about him? Did she think about him as much as he thought about her? She had won him, he knew. He was willing to discard Sharon for her. The dealer dealt him his second card which was also a picture. It was a King.

'Hit!' Said the man to his right. The dealer dealt the man another eight to go with his existing eight and his first card which had been a six. The dealer promptly relieved him of the small pile of chips.

Suddenly the words struck home to Michael. The hit had made the man bust. That was how quick it was. The wrong decision and it was all over. What if he got it wrong with Sharon? He could be busted for a very long time.

The dealer looked towards him. Michael looked at the dealer's nine, and then back to the dealer who was still looking at him and waiting for a reply. The answer should have been, or was, a foregone conclusion, but etiquette demanded that Michael answered in some way, as he could have taken a Hit or even Split the cards. Michael held up the palm of his hand. 'Stand!' He smiled. Obviously he would be allowed to split the cards and bet on each card separately. He had seen others do it. Why? He was never sure. For the sake of doubling their bet they would put both cards at risk. The King and Queen together provided a strong hand. A very strong hand. Together they stood. Together they would stand. They would not be divided. That was the way it was. That was the way it was going to be. He would only have to wait a short time.

The dealer played out the hand with the man in the Hawaiian shirt next to him, and he also busted. The dealer then showed the table that he had an Eight and was forced by the rules of the table to Stand. Michael was the winner. He had won. He was lucky. He felt lucky, and he knew that he had it all planned to back up his luck. He picked up all his chips from the table and flicked them from one hand to the other, and left the table. It was time to go back to the cabin. Time to see Sharon.

Michael took the glass lift up to the ninth deck. These lifts were so slick and fast and he felt his stomach churn. Was it the lift he asked himself or was it simply his nerves? He jiggled the chips in his pocket as he walked along the corridor. His winnings had put a spring in his step. He had not wanted to cash the chips in knowing that he would be back on the tables later. Nevertheless, he could still feel his stomach as he walked past all the closed doors to all the other cabins. It was like living in a little terraced street and not knowing your neighbours. Michael took the plastic key card from his wallet, as he approached their cabin. He guessed Sharon would be back already from her massage and suitably relaxed. She would probably be off guard as she decided what to wear for dinner.

Michael slid the card into the slot, opened the door and stepped into the cabin. At first he thought she was not in the cabin, but then he heard the music. It was coming from a small speaker that she plugged into her mobile phone when she was getting ready. He immediately recognised the soul music. To him it sounded old, but Sharon had always liked it. His eyes searched the room for her, and he opened the bathroom door. Finally he spotted her through the net curtains out on the balcony. The patio doors were open. She was standing looking over the railing down at the water. She had obviously not heard him come back.

Michael smiled to himself as he walked quietly towards her. Was this the opportunity that he had been waiting for? It was a couple of days or so early and it was still daylight. Not the ideal scenario, but she was exactly in the right place. Michael's mind raced. He needed to make a decision. Almost a split second decision. It was like being in the casino when everything depended on one quick turn of a card. His mind raced as he walked quietly towards her. Sharon still had her back to him. She still had not heard him. Was it the sound of the sea, despite being so far below, masking his movement? Michael got to within a few feet of her when Sharon suddenly turned almost instinctively. By then Michael had his arm out parallel with her shoulders. He quickly put his arm around her.

'Good evening,' a strange man's voice drifted towards them.

Michael turned suddenly to where the voice came from and saw the ruddy face of a man leaning around the balcony partition that separated their cabin from the next one.

'Thought I would introduce myself,' the man continued. 'I'm Darren, and my wife Laura is just getting ready. She's tried four outfits on already.'

Michael tried to smile at the man, and tried not to show his devastation at the uninvited intrusion, sure that the colour had drained from his face.

~

The next morning Michael stood on their balcony looking out to the calm sea. He could not sleep any more. It was D-Day + 4. He had originally thought that the event itself would ideally be D-Day + 6. With so many things running through his head he found it hard to sleep. He gazed across at Sharon who had been sleeping soundly unaware of his torment. The beauty of the large bed was that you were not even aware that another person was in it, and that you were certainly not forced to sleep like spoons.

He rested his head and gazed at her as she slept in a way that he had not done for many years. She looked so peaceful. Would she look like that when she was laid to rest? Didn't they say that a person who had been prepared for burial just looked like they were asleep? Although Michael remembered reading accounts of what a person could look like, and how bloated they might be, if they had drowned. He tried to put the thought out of his head. He had wanted to reach out and touch her. Why? He wasn't sure. Would he have wanted to do that if she had been stone cold? He hadn't wanted to touch her like that in years. He was confused. Last night had really scared him. It had been such a shock when their neighbour had poked his head around the partition just as he was coming up behind Sharon. Would that have been the moment? Even he was not sure, but it was certainly as good a practice run as he was likely to get. Michael's head began to spin with the contemplation, and he found himself sweating so he got out of bed.

Standing on their balcony his mind began to race. It was

early morning and before the sun had any heat. He could see the Italian land mass as they neared. Today it was Florence. Today was Sharon's day. It was Sharon's day in more ways than one. Today was her birthday, and it was the big Five O. The day that he knew she had been dreading. Michael had done all he could to make it a special day. He had done it to show the world, or at least their table, what a caring, loving, husband he really was. He was sure that some of the couples on their table would be very impressed by the lengths that he had gone to in order to make sure her birthday was a success. It had been a very important part of his master plan. A plan that was very much coming together.

He gripped the rail with a mixture of nervousness and excitement. He would present her with her major present when she got up so that she could show it off to the other passengers as they met or at dinner tonight. He could imagine her presenting her hand as she showed it, and telling the others what a lovely day they had had in Florence. Yes, it was her day. He was taking her to see Ghiberti's Gates of Paradise. Michael smiled to himself. Wasn't it ironic really? She would be seeing the real gates very soon if there was ever such a thing. Would Saint Peter be there to meet her if the story was true, and if it was, Michael knew he was certainly going to a hotter place. Michael thought he had enough to worry about in this life without bothering to worry about the next.

He took a sip of his green tea and looked thoughtfully towards the shore. He almost begrudgingly had to admit that this cruise had actually been quite enjoyable up until now. In fact surprisingly so. It had been a bit of give and take. Normally within their relationship he had been quite selfish and he knew he liked to get his own way. Really they both did. He had been quite controlling and in return Sharon had rebelled and could be very cruel. It had made it an impossible battle over the years.

This cruise seemed to change all that. He had been more relaxed. More relaxed because initially he had a purpose. There was method in his madness. He had a plan and he was sticking to it. Surprisingly Sharon seem to respond to it differently as well. There was less tension. Less stress. It was more a case of, 'We will do what you want today, and then tomorrow we can do what I want.' He thought back to the day when they had docked in Provence. It really had been very enjoyable especially from his point of view. It had been a historic day in more ways than one.

Sharon was aware that he always loved history and especially naval and military things. The day had been ideal as they had visited the Allied Landings Museum which displayed memorabilia of the Second World War. He could have spent hours there, and he had to admit that perhaps they had spent a bit more time there than Sharon would have liked, but she had been very patient. It was a quality that he never noticed of her before. He had thought little of it as they walked around and he became engrossed in the exhibits. Thinking about it now he thought that it was almost as if they were two different people on this cruise and not the warring couple that they were.

The actual high of the trip had been the cable car ride which was a five minute walk from the museum, and he had enjoyed it immensely. It had reminded him of the film *Where Eagles Dare* where there was a castle at the end of the cable car run. It had been a very exciting film and he was quite young when he saw it, but he would always remember the fighting on top of the cable car and how Richard Burton had pushed one of the Germans off. He had looked at Sharon as the car climbed and made that connection and smiled to himself. That film was just a boyhood memory with its fantasy scene, as he knew in reality the cable car did not travel to a castle in the sky. That was just the imagination and the skill of the filmmaker. It was just made up and superimposed. The reality of it all had shot home. This was not a film he was in. This was real life, and it would be a real death.

Michael glanced back inside their cabin. Sharon seemed to be stirring. It was time to execute the plan. Well part of it in any case. He quietly slid open the patio door and went back inside. Let the spoiling begin. He made a cup of coffee with the help of the machine in their cabin that the cruise line provided, and also charged them for every capsule used. He then retrieved from his hand luggage the card and small box that he had wrapped before they had departed.

'Morning,' he said as he gently shook her shoulder. 'Happy Birthday.'

Sharon opened her eyes and within a few seconds she was awake.

'I've made you a coffee.'

Sharon sat up and a few minutes later she was opening the small neatly wrapped package. Slowly she opened the lid of the box to reveal the 9ct white gold diamond eternity ring.

Her expression was one of surprise, and even shock.

Michael stood by the bed looking down at her. 'Do you

like it? It's an eternity ring.'

'Yes............Yes, I know.' Sharon's voice was shaky.

Michael smiled. 'I hope you like it. Slip it on. You can show everybody at breakfast.'

THIRTY TWO

Sharon closed her eyes, as Katie ran her hands through her hair. It had been a long hot day, but nevertheless very enjoyable. She could not remember when she had done so much on her birthday, and the tour of Florence had been the icing on the cake. Now, before the evening began, it was nice to relax. It was so nice to be pampered. It was something that Sharon could have got used to if she had allowed herself the time. The cruise line worked hard at giving their passengers a dreamlike holiday as the customers travelled the world to forget the troubles of the world.

Michael had told her there were some rich couples, and singles, with money that virtually spent their lives on cruise ships. Some on the same ship, and if not on the same ship, then probably with the same cruise line. Most cruise lines operate a loyalty scheme that rewards passengers who sail with them regularly. Nevertheless, these passengers took that to another level. They had the money and generally due to their age they had the time. They could choose not to live in the real world. They did not have to. They could live in an almost permanent Disney World existence. Sharon could understand why. Life was so simple. Life was so easy.

Everything was done for you. You could sail around the world avoiding all the nasty hot spots, and never even have to look at a newspaper or news channel if you did not want to. Sharon found that sitting in the hairdresser's chair it was certainly very easy to forget. Well, at least for a few moments, then all the images flooded back. All her troubles came to the fore. Troubles that even if she travelled to the other side of the globe or even the other side of the moon, she could not forget or escape from.

'You are lucky,' Katie said.

Sharon opened her eyes and smiled. 'Yes. Yes, thank you. Perhaps I am.' She so desperately wanted to change the subject, and decided to try to switch the topic. 'So how long do you want to carry on this life working on the ships?'

Katie looked thoughtful. She was quite short with blondish, reddish, unkempt hair that would have any observer disbelieving that she was a hairdresser. Katie had quite a high pitched voice, but Sharon had already learned that not only was she funny, but that she was also extremely well read, and had obviously travelled extensively. Some of the stories that Katie had just told her about her escapades on the high seas had been truly amazing, and very amusing. Yet here was Katie wanting to give it all up and settle down, and still hoping to find a nice man to do it with.

Sharon had wanted to tell her not to bother. It really was not worth it. She would probably have to sail each of the seven seas to find a decent honest man. There were no heroes left. No real life heroes anyway. Katie had earlier asked her what her favourite film was, and Sharon had immediately said that *Gone with the Wind* was up there, and very near to top of her list. Both had agreed how dashing Clark Gable had been, and how well cast, but of course it was only a film. Katie, who was like a walking encyclopaedia, had told Sharon that after the death of Clark Gable's wife in a plane crash on a War Bond Tour, Clark had gone on to enlist, despite both his advanced age and status. Further, not only did he want to promote the forces, but he had flown in combat, including flying over Germany, and had been awarded the DFC.

Both had agreed that men like him did not seem to exist anymore. If it was loyalty that they wanted nowadays they were better off getting a puppy. Sharon had always prided herself on being a loyal person, and she thought that all of her friends had been loyal as well. What a laugh that had been, and what a mistake. She knew she could not help being loyal. Perhaps it was a quality you were born with, or if not, certainly brought up with. Her mother had been loyal and a fat lot of good that had done her. Sharon had automatically followed suit. What a fool she had been too. How misguided and trusting she had been, and look how she had been betrayed. She had been kissed on both cheeks, not only by her husband, but by one of her best friends as well. It had devastated her. It had almost destroyed her, and now it was time to destroy them.

She took a sip from her glass of water, and then put it back on the glass shelf. She wasn't silly or stupid. She knew that Michael was not that happy. Did he really think that she was happy? He would have argued rightly or wrongly that there were unwritten rules between them. Unwritten statements and actions that both had been ignoring for years. Did Michael not think that she had not been tempted? Of course she had been tempted. Did it not come with any marriage?

Did he not think that she wasn't attractive? She could have showed him. She could have showed him with men that were quite a few years younger than he was. Although, she was not the one having a middle aged crisis like the cliché it had become. She had been tempted. She had been tempted more than once. The Muscles from Brussels had been one example. She could have almost acted out a fantasy from one of the romantic books that she once read. It would not have been hard to let herself be seduced. She had to admit that she had been near. Very near, but she held back.

It was what she did. She always held back. Never different. There were lots of different things that she did in her leisure time. Probably high on her list of favourite pursuits was shopping. She loved to shop. Michael would have said that she was very good at shopping. She could have won medals shopping for England, but shopping for men was one thing that she did not do. Yes, she might have been window shopping. What woman or man does not look twice at a member of the opposite sex occasionally? Was that not natural? She had looked. She had been tempted. What woman who had been married for as long as she had, and especially in her situation, would not have been?

It was like going to the same restaurant every night with the same menu. You were bound to become a bit bored even if the food was of high quality. Was it not like that with every couple when they were first together, and it was all fresh, and they could probably say that it was fine dining with Spode china and tablecloths. Sharon's love life had then moved to a quick take-away each week. Then almost a drive through grab and go, and then even that had stopped.

It always astounded her how sex was so important to

some people and how unimportant it was to others. Was it an age thing? Was it a gender thing? Was it nature saying that you have had children so now take a rest, and you do not need to do that anymore? Therefore, was it not obvious that one or the other would go off with someone else? Was it not to be expected? The sad thing was that it did seem as if it did not matter how nice or kind the partner was. Perhaps the nicer the partner the more likely they were to be cheated on. Bob was a prime example. Even she had thought of him as 'Boring Bob.' Despite him spoiling Mary it had not stopped her going off with someone else, and from what Bob had said it wasn't just one. She might even have been having it off with the whole of the Coldstream Guards, but perhaps more importantly it had still not stopped her from going off with her husband. Betraying both Bob and herself, just for her fun. She could picture them together. She did not want to, but she could not stop herself.

The images of the two of them kept creeping into her mind. She tried to stop them, but she couldn't. It was not the fact that Michael was with another woman that bothered her. It was the fact that it was Mary. It might not have mattered if Michael had behaved like some French politician and taken a mistress. A mistress that she did not know about. A faceless woman she did not know, and a faceless woman that she did not even know about. That would have been entirely different. With Mary involved it was different. Very different. It was particularly all the creeping around behind her back that did it. Then there was the plotting and scheming. For that words failed her, and here was Katie saying she was lucky. Katie did not know the half of it. Why should she? How could she? All Katie knew was what she had been told or seen, and to the outside world they must have seemed to be a happy couple.

'Well I suppose if the truth be known,' Katie continued. 'I would give it all up in an instant just to settle down and have children before it's too late. How many children do you have?'

Sharon looked straight in the mirror at her reflection and then up at Katie. Why do people always presume that women of a certain age always have children? It was a question that she had often been asked. It got easier to answer, but nevertheless it was still painful. She guessed it always would be. Time would dull the pain. Time did dull the pain and obviously as she had got older and nature dictated that she would definitely not have children the pain turned into regret. 'None,' Sharon answered quietly. 'We just never got round to it.' She smiled softly. It was the best answer to give. It was always the answer that she gave, especially to strangers. It was easier. It was much easier than telling the truth and going into long explanations.

'Oh dear,' Katie exclaimed. 'I just thought you would have. Put my foot in it again. Sorry.'

'Yes everybody does. Everybody always presumes you have children, I mean,' Sharon answered distantly. 'No matter. No offence.'

'Still at least you have a husband that obviously absolutely adores you. How romantic that even after being married all these years he bought you an eternity ring for your birthday.'

Sharon smiled, but did not say anything. Yes it might look like that to others. It even confused her.

'He is obviously still proud of you and booking for you to have your hair done for the big day. Are you looking forward to the formal night? I bet you have a nice dress.'

'Yes. You could say it's a one off. It's red, and I did choose it specially.'

~

Sharon wandered through the ship from the Olympic Spa pampering section and past the inside swimming pool with its ornate glass roof. The area continued the ship's Greek theme with its great Ionic pillars, and there were plenty of lush green plants making a warm and almost erotic atmosphere. Sharon pictured how it might have been in ancient times, and how it reminded her of the historical dramas that showed bare breasted nubile women falling out of their togas before the orgies started. It appeared that sex for pleasure was not something that was a modern invention, but had been enjoyed for a couple of thousand years or more. She remembered Michael telling her earlier in the week, as he looked at a painting of the old Olympic Games, that the athletes actually competed naked. He had told her that the literal translation of the word gymnastics was to compete or train naked. Michael loved his history and he was always coming up with facts. Sharon was never good at it at school, and as she walked passed one of the sunken Jacuzzis she pondered that perhaps she might have been mistaken about the Greeks having orgies, and she might have been thinking about the Romans?

In any case the thought of writhing bodies brought back the image of Michael and Mary. She could imagine Michael's hand creeping over Mary's white flesh. She knew that what she really wanted to do was let her hands creep over Mary's neck.

Sharon reached the Ambrosia Chocolate Cafe and sat on

one of the brightly coloured velvet high backed chairs after she had ordered a white hot chocolate and two strawberries dipped in chocolate from the fountain. She looked up and saw Camilla and Nevin from their dining table walk past.

'Happy Birthday,' they both said in unison. 'See you at dinner later.'

Sharon smiled. Their whole table seemed to know it was her birthday. She hoped they were not planning anything. She hated being the centre of attention. She put one of the strawberries in her mouth and sucked the chocolate from it. It melted almost instantly. It tasted so good. It felt so indulgent, but that did not matter. Normally she would have refrained as she would have been conscious of her weight, and how such luxuries might add to it. It seemed to be a curse of cruises because not only was the food high quality cuisine, but there was always so much of it. Most of the other passengers always seemed to indulge themselves to an almost grotesque level, and they would only worry about the new diet they needed to go on when they got home. Sharon had to admit that she thought it almost vulgar when she considered all the starving in the world. Many times she had watched others approach the buffet style cabinets at breakfast or lunch and cram their plates with as much food as they could get on it. Perhaps it would not have mattered if they had taken it to their table and enjoyed all the food as they gazed out at the sea through the large floor-to-ceiling windows. No, they didn't. Generally they would get up when they had eaten barely half of it, and walk away leaving the leftover food for one of the hardworking crew members to clear up.

She picked up the remaining strawberry and popped it

in her mouth and laughed to herself when she remembered the old adverts that would show a young woman seductively eating a Cadbury's chocolate flake. Usually the young lady was in a poppy field or an exotic setting, and the girl would not tear the wrapping, but unwrap it or even undress it in a way that told the viewer that chocolate was the most important thing in her life. Well Sharon thought she had just had such a moment. She looked at her watch. There was time enough before the sit down dinner. She would treat herself to a couple more before she went back to her cabin and started to get ready. What did it matter? What did it matter anymore? She certainly knew that she did not now have to bother about putting any weight on.

The dinner had gone well. Sharon had started with a fan of sweet summer melon with berry and cassis jelly, and continued with a main course of dairy cream cheese and chive stuffed chicken breast with Caesar pasta and Milanese crumb. Now she was waiting for her dessert, and she had chosen Pavlova topped with kiwi and a passion fruit nectar. Everybody around the table had wished her a happy birthday and everyone, especially the women, had admired her ring. Erin, a tall lady with a rich Irish accent to her left, had been absolutely taken with it and told her how lucky she was, and how lucky she was to have Michael, who so obviously still found her the most precious thing in his life. Sharon had smiled politely and had been amused by Erin using the word, 'Precious'. She had laughed to herself as she pictured Gollum in *The Hobbit* and *Lord of the Rings* holding on to his little precious which interestingly had turned out to be a ring.

Michael obviously appeared to be fooling a lot of people.

He was even fooling her. Now at least two members of staff had told her how lucky she was to have him and all their table was of the same opinion. She studied him quietly as if he were a stranger while he talked to Steph. Perhaps 'Gollum' would be a better nickname now for him rather than the 'Erinaceous' one. Alternatively she could call him 'Her precious'. It certainly made her smile, but the time for nicknames had gone. Perhaps she had even given them to him in an almost affectionate way. It was strange really, but perhaps she did not know him? Perhaps she had never known him? She had to admit that she was beginning to like the man that she had come on the cruise with. It was as if a different man had come on board with her. If only he had been like this towards her from the beginning it could have been so different. Anyway, it did not matter now, it was far too late. Surprisingly she probably had the best birthday of her life. It was a shame that they still seemed to be playing games with one another. Maybe she was just as guilty. She thought back to the Café earlier in the day when she had eaten the strawberries, and knew that she did not have to worry about putting weight on. Nevertheless, she still wanted to look her best, and perhaps importantly she still wanted to feel like a woman. Earlier in the evening she had put on the new green basque she had bought from Ann Summers, before she put on her dress. Why she had bought it and exactly what had been on her mind in the shop she wasn't sure? Michael's face had been a picture when she had, accidentally on purpose, let him catch a glimpse of her in it complete with the stockings attached to the suspenders. He might not have wanted to sleep with her, but it had made her feel good. It certainly showed him what he had been missing. He had certainly looked like a confused man.

Suddenly, music started and she was aware that members of the crew were gathering around their table. Some had even come out of the kitchen and they all lined up with each one wearing a badge with their name and nationality on it. Sharon saw a cake being carried towards her from the kitchen. The cake had giant sparklers on it that were fizzing, and could have probably been used as distress flares. Captain Tim Corbett left his table and strolled towards her with a glass of wine in his hand. Sharon had only ever seen him sitting down at his table from a distance, and she had also heard his announcements as they came over the ship's public address system. Sharon thought he was shorter than he sounded.

Captain Corbett raised his glass, and one of the kitchen staff began to sing. Quickly the whole dining room joined in and all the diners waved their napkins around in circles as they all sang, 'Happy Birthday'. Sharon felt a tear in her eye. She ignored the pain in her back. She had to admit that Michael had done it again. She looked around the table at all the others and smiled. They had all become her new best friends. At least for a week anyway. Sharon realised just how shocked they would have been if they actually knew what she was thinking, and what was on her mind.

THIRTY THREE

Michael had awoken early. He could not sleep. He had left Sharon sleeping soundly. She seemed more relaxed than he ever remembered. She had gone straight to sleep when they had got back from a few drinks with the rest of their table after dinner last night. He had to admit that it had been a good evening. Everyone had had plenty to drink including him and Sharon. Now it was time for a detox. Now it was time to clear his head and think.

Michael reached forward and adjusted the speed timing on the running machine. He had already tried to run around the top deck with its designated running track, which in reality was two lines marked on the decking. It had been nice to be out in the air, but dodging the early morning strollers meant that he could not get up to the pace that he wanted so he had retired to the ship's gymnasium. The gym always appeared to be a well-advertised feature of any cruise ship, but he found that it was probably one of the most underused facilities. Common sense would have said that it would have been ideal for everybody to work off the extra food that they put on during the cruise. In practice, Michael suspected that it was more likely only used by persons that actually attended a gym regularly when they were at home. Michael preferred to jog in the open air, but he could see the advantages of using a gym, especially when it was bad weather. Besides, this gym had spectacular views as the running machine faced the sea and the gym had floor to ceiling windows. The gym was equipped with mats, balls, weight machines, and other apparatus, but he was the sole occupant.

That was good. Michael did not want to be distracted. He thought about Sharon sleeping, and how over the years they had done less and less together. Even their own fitness had been an individual thing and something that they did on their own. Yet he found he was enjoying this treadmill. He had never really wanted to use them before, and he could have gone to the gym with Sharon. It was something that they could have done together. Maybe they could have faced the daily treadmill together more? Maybe life would have been a bit more enjoyable? It would certainly have been easier if he had had someone he could have shared things with, including his problems. Michael would certainly have liked it if he felt the burden of all the day to day things, and all the bills were not just his, and his alone.

Michael felt a trickle of sweat drip down from his forehead, and he used his wrist sweatband to wipe it away. He wanted to congratulate himself on how successful the cruise had been so far. He acknowledged that he would not normally have been so attentive, and he had planned everything to a fine detail, but it had been necessary for his plan. A plan that was coming together very successfully. Last night had proved that, as all of their table had retired to the Acropolis Bar with the two of them to celebrate

Sharon's birthday. Sharon was certainly very popular and it was obvious to all how happy they were as a couple. What Michael found a bit alarming was that he also felt happy.

In Brighton Mary was never far from his mind. He lived for her saucy texts. He lived for his quick visits to her with her highly inventive ways. On the cruise he had received a few texts from her, but they appeared to be a bit distant. Of course, he could have misread them. That was so easy to do with texts. It was so easy to misjudge both the tone and content. Was it Mary being distant or was it him? Was it just the distance between them in miles or was it more than that. Mary was probably the only woman that had controlled him. It was her that had done all the running, and not in an athletic way. Yes they had had their exertions. Sex had played a big part. To be honest he wasn't sure if it was the only part. Did they have anything else? He had been like a horny marionette, and she had simply pulled the strings when she felt like it. He was sure that he had not been the only player in her theatre of dreams. He was sure there had been others before. Probably more than he cared to think about, because Mary was very good at what she did. Perhaps this interval was good? He had been looking forward to the next act. Now he was not so sure. Was it time to bring the curtain down?

Michael wiped his brow again and his legs begun to feel a little bit weak. He felt unsteady. He felt unsure of himself. Michael was confused. Sharon, he realised, was adding to that confusion. Last night he had been astounded, but he had tried not to show it when he had seen her in that green basque. Had she done it on purpose? Had it been a trap? He was a man. He was red blooded. What did she expect? It had come as a shock. He was aware that she was a woman that took care of herself. He was aware that she was a woman that always tried to look her best. Well, on the outside anyway. He had never considered what she might wear underneath. He had not considered that for a very long time. So what the hell had the green basque been all about? The green basque complete with stockings and suspenders. Didn't most women only wear that sort of thing as a treat for a man? Surely it wasn't what they would normally wear even if they were going out, and dressing up to the nines?

Michael realised he was sweating quite heavily. His pace had picked up, but so had his pulse, he suspected, in more ways than one. Was it picturing Sharon in sexy underwear that had done it? She was his wife. They had been married for years. They hadn't had sex for years. He didn't look at her like that anymore. Well he thought he didn't. Although there was also something else worrying him. Something that he could not put his finger on, and then he remembered. It was the actual Basque in its unique green. A racing green was probably the best way to describe it, and it had certainly made his mind race, but perhaps not in the way it was designed to do. He had seen it before. He had been up close and personal. He could remember its touch. He could remember the little black bows. He could even remember who was wearing it, and it was not Sharon. It was Mary. Mary, sweet Mary.

Michael stopped the machine. His head was spinning. He did not want his legs spinning from underneath him as well. He picked up the water bottle and took a swig. How? What? Could it just have been a huge coincidence? Surely it was too much of a coincidence? He did not want to go back to the 'Stranger things happen at sea', scenario. But how come both the women in his life had ended up wearing exactly the same sexy underwear? Was someone playing with his head? His mind was scrambled. Why had Sharon put it on, and for what purpose? How did she end up having exactly the same one as Mary? Which one was playing games? Were either of them playing games or was it really just an amazing coincidence? Michael picked up his water bottle, grabbed his towel and wandered out of the gym. He needed to get to the top deck. He needed air.

Michael stood on the open deck with both hands gripping the handrail and his mind began to drift as he gazed out at the calm sea, but he felt anything but calm. He needed to think. Had he got it wrong? Had he even got the wrong woman? Did he want the wrong woman? Was he actually married to the wrong woman or was she actually the right woman for him? He needed to be sure. He had thought he was sure. He shook his head then heard the large heavy door behind him open and then footsteps.

'Morning Michael.' Michael looked over his shoulder to see Nevin standing there smiling. 'Are you looking forward to going to Rome?'

Michael nodded, and turned towards Nevin with his back against the deck rail. He did not really want to talk, but he did not want to be that unfriendly either. He turned towards Nevin who was actually quite a few inches shorter than him. Nevin, he guessed was probably approaching forty, although looking quite good on it. He had quite close cropped hair with a small quiff, and looked as if he might have been hammered on the head at a young age, thus reducing his height, but making him stockier.

'Yes. Yes we are,' Michael answered. 'We've not been to Rome before. I'm looking forward to seeing the Coliseum.'

'Oh do you like films about gladiators?' Nevin asked quickly, and with a big grin on his face.

Michael laughed. He presumed it was a direct quote from the film, Airplane. For some strange reason the quote seemed to be one that most men of a certain age knew. There were quite a number of quotes that Leslie Nielsen had made famous from the film. The gladiator quote was a question that the small boy was asked by one of the pilots. The pilot then went on to ask him if he hung about outside gymnasiums. It was a film that Michael had seen many times over the years, and each time he had seen it he had noticed something that he had not noticed before. It was extremely funny, and an often quoted film. Generally Michael liked more serious films including all the epics. He had always loved the swords and sandals films such as Ben-Hur, Spartacus, and ironically Gladiator.

The Coliseum, Michael guessed would be the best bit. It would make the films seem real. He knew it was on the itinerary, and for all the other stops the tour guide would decide what they would all see throughout the city, although he knew that they would get free time to do their own thing. Michael wanted to change the subject. If he were honest he did not want to talk. He needed time to himself. He needed time to think. 'To be honest I'm really looking forward to Pompeii just as much. Should be there a decent amount of time and long enough to soak it all in.'

'Are you looking forward to seeing the bodies?' Nevin asked.

'Bodies?' Michael asked. The question caught him by

surprise. He could only concentrate on one body at a time.

'Yes. The ones that were unprepared and caught unaware, and that are now frozen in time.'

'Oh yes. Of course. How could I forget?' Michael laughed, as he pictured seeing the pictures that were probably the most well-known images of the eruption. Men, women, and children, who had stayed where they had fallen, and although the body had decayed below, the lava had formed a perfect image for all to see for eternity. He just was not thinking straight. What was he thinking?

'Yes it should be a good day. See Naples and die,' Nevin said with a large grin. 'See you later.'

Michael gripped the rail and looked down to the sea. The world was going past. His world was going past. Nevin's words seemed to have hit home. It was the talk of bodies, and then the Naples quote. Of course, they would be docking in Naples to go to Pompeii. Michael had heard the quote before, and the bit about dying was not as sinister as it seemed. He always believed it meant that when you saw the beauty of Naples it would take your breath away. He also read that it could mean that you had to experience Naples before you died. That would certainly have fitted in with his plans for Sharon. It was ironic that it almost fitted in to the day. Just another one of those coincidences he mused, or was it a sign?

Michael stared down at the sea. It was a long way down. A very long way down. He let go of his water bottle and watched it as it twisted and tumbled as it hurled towards the sea. It seemed to take ages before it hit the water. He nervously glanced to the left and then to the right. Nobody had seen him. It was only sea pollution, but the principle was the same. There were no cameras on their balcony, but there were cameras on the open decks. They might have picked it up. He remembered reading the case of the woman that had fallen off the Island Escape, and how a camera had picked up her body going past. However, as it could not pick up the beginning of her plight it did not prove foul play. It was as easy as that. But was it? Would it be as easy as that if he pushed Sharon off? Planning it had seemed so easy.

Could he do it when push came to shove? Did he want to do it when push came to shove? Michael smiled at the irony of his thoughts. What was the difference between a push and a shove? How exactly would he dispatch Sharon? Did he actually have the guts? Did he actually want to have the guts?

Michael paced the deck. To say that he was having second thoughts was an understatement. He was having third and fourth ones as well. He looked at his watch. Sharon would probably be awake by now. She was probably wanting to go down to breakfast, and then they would start the day. This could actually be the start of their life together. It did not need to be the start of the end of it. Maybe. Just maybe, he was making the biggest mistake of his life. What would he gain? He had it all to lose. He could lose it all if the police got any indication that foul play was at hand. He might never get that insurance pay-out. In fact, he might even get life. Was it worth the risk? It was high stakes. Higher stakes than he had ever played with before. Was the risk worth the reward? He wound the towel around his neck and walked towards where the lifts would take him down to their deck.

The sun was beginning to get stronger. It was going to be a nice day. In fact it could be a great day. It was like all of the clouds had lifted from him. He started to feel better. All the effort that he had done would be wasted, but he realised all of his efforts had been misplaced. Mary had simply been a distraction. Most men would have been attracted to her. They certainly would have been in a sexual sense. That did not seem to matter now. Sharon was his wife. His legal spouse. It was her that the law said he should be with, and the cruise had shown him that. The cruise had shown him that they could be good together. That they could get on and do things together. They could even enjoy each other's company. They just had to show a bit of give and take towards each other. With each of them putting in a bit of thought he was sure it could work. He would make it work. It was just a question of building on the cruise, and working with what they had got. Sharon would be shocked. He was sure of that. Though, Michael was sure that she would be pleasantly surprised, but he did not want to put any immediate pressure on her. He would take it carefully. He would take it one step at a time and slowly build on what they already had. It would be fun falling in love with his wife all over again, and this time he would not be as selfish. He was older and wiser, and he had come to within a whisker of making the biggest mistake of his life.

Michael reached the lift and pressed the call button. He was going back to Sharon. He had been such a fool. Thank goodness she did not know anything different. She would never know. She would just be happy how he treated her from now on. He hoped it would make her forget some things of the past. He would really try. He would try as if his life depended on it. He had to make it up to her. Mary did not matter. He knew that now, and he doubted that he really meant that much to Mary. Surely it was just sexual attraction. That was what it was. He was sure that Mary would easily forget him. Mary would move on. He had had a lucky escape. Sharon had had a lucky escape. How could he have been so stupid? At least it was not too late. He had come to his senses in time. Thank God for small mercies. He felt as if a great weight had been lifted off his shoulders. He felt such a sense of relief. His spirits lifted as the lift arrived and made its customary ping sound as the lift doors opened.

Michael thought that he would play it cool today as he travelled down in the lift. He did not want to overpower Sharon all at once. If he shocked her too much she might put up her guard and be suspicious. No it had to happen almost organically and not seem forced. Besides they had been together over thirty years so what was the rush? They had the rest of their life together. It could be better than it had ever been. Slow but sure that was the way, but he was sure he would win Sharon over. Tonight he would bring up champagne to their room as a surprise before they went to bed, and settled down. It would be a celebration of a new beginning, and if she was wearing that green Basque then so much the better.

THIRTY FOUR

'Come on. Hurry up and finish that beer, please,' Sharon called out to Michael who was standing on their cabin balcony. 'We will be late for dinner'.

It was time to put the dirt, dust, and heat of Rome behind them. It was time that she put a lot of things behind her. The day had been very enjoyable. The cruise had been very enjoyable. If only life had always been like this holiday. The trouble was that holidays did not last a lifetime. Well not generally.

Michael placed the beer bottle on their table on the balcony, and came back inside.

'Oh Michael,' Sharon urged. 'Don't leave it out there. Bring it in otherwise if it blows over the side you would be the first one to moan about sea pollution.'

'I could put a message in it. In the hope of being rescued,' Michael replied quickly.

Sharon did not hear his remark, as she added a last minute adjustment to her make-up. She pouted into the cabin's full length mirror, and decided that her outfit had just the right sense of occasion to it, and tonight was going to be an occasion. It was a formal night, and Michael was sporting a black bow tie with a wing collared shirt. He had stopped short of wearing a frilled one or a cumberband. Sharon was wearing the red dress that she had chosen for just this occasion. It had been expensive, but what did that matter. She was only going to wear it once. She gazed back in the mirror and was pleased with her choice. Red suited her, she had been told. She nodded in agreement. Sharon picked up her clutch bag, and walked out of the cabin with Michael following a few feet behind.

The dinner passed without event. Michael seemed to be in a good mood, as indeed was everybody at their table. Although Michael was not a big drinker he did enjoy a glass of red wine with his meal, and Sharon was keen to ensure that his glass was topped up, but not in such a way that it was noticeable by the other diners that she did so.

After dinner they made their excuses and retired to the piano bar. Sharon sat in one of the comfortable armchairs dreamily listening to the piano player. Michael returned from the bar with a beer and a glass of red wine, and sat in a chair opposite her.

Sharon went to pick up her wine glass, then stopped. 'I've got a bit of a headache. Think I'll nip back to the cabin, and take a couple of tablets.' She rummaged through her clutch bag. 'Oh, I think I've left my key card in there. Can I borrow yours?'

Michael took out his card from his CK wallet and went to hand it to her.

Sharon offered up her open clutch bag. 'Just drop it in. I won't be long.'

Sharon made her way back to their cabin. When she got outside their cabin door she glanced both left and right to ensure no one was about. She was grateful that there were no security cameras in the corridors, as she took out two plastic surgical gloves from her handbag. Carefully she peeled them one onto each hand and took out Michael's electronic key card from her handbag. Looking both left and right again she swiped the card key in the electronic lock and opened the door, but did not go in. Sharon then ensured that the door looked like it was closed from the outside, but in reality a push would open it. She then placed the card back in her bag, peeled off the plastic gloves and zipped them in the inside compartment, turned and walked back down the corridor to re-join Michael.

Michael was sitting there quietly when she returned. He had drunk half of his beer. Sharon sat down opposite him.

'Did you take them?' Michael asked.

Sharon nodded gently. 'Yes. Hopefully they will kick in soon. Oh, before I forget let me give you back your key.' She opened her clutch bag so that it was visible and Michael reached across and took it, and then placed it back in his wallet.

'Thanks,' Michael answered. 'What do you want to do next? Do you want to go up to the Acropolis Bar?'

Sharon took in the opulence of her surroundings. What did any of this matter she thought to herself? She had enjoyed the day. In fact, she had had a great day. The days on the cruise had just kept getting better and better. Michael had been so polite and accommodating. She could really have been fooled into thinking that he cared. He was very convincing, if she hadn't known him better. She shook her head. 'Sorry. I think this headache is getting worse, and I'm very tired. It's been a long day. Do you mind if I go back to the cabin? Think I might crash out.'

Michael looked as if he was genuinely disappointed and nodded. 'No not at all. I'll have a quick wander, and maybe have a drink in the Myrtos Beach Bar, then perhaps a little visit to the Casino. Won't be that long.'

Sharon managed a smile. 'Take your time. No hurry. Just don't wake me up when you come back.'

Michael smiled and Sharon stood up, and then turned to walk away. Suddenly she stopped and turned back towards Michael. 'On second thoughts can you give me time to take off my make-up, say, about thirty minutes then bring me up a hot chocolate, please? Then you can go back to the Casino.'

Sharon wandered back to their cabin. She knew that Michael would be more than happy on his own for half an hour or so, but in half an hour he would be on his own. She reached the cabin door that was already unlocked and gently pushed it open. She went in and pushed the door shut. The cabin was very tidy as the Cabin Steward, who was called Anna, a Polish girl, who worked very hard, had been in when they were at dinner, tidied up, and then turned down their bed. The soft lighting had been turned on. The ship's daily newspaper with the itinerary for the next day, planned events, and shows, had been placed on the bed. Either side of it were their two fresh, clean towels that had been folded into the shape of two swimming swans, that also combined made the shape of a heart. Sharon managed a thin smile as she looked towards the love tokens. It was too late for that. She had thought once that Michael had loved her. She wanted to be loved. She needed to be loved. Love though had seemed to have evaded her all her life. It did not matter anymore. Nothing mattered anymore. She knew what she had to do. She had to stay focused.

Sharon placed her clutch bag on the bed and took out the two plastic gloves and put them on. It was now or never. There was no turning back. She walked over to the padded chair that sat in front of the desk that doubled as a vanity unit. Sharon pulled it towards her so that it fell on the floor. She undid the patio doors to the balcony and slid them open. Sharon found herself taking a deep breath. Was it really going to be this easy? No. She knew she did not have time to think. She had thought it all out a thousand times before. It had all been planned in her head for so long now. It was always going to be easier a few days into the cruise and nearer the end of the week. Did people who planned to jump in front of a train ever have second thoughts? Did they ever miss their train? She did not want to miss her boat. What was the alternative? Was there an alternative? The alternative, she knew, would be both painful and drawn out. This way she would kill two birds with one stone. She laughed at the thought, but felt a bit of an idiot. What fool would laugh at a time like this. A serious one she told herself. Two birds at the same time. Well not exactly. One dead and the other in hell, she hoped.

Her breath seemed short, and she gulped. She could feel her hands beginning to sweat in the plastic gloves. She glanced around the room. What did she need to do next? One mistake and it could prove costly. Not that she would ever know. She walked over to patio doors and looked out. Obviously no land could be seen. They were far out to sea. It looked cold and dark out there. Not even any illumination from any other passing vessels. It was now or never.

She glanced at her watch. Why, she did not know. The

time did not matter. Poor Michael expecting to pop back with her drink, and then go back to the gaming tables playing blackjack. Well his luck was going to change. He was going to go bust. She was pleased that she had asked him to pop back, as she knew that there was probably a camera to record Michael's presence in the casino, and perhaps more importantly the Pit Manager would almost certainly have recognized Michael by now, and remember that he had been there. The request for the hot chocolate had been a good one. It would immediately connect Michael to the cabin, and at the right time. She smiled to herself, but realised there was no time to congratulate herself as the self-imposed time bomb was ticking away.

Her stomach fluttered, and she knew that nerves were kicking in. 'Get a grip, girl,' she said under her breath. 'Pull yourself together, and then you can have that well-deserved rest.'

She walked over to the glass beer bottle that Michael had left earlier and picked it up by the neck. Like she was about to swat a fly she raised it above her head, and with as much strength as she could muster she brought it down on the back of her head. The bottle shattered and all the pieces fell onto the bed. She threw the jagged edge of the neck to the corner of the room. She was starting to feel dizzy and the strength appeared to go from her legs. She knew she had to hold herself together. Just a little while longer and then it would all be over. Then she could have a well-deserved rest. Quickly she peeled off the plastic gloves, and inserted one inside the other. With a great effort she opened the patio doors went out on to the balcony, and then threw them out into the wind. Quicker than a shooting star they were gone.

Sharon went back into the room. She was feeling less steady with every step. She put her hand to the back of head, and she felt the blood on her palm warm and sticky. She put her hand down to steady herself on the bed and the white bed cover immediately took on a red stain. Sharon managed a smile. Her head was beginning to spin. She wanted to lay down. She needed to rest. She was beginning to feel so tired. She needed to sleep.

'Not too much longer,' she told herself. 'Soon I can rest. Soon............'

She noticed that her head was starting to bleed quite heavily, and there was more blood on the cover. She knew she did not have long left. Not long in any sense. She had to be quick. Soon it would be over. The game would be over. The game that they had played for the last thirty years. Thirty years. Where had it all gone? For some strange reason the words to the Abba song came to her head, and she started to sing, 'The Winner Takes It All.'

Although were there any winners? Only one loser, she thought, as she walked over to the curtain, and with her blood stained hand gave it a hard pull so that it came away from the curtain rail at the top. Then as she walked through the patio doors and out onto the balcony she grabbed hold of one of the net curtains so that the edge took on a red tint.

She ran her hand along the wooden balcony rail. Yes it was the standard recommended height that was supposed to help prevent accidents or even one member of a loving or eager copulating couple falling over. It did happen, or so the insurance reports often said. Michael's research had shown that. Did he think she was a complete fool? 'That one is too clever by half', her mother would have said, and now she was going to see her mother again. Soon the pain would be gone. The deceit. The hiding. The worry. It would all be gone. The sleepless nights she had worrying about her future. Worrying if she had a future. Now it was in her hands. She had never wanted it to end like this. We all have to die sometime, she reasoned, but how many of us actually choose our exit? Perhaps we should be able to, especially in certain circumstances, but that was a different argument, and not one for this lifetime.

Voices appeared to be in her head telling her to do it. Now was the time. It was easy. Very easy. She would be welcome. There would be no more pain. There would be no more stress and worry before the eventuality took control. Death would come. It was only a question of time. She could hear her mother's voice calling out to her as she had done when she was a small child. 'Come in now Sharon. It's time to come in.'

'Coming Mother,' she heard herself say automatically. 'Coming. Just one minute more. One minute I promise.'

She was a small girl again looking up at the night sky. It had gone dark. She should be in. Playtime was over. Her mother wanted her. It was time to go in. The stars seemed to sparkle at her. They seemed to wink at her like old friends she had known, but were now departed. How her head ached, but she felt absurdly calm. She briefly looked down at the sea nine decks below. It looked hypnotising. It looked soothing. She would slide into the great water, and her troubles would be no more.

'I'm not going to my death,' she said quietly to herself. 'I am just actually changing worlds.' She glanced over her shoulder towards their cabin. 'Goodbye Michael,' she said quietly. 'I hope you get what you deserve.' She lifted her leg up on to the rail and then straddling it she lifted up the other. For what seemed an eternity, but was in reality only a few seconds, she stared downwards towards the welcoming water. It was time to go.

Sharon closed her eyes and launched herself. She was in free fall. Her head felt heavy. 'Coming Mother,' she shouted into the wind. It was the last words she was to utter.

THIRTY FIVE

Michael knew that Sharon was sleeping with the fishes. But he also knew that he had been done up like a kipper. How could he have been so naive? How could he have been so stupid? How had he missed it? He had been blinded by his own wants. All that planning. All that planning for nothing. No, not for nothing. It was worse than that. It was much worse than that. All he really needed to do was sit tight, and he would have got his wish. He could have had it all. All he had needed to have done was waited. Even the insurance money would have kicked in. He would have been single. He would have been free to start up with Mary. Wasn't it ironic that that wasn't even what he wanted in the end? Now, he had nothing, or less than nothing if that were possible. A month ago he had a life. Now he had no life.

Michael placed his head in his hands. The cell bed was hard, and he stared up into the recessed light in the ceiling. Even they controlled that. He could not even turn off a light in his life anymore. He had no control. Sharon had seen to that. He had thought he was the chess player, but he had been outplayed. It was checkmate to her. She had played a blinder. She had been moves ahead. He had not seen it coming.

He replayed it back in his mind. The way he had done for many games he had previously played. The clues were there. He had just not been looking. He had been far too busy concentrating on what he wanted to do, and how he was going to achieve it. The first rule he learned in Primary School, when he was first taught chess, was to always keep an eye on what your opponent was doing. Don't push forward so eagerly, and overlook what the person in front of you was thinking. Like a child he had forgotten that. It was a schoolboy error. It was checkmate. It was all over. The king had been toppled. The queen was dead, but she had taken the king with her. His life with Sharon had almost been like a game. A deadly game with deadly consequences. Now the game was well and truly over.

Michael glanced towards the door. He knew that soon they would be coming for him again. It would be yet another pointless interview. They knew they had him. He knew they had him. What would be the point of trying to prove his innocence? Was he guilty by association or any other such law? Could you be done for murder if you had planned it, but had not actually carried it out? Of course, it looked like he had done it. Any fool could see that. The evidence was far too strong. No jury in the world would believe him if he told them he had not done it. They would certainly not believe him that he had been framed. He couldn't believe it himself let alone anyone else.

He was thankful that capital punishment had been abolished. Nevertheless, he could almost feel the noose tightening around his neck. He was a dead man walking. He pulled himself up and stood looking at the bare walls. His barren cell originally reminded him of an inner cabin on a cruise ship. Inside cabins were always the cheaper option to cruise because they had no window or port hole. Many passengers preferred not to purchase them, but at least those that did could avoid having to spend much time in them. They were more bearable, given the thought that they were used just for sleeping, washing and changing really. How different his cell was, and for many more years than he cared to think about, he could be spending up to twenty three hours a day in one.

He tried to think what might save him. Could they convict him if they did not have a body? He knew from his research that over seventy five per cent of bodies lost or missing at sea were never recovered.

So they didn't have a body, but they did not have to try too hard to find a reason or the evidence. It was shouting at them. A great long list that he could not argue against. The ice queen had seen to that. His fingerprints on the broken bottle. Her blood everywhere, and of course they had not believed his surprise when he had returned to the cabin. Had he not been waiting for her? Didn't the electronic door key card log for the door entry record prove that he had opened the door to their cabin, and was therefore waiting for her to come back? He must have opened the door to let her in or they could have even gone back together. Sharon had not used her key card to get in to their cabin that night. The records and logs showed she had definitely not used it to gain entry, they told him. It proved she was never on her own in the cabin. Was it not obvious that he did the evil deed, before going back to the bar pretending to return with the drinks, then letting himself in with the key card again.

Michael stood up and kicked the bench in frustration.

He knew he would be kicking himself for the rest of his natural life. Why had he not picked up the signs? How could she have kept it so secret? He slumped down on the bed again. The signs were all there. He had just not read them. He had thought she was seeing someone else. Had there not almost been an unwritten rule between them? They were not actually sleeping together. Yes, they shared a bedroom, but the physical side had died a long time ago. He must admit he had been a rat. There were really no other words to soften that, but he could not resist her friend. Well, Sharon had not wanted him, and he needed to be wanted.

The amount of times he had caught Sharon talking on the phone, and then she quickly terminated the call when he had come within range. The times when she had been out, and he had had no idea where she was, especially during the day. Now it was clear who she was talking to and why. Now it was clear where she was visiting on those days out. Bob had been the only person that Sharon had shared her news with. She had not shared it with him or her friends, or so he thought, but certainly not Mary. Now he knew why. Revenge, they said, was a dish best served cold. She had been more cold and calculating than him. Of course he had asked for it. He couldn't argue with that. Now he was to pay the price.

Originally, Michael had been dumbfounded when he had returned to their cabin. He had been carrying a tray with the hot chocolate that Sharon had asked for. He also had on it a bottle of champagne, and two glasses. That was what he originally planned to do in the hope that they might have rekindled their relationship. He had come to his senses, and discovered that it was Sharon he wanted to be with, and not

Mary. He realised that Sharon had a headache, but he was hoping she felt a bit better, and that he could turn it around. He hoped it would be a nice surprise. Surprise? That was a laugh. He had had the surprise, and she had the last laugh. He had never been more surprised or shocked in his life.

Michael remembered putting down the tray whilst he got out his key card, and then opening the door. Almost, immediately the bedlam hit him, but strangely what he recalled was not dropping the tray, as if he was in some cheap movie, but actually placing it on the vanity or desk unit. The patio door was still open with the net curtains flapping in the wind. There was glass all over the bed, and blood seemed to be everywhere. At first he had simply been stunned. It was obviously a crime scene, and he thought that Sharon had been attacked, and possibly even killed and thrown overboard. He had felt the panic rise through him. She might have managed to escape and run back into the body of the ship. What could he do? What should he do? He immediately picked up the ship's telephone and called the operator, who sent security straight away. The rest now seemed a bit of a blur. He presumed that Sharon's attacker was loose on the ship. There was a dangerous man still at large. A dangerous man they should still have been looking for, and not asking him stupid questions.

He knew that she had been attacked. How could they not see that? So the immediate evidence might have pointed to him? Yes, he could concede that, but he knew differently. He knew he had not killed her. He had not for one second considered that she had committed suicide. What? Not only had she topped herself, but she had done it in such a way as to frame him. Never. Not in a million. Although what the truth was had been eating him away. He had almost felt her teasing him from her watery grave. It had only become clearer when Bob had paid him that very brief visit a couple of days ago.

~

Bob sat down opposite him with a sardonic smile on his face. 'You are going down for a very long time Michael, he had said. 'A very long time indeed.'

'But I did not kill her,' Michael had tried to protest.

Bob had held up the palm of his hand. 'Yes. I think we both know that. However, we are probably the only two people left in the world to believe that. You might have well had. You were planning to. But she got there first. You see, what you didn't know, what nobody else knew, was that Sharon had cancer.'

Michael went to speak.

'No I don't want to hear anything you have to say.' Bob lowered his voice even further. 'Yes, she looked so well didn't she? She only had a few pains up until then. She had not felt that bad at all. It started with a back pain, I believe. She had no idea as to the extent of how ill she actually was. None at all. Amazing. You wouldn't believe it. But she only had months. A year at most, to live. That's what they said. That's what they told her. Only months, but months to die in great pain, and without dignity. She had no future to look forward to. She would have had no future anyway if you had had your way. Strange isn't it? She told me that when she found out about the Big C she actually felt closer to you. She wanted to make a go of it. She wanted to make up for all the wasted time, and the wasted years. Then she discovered that not only were you shagging my wife, and her so called best friend, but that the two of you actually planned to kill her. Yes, I knew about you and Mary some time before. Call me stupid, but you are not the first person that Mary had been seeing. I knew that she did have dalliances. Although I pretended not to know. What I could not pretend was to ignore you and her. So together Sharon and I did some investigating. I wanted to prove to Sharon that you were seeing Mary. I wanted concrete proof. So we broke into your computer expecting just to prove the affair. Then we discovered your research and emails, and looked at what sites you had been on. You had made a list. A sort of DIY Guide on how to kill off your wife on a cruise. To say we were both shocked is an understatement. By then Sharon had an idea that she was ill. She was going to all these appointments trying to find out how ill she actually was. Then she got the news. The devastating news of the full prognosis, and the prediction of her life expectancy. That's when the plan was hatched. That poor woman wanted to die with dignity. However, she was so shocked that you were planning to kill her, the lengths that you were prepared to go to, and the effort. She was so angry, and so was I. Certainly then she did not want you to have it all. She did not want you to have anything. Now she knew that she was going to die anyway so she thought she would make you pay. She thought she would play you at your own little game. I think she very much succeeded. I would say with all your research, emails, and evidence on the boat, you are bang to rights. You shot yourself through both feet. They don't need Columbo to solve this one. You even had a DVD, I understand. Deadly something or other, she remembered. Did it give you a few ideas? You really are not as clever as you think, Michael.

But remember all of this is just a little secret between you and me. The Authorities already know you are guilty, and obviously I could not possibly disagree with them. Besides, it is payback time. You are the one with no future now. I don't think they are going after Mary. There really is not enough proof and evidence that you were in it together, old boy. Just you on your own now. That's all it's going to be. That's all it's ever going to be. Good luck. Enjoy.'

~

Bob's words had hit home. The whole conversation haunted him, and Michael could practically recall it verbatim. He pictured their cabin and the devastation he had found. It was the scene that he kept playing back in his mind time and time again, like an old video tape that was stuck on replay. It all made sense now. He had been fitted up. Should he confess to a crime that he had not committed, but a crime that he had been committed to. Either way it didn't really matter much anymore. He knew that he was going down. He knew that he was going down for a very long time, and he was going to be a very old man before he saw the sea again.

AFTERWARD

Thank you for reading this book. I hope you have enjoyed it. If you have, why not visit my website www.wifeoverboard.com where you can read my blogs. You can also give me a tweet.

Further, I would appreciate it if you took the time and trouble to leave an honest review on one of the relevant sites to encourage more readers. Thank you in advance.

Happy Cruising
Steve Colbourne

www.wifeoverboard.com
Follow Steve Colbourne: twitter.com/WifeOverboard
On Facebook: www. facebook.com/wifeoverboard

FURTHER READING

A big thank you to Cruise Bruise who gave their Editor's Choice Award to *Wife Overboard*. Cruise Bruise called my book, "A Blueprint For Cruise Ship Murder At Sea" and they now provide a Cruise Bruise Companion to Wife Overboard on their site. This guide briefly details and then links directly to the overboard cases that I mention in Michael's research throughout my book.

Cruise Bruise is the largest collection of sites that detail each case overboard in the world, as well as many other amazing facts and distressing statistics about the cruise industry. Sites include Cruise Ships Missing and Cruise Ships Deaths. They are often the only hope that a family might still have of proving that their missing relative might have been a victim of foul play. Yes, my book is fictional, but here you will read case after case and see the photos of the numerous poor, unfortunate souls that have been lost at sea but not forgotten. Go to **www.cruisebruise.com** and see the great work they do.

ABOUT THE AUTHOR

Steve Colbourne used to write a regular column for the *Brighton Evening Argus* newspaper for their women's magazine. He has also written regularly for Baby Magazine and has had a number of features, articles, and stories published in national magazines. *Wife Overboard* is his first published novel. Steve also runs a Support Group for Leukaemia sufferers and their families and carers. Please contact him for further details. Steve currently lives in Brighton, England with his wife, daughter Olivia, and son Ben. He is an avid supporter of Brighton and Hove Albion.

Printed in Poland
by Amazon Fulfillment
Poland Sp. z o.o., Wrocław